THE A

RODERICK MANN

The Account

HarperCollins*Publishers*

HarperCollins*Publishers*
77–85 Fulham Palace Road,
Hammersmith, London W6 8JB

Published by HarperCollins*Publishers* 1994
1 3 5 7 9 8 6 4 2

Copyright © Roderick Mann 1994

The Author asserts the moral right to
be identified as the author of this work

A catalogue record for this book is
available from the British Library

ISBN 0 00 224359 8

Set in Linotron Palatino

Printed in Great Britain by
HarperCollinsManufacturing Glasgow

For Anastasia

From the *Daily Mail*

SOCIETY WOMAN MURDERED

The body of Jane Summerwood, 27, of Connaught Square, London, was discovered by an early morning jogger yesterday in a clump of bushes in Hyde Park.

Police described the condition of the body as appalling. 'She had been brutally beaten,' a spokesman said. 'It was the work of a maniac.'

Miss Summerwood, daughter of Colonel James Summerwood of East Grinstead, was well known in London social circles and was an accomplished horsewoman. She is known to have been in the company of American billionaire Robert Brand, and was a frequent guest on his yacht in Monte Carlo. Mr Brand, now in America, could not be reached for comment yesterday but his secretary described him as 'devastated'. Police inquiries continue.

Chapter 1

It was raining hard. Driving along the Quai du Mont-Blanc in his black Renault, Paul Eberhardt glanced idly towards Lake Geneva, sheathed now in a fine mist that rendered the mountains beyond barely visible.

The man sometimes called the most astute banker in Europe was deeply depressed. Usually on Thursdays his spirits rose. This was the evening he set aside his worries and drove along the lakeside to spend an hour at the house of Madame Valdoni.

Relaxing. Taking his pleasure. Watching the film that now lay on the seat beside him.

But events that afternoon had dampened his enthusiasm for the evening to come. First there was the memo from his partner, Georges di Marco, demanding a meeting. Eberhardt knew what di Marco wanted to talk about; what he had been threatening for weeks now. It could no longer be postponed. Then, to make matters worse, Robert Brand had arrived unexpectedly at the bank. Eberhardt's relationship with the American billionaire had always been polite. They were, after all, locked in a tight financial embrace that could not easily be broken. But the meeting that afternoon had been unpleasant. Brand, in a bad mood, had queried everything and had barely been civil. Eberhardt, who had always prided himself that he could handle the American, was now not so sure.

He swore and braked hard as a woman, her view hidden by an umbrella, stepped out suddenly to cross the street. He must pay attention. This was just the sort of day when accidents occurred.

Leaving the city he adjusted the speed of the

windscreen wipers and switched on the heater to demist the glass. There were few other vehicles about. That suited him fine. The drive along the Lausanne road normally took him forty-five minutes. Today it would be quicker.

An impatient horn behind him interrupted his thoughts. Pulling over he saw he was near the lakeside hotel where he occasionally dined. He drove into the car park and switched off the engine. A drink, he decided, would make him feel better; would calm his nerves. Otherwise the seductive ministrations of Madame Valdoni's girl would be wasted.

The bar of the hotel was quiet. Relieved, he perched himself on a stool and ordered a double Scotch. The warmth of the drink in his throat made him feel better. Glancing around he caught an unwelcome glimpse of himself in a wall mirror. How pale he looked; how old. Yet he was still an aristocratic-looking man, tall and distinguished in a formal way. Anyone seeing him sitting there nursing his drink would have found it hard to guess his profession. A diplomat perhaps. Or a doctor. He was not an easy man to place on looks alone.

Finishing his drink he paid his bill and left. Outside, he stood for a moment protected by an awning, breathing in the chill late afternoon air. The smell of the lake was quite strong; tangy and pervasive. As he hurried to his car he stepped in a pool of rainwater, soaking one of his highly polished shoes. Damn! Could nothing go right this day? He held the shoe out of the car window, upside down, shaking it.

Just past the town of Nyon, Eberhardt turned up a private road that wound its way through several acres of woodland and pasture. Faded signs warning against trespassing stood alongside the road. Eberhardt knew the road well. It was the landscape of his other self, not the severe banking mandarin of Geneva but the private pleasure-seeking sensualist. At the end of the road was a large, wrought-iron gate. And, beyond, a half-moon shaped driveway fronting a two-storey mansion. The house, which had once belonged to a wealthy Swiss industrialist, had been bought by Italian-born Madame Valdoni twenty years earlier and turned into a *maison de plaisir* catering to an exclusive clientele of men from Geneva and Lausanne who were prepared to pay 500 Swiss francs for the services of any one of half a dozen spectacular-looking girls.

Eberhardt's friend, the lawyer Maître Claude Bertrand, the only man in whom he ever confided, had often suggested that the banker take a permanent mistress. But the sense of illicit, furtive adventure stimulated Eberhardt's libido in a way he knew a regular woman could not.

Anyway, he had lived alone since the death of his wife, Hilde, ten years before, and now had no intention of sharing his life with anyone. Coupled with this was the fact that Geneva banking circles, prim and censorious, would frown on any such liaison.

As he drove through the gates Eberhardt was relieved to note that there were no other cars outside the house. Highly secretive by nature, he preferred to keep these visits private and always used an alias.

Holding the can of film beneath his jacket he hastened towards the front door, which was opened almost immediately by a maid.

'Good evening, Dr Weber,' she said. 'I will tell Madame you are here.' A moment later she returned with a woman in her mid-fifties, elegantly and expensively dressed in black.

'My dear doctor.' Madame Valdoni proffered her hand. 'What a pleasure.' She turned to the maid. 'A drink for Doctor Weber.' She glanced at Eberhardt. 'The usual?'

Eberhardt nodded. He pointed to his shoe. 'Look at that. Soaked. This damn rain. Perhaps you could dry it?'

'Of course.' Valdoni motioned to the maid who knelt before Eberhardt and removed both his shoes and socks.

'I will have them ready by the time you leave,' she beamed.

'Is everything arranged?'

'As soon as you telephoned. We have someone quite special for you tonight . . .'

'Not Genevieve?' He felt a pang of disappointment.

'She is away. Her mother is sick. But you will not be disappointed.'

When the maid returned with a glass of chilled white wine, Eberhardt, barefoot, followed Valdoni up the sweeping staircase. At the top she took the can of film he handed her and led him down a hallway to a thickly carpeted dressing room complete with day bed and wardrobe. A door led to an adjacent room.

A young Oriental girl stood there. She was perhaps sixteen years old and so incredibly lovely that Eberhardt was astonished. She was wearing black panties and a black brassiere. She too was barefoot.

'Jasmine,' the older woman said, handing her the can of film, 'this is Dr Weber, one of our special friends. I am relying on you to take care of him.'

The girl nodded. 'My honour, sir.' She bowed and retreated into the other room.

Valdoni smiled. 'Enjoy yourself, dear doctor.' She went out closing the door.

Eberhardt undressed completely, hanging his clothes in the wardrobe, and stepped into the next room, which was in semi-darkness. Uncarpeted, it contained nothing but a wooden chair with a bell push on one arm, a screen some six feet square, and a film projector on a table at the opposite end.

Eberhardt sat in the chair facing the screen. A moment later Jasmine came in. She was naked now, her body and hands slightly oiled. She was carrying two glasses, one filled with hot water, the other with ice cubes. She put these beside the cushion at the foot of the chair. Reaching for a packet beside the projector she took out a crumpled cigarette, lit it and inhaled deeply before passing it to

Eberhardt. She watched as he drew the smoke deep into his lungs. He passed the joint back to the girl, who again inhaled. Soon the small room was pungent with the smell of marijuana. Eberhardt began to relax. He stubbed the joint out on the wooden floor.

'Ready,' he said.

The girl knelt before him, her tongue flicking across her lips. She took a swallow of hot water and enveloped him with her mouth. His erection swelled. She curled her tongue expertly, making him groan.

Soon she stopped and slipped two ice cubes into her mouth. When she again enveloped him his erection began to subside. He moaned, looking down at her. But with the second mouthful of hot water his erection swelled even more. Three times the girl repeated the process, fingers teasing, tongue flickering, writhing, twisting, hair swaying, each time driving Eberhardt nearer to climax. Finally he pressed the bell push and a beam of light stabbed the gloom. The film began unrolling. Clasping the girl's head in his hands, pulling her further to him, Eberhardt leaned forward, his eyes fixed upon the screen, reading every word of the German subtitles although he knew them by heart.

The print, old now and scratched in places, never failed to excite him. It was one of many made by the Nazis. The film, much prized, had been given to him by a German friend. 'Something to warm you on those cold Geneva nights,' he had joked.

The film depicted a chilling scene. There were four people in a small, cell-like room. One of them, a young dark-haired man, his face and torso bloodied, was in a chair, his hands tied behind him. Two other men, both in black SS uniforms, were taking turns beating him with truncheons.

On a single bed in the background lay a young woman, naked, her hands also tied. She was screaming. When the beating finished the SS men turned the young man's chair around so that it faced the bed. Removing his tunic and boots one of the SS men dropped his breeches and approached the woman on the bed.

While the Nazi forced himself into her, the young man, struggling violently, tried to look away. He could not. The other captor held his head tightly, forcing him to watch.

Hypnotized by what he was seeing, his pulse throbbing, his breath laboured, the blood pounding in his ears, Eberhardt suddenly groaned and came with such force that he almost slid from the chair. After a moment the girl rose and tiptoed from the room.

When Eberhardt looked at the screen again the other man was on the woman. The prisoner in the chair now sat without moving, apparently in shock. As the SS man climaxed, his body shuddering, the woman beneath him spat in his face. Rearing back, the man struck her savagely causing blood to gush from her nose. He continued striking her.

When his companion finally rose from the moaning woman, the first SS man, dressed now, took out his revolver and fired once into the head of each victim.

Transfixed, Eberhardt watched until the film ran off the spool. He rose shakily. Taking the film he went next door to dress. His shoes and socks, now dry, awaited him. Before leaving he placed an envelope on the day bed.

In an upstairs room Jasmine watched as he accelerated away down the drive. She turned to her employer. 'That film.' She shuddered. 'He's sick, that man.'

'You saw it?'

'Genevieve told me.'

'He's a good customer,' the older woman said.

They stood together watching the lights of the Renault as it reached the end of the drive and turned down the private road.

Madame Valdoni shook her head. 'And he still thinks we don't know who he is.'

She laughed softly.

Chapter 2

Eberhardt arrived early at his office the next morning. He had slept well, relaxed after his visit to Madame Valdoni's. But he was apprehensive about the meeting he had arranged with his partner, Georges di Marco. Confrontations of any kind were not to his liking.

Sipping the first of the many morning coffees his secretary, Marte, brought him, he let his eyes wander down to the street below.

Even the most chauvinistic citizens of Geneva agreed that the rue de Hesse was an unremarkable thoroughfare. But Eberhardt had loved it ever since he first stood on the corner by the Café des Banques trying to decide whether to move his bank there from its original location in the rue du Rhône. It was that or the rue de la Corraterie, supposedly the most respectable financial address in Geneva. In the end he had opted for the rue de Hesse – already the home of the Banque Privée de Edmond Rothschild – and he had never regretted it. There his bank had grown and prospered to the point where it was now a major player in the world's money markets. And he, at the age of seventy-seven, was one of the most respected bankers in Europe.

Many foreigners, Eberhardt knew, thought of Switzerland as a land of watches, chocolates and cuckoo clocks. But what made Switzerland work, what gave it its independence and its prestige, were the banks. There were the three great commercial banks, Credit Suisse, Union Bank and the Swiss Bank Corporation. And there were the private banks – Lombard Odier, Pictet, Rothschild, Darier, Hentsch and Eberhardt.

The private bankers of Geneva thought of themselves

15

as an élite group. They belonged to the *Groupement*, the association of Geneva private bankers, the most exclusive sector in the Swiss financial system. And they had something else in common. They were all, without exception, paranoid about secrecy, fearing rightly that its abolition would lead to a wholesale withdrawal of the trillions in marks, dollars, pounds, lire and yen invested with them. Secrecy, in fact, was the law. Clause 47(b) of the 1934 Banking Act set out stiff penalties – fines and a jail sentence – for any bank director or employee who gave away secrets.

Foreign bankers liked to point out that Swiss bankers had a poor record in forecasting movements in the stock markets. The Swiss argued back that with them the emphasis was on security rather than spectacular performance in portfolio management. And bankers like Eberhardt were quick to reiterate how much more prudent they were than American bankers, who, in his words, 'seemed intent on throwing away clients' money'.

But Swiss bankers could no longer afford to be smug. A billion-dollar money laundering racket had resulted in the resignation of Switzerland's Justice Minister. And the scandal at Credit Suisse, which had written off $700 million after fraud at its branch in Chiasso, had thrown doubt on Switzerland's reputation for prudence. Then came the jail sentence handed out to Robert Leclerc, whose private bank collapsed. No one was particularly surprised at the judge's decision; malpractice by a partner in a private bank rated just below murder in the eyes of the Swiss authorities. Eberhardt had no concerns about his own establishment, which was the third most prestigious private bank in Switzerland. His worry was the shadow that lay over the life he had built for himself in Geneva. And the fact that the man on his way up to see him knew what it was.

Georges di Marco had joined the Banque Eberhardt just before the Second World War, leaving the prestigious firm of M. M. Warburg and Co. And he had stayed with the bank as its fortunes rose, despite attractive offers to go elsewhere. He was a good banker with the right attributes: boldness, instinct, judgement and knowledge. And because Swiss law required at least two partners to head a private bank, Eberhardt had eventually elevated him to full partner.

Now this.

When di Marco walked in, Eberhardt rose to greet him. He was a small man with a long mournful face and wispy white hair. Eberhardt had often thought he looked more like an undertaker than a banker.

'You know why I am here, Paul . . .' Di Marco took a chair on the other side of the desk.

'A friendly talk, I trust.' Eberhardt forced a smile.

'Paul, I am due to retire soon. I have been with the bank a long time – almost as long as you. I have served it well – '

'You have served it brilliantly.'

'I cannot leave without a clear conscience.'

Eberhardt mustered another bleak smile. 'Georges, we have been through this so often . . .'

'And I have always given in to your wishes.'

'Come now, Georges.' Confronted by the frail little man, Eberhardt felt some of his confidence returning. 'It's not a question of giving in. We are friends; partners. I respect your position. You know that. But we're talking about something that happened years ago. It's dead; forgotten. What you are suggesting would ruin the bank.'

'We would survive.'

'Survive?' Eberhardt said heavily. 'Georges, I have not come this far merely to survive.' He picked up his gold pen from the desk and toyed with it. 'Next year I will chair the International Bankers' Conference in Vienna. I have a reputation to protect.' He leaned forward. 'Dine with me tonight. We will go to the Lion d'Or. Talk it over. Like old times . . .'

'I'm sorry, Paul.' The little man looked at his hands. 'I

have made my decision. I am going to talk to the authorities.'

Eberhardt tried to ignore the uneasiness in the pit of his stomach. A *frisson* of anxiety made the side of his mouth twitch.

'Georges, please, what kind of talk is that among friends?' He paused. 'What you need is a break. Take a few weeks off. Somewhere warm.' He tried to inject some enthusiasm into his voice. 'Friends of mine have a house in Puerto Vallarta. I could call them. You'd like Mexico.'

'You don't understand,' di Marco said. 'What I'm looking for is peace of mind.'

'But what you're suggesting would make everything worse. It would destroy the bank's reputation . . .'

'It would enable me to sleep,' di Marco said quietly. He looked straight at Eberhardt. 'You made a decision forty years ago to say nothing to the Government when enquiries began. I begged you then to speak up. You refused. Out of loyalty I have kept quiet all this time.'

'I appreciate that,' Eberhardt said. 'Even so – '

'We are partners,' the old man said. 'I have some say.'

'My dear Georges,' Eberhardt leaned forward, 'of course you do. But you must think of the consequences.' He shook his head slowly. 'When I started this bank there were 150 private banks in Switzerland. How many are there today? Twenty. Look at the clients we have – Robert Brand, Marie de Boissy, Francine Rochas, Max Schröder. World-famous names. We have survived because we are a fine bank, widely respected. Much of that respect was earned by your good work. You are a great banker, Georges. How can you think of throwing it all away now?'

'I won't change my mind, Paul.' Di Marco got to his feet and began to walk towards the door.

'I ask you again to consider the consequences,' Eberhardt tried as a last shot. 'Our reputations – '

'Our consciences would be clear,' di Marco said. He opened the door and went out.

Watching him go, Eberhardt knew he had lost. He had hoped to prolong the meeting, to reason with di Marco, make him see how foolish it would be to throw away the work of a lifetime. But the old man had already made up his mind. Like the good Catholic he was, he was going to confess his sins – but not to a priest. In doing so he would ruin the reputation Eberhardt had built up over fifty years. He rose wearily and crossed to the window, staring again at the street below. Raindrops were bouncing off the roofs of the cars parked on either side. He stood there for a long time.

Eventually, Eberhardt buzzed his secretary.

'I'm leaving in a moment, Marte. Have the garage bring round my car.'

'Immediately, Monsieur Eberhardt.'

He sat down in his chair again. He had been through this all before with André Leber, one of his account officers who, through diligence and hard work, had graduated to the bank's executive committee before retiring. Leber had been after money, of course. And Eberhardt had been unwise enough to pay him. Ten thousand francs a month for five years. Just thinking about it upset him. It would have gone on and on had he not finally mustered enough courage to end it.

Now he would have to do the same thing with Georges di Marco. Crossing the room he opened his private safe and removed a black address book. Tucked inside was a slip of paper with a name on it. Eberhardt looked at it for a moment before putting it in his jacket pocket and closing the safe.

He would call the man from home, he decided. He prayed he was still available.

Chapter 3

At the same time that Paul Eberhardt was heading for home, Robert Brand's Gulfstream IV was landing in the rain at Paris's Charles de Gaulle Airport.

Staring out of the window at the glistening runway Brand had begun to feel better. That morning, getting out of bed in Geneva, an attack of dizziness had made him sway on his feet. Alarmed, he had waited until noon and called his doctor in New York.

'Look,' Rex Kiernan said, 'it's probably nothing serious. Maybe you got up too quickly. How's your hearing?'

'Fine. Why?'

'Could be an inner ear problem. Want me to recommend someone over there?'

'I haven't the time. Anyway, I'll be home soon.'

'You should slow down,' Kiernan said. 'I keep telling you that. What is it – a year since your attack? All that trauma? Takes time. At our age the body heals more slowly . . .'

In Robert Brand's opinion he had slowed down since his heart attack. At that time Kiernan had advised complete rest.

'This is your life we're talking about,' he said. 'You're sixty-three years old. You've been through a terrible experience. Why don't you use that damn great yacht of yours and take a long cruise, do nothing for a few months?'

Brand had agreed that he would. But the month-long cruise of the Mediterranean with a couple of business friends had only served to increase his sense of loss.

Trapped in a sterile and unhappy relationship for

many years, Robert Brand, a handsome, energetic man, had almost abandoned hope of ever enjoying a romantic and emotional relationship with a woman. Instead he had allowed himself a succession of brief affairs, most of them unsatisfactory. Then one evening, in the bar of the Athenaeum Hotel in London, he had been introduced to Jane Summerwood.

The attraction had been immediate. She had left with friends that evening, but he had managed to track her down. And, in the ensuing weeks, they had fallen in love.

Within three months he had made up his mind. He would ask his wife for a divorce – regardless of the consequences – and marry Jane, a decision hastened by the discovery that she was pregnant. He could still remember her face, flushed with happiness, when he took her down Bond Street to buy the engagement ring.

He had told only one person of his plan, his friend Bobby Koenig. Koenig had encouraged him. 'Go for it,' he said. 'You have one life. Don't waste it.'

A month later Jane was found dead in a London park. The police, with no clues, had put it down to another senseless random murder.

And within weeks Brand, almost immobilized with grief, suffered a heart attack. At first he was forced to rest, but then, ignoring Rex Kiernan's warnings, he had plunged back into work. And, until that morning in Geneva, felt reasonably fit.

According to the latest *Fortune* magazine, he was now the sixth richest man in America. A workaholic, he spent most of his time on the top floor of the thirty-storey black glass building on Madison Avenue where the Brand Corporation was based. There, he put in a fourteen-hour day, overseeing a business empire with interests in oil, shipping, hotels, food processing and drugs.

'The Man Who Has Everything', *Business Week* dubbed him in a piece that was laudatory but glaringly short of facts, for Brand never gave interviews and provided no biography for inquisitive journalists. Even the accompanying photograph was an old one.

Brand knew that success usually came either through an accident of birth or the sheer power of will. But in his case it was both. At twenty-two, with $50 million inherited from his father, he had tasted the heady fruits of power and found them to his liking.

Calculating risks to the nth degree he flew in and out of the world's capitals making deals and increasing his fortune. He took gambles that even the biggest banks balked at. With the Pacific Rim booming, he waited until Indonesia's currency became convertible and then invested heavily, knowing the country was rich in natural resources. Within two years his investment had tripled. He then moved into the Finnish market, which was underpriced, and doubled his money within a year. Then, anticipating the dollar's fall, he invested heavily in other currencies.

Since Jane's death, however, he found himself deriving less and less satisfaction from the mere making of money. He wanted someone, or something, to change his life, to set him on a new course.

Speeding down the neon-lit autoroute into Paris he lay back against the chill leather of the limousine and closed his eyes. He realized he had never felt so lonely in his life.

Georges di Marco awoke suddenly. He glanced at the clock by his bedside. It was 2.30 a.m. He had been asleep less than two hours. Touching his forehead he realized it was damp with perspiration. The dream. It was always the same. Ghosts from the past, jeering, pointing fingers. And money, stacks of it, scattering in the wind as he tried to count it. He sat up, switching on the bedside light. I'm an old man, he thought; I should be sleeping soundly. My conscience should be clear. Instead I awake in dread.

For a moment, as a spasm of nausea assailed him, he

feared he might be sick, and reached for a handkerchief. What's the matter with me? he thought, on the edge of panic. Why is this happening? He took a drink of water from the glass on his bedside table.

I must tell someone, he decided. That man with the Federal Banking Commission – Albert-Jean Cristiani – I will call him. Take him to dinner. Ask his advice. Produce the diary, perhaps. He will know what I should do. He will realize I am an honourable man.

He bunched the pillows beneath his head. Switching off the light he closed his eyes, hoping for sleep.

Chapter 4

Julia Lang had thought herself prepared for the encounter, for the time when she would have to face him again, but now that the moment had arrived, now that he was standing there in the lobby of London's Burlington Hotel talking to one of the guests, she was swept by a feeling of such revulsion that for a moment she feared she might be physically sick.

It had been sixteen years since their last meeting and seeing him again it seemed to her that he had not changed at all. The same aristocratic stance, hands behind his back; the same black hair brushed straight back; the same rimless spectacles. And the same dark grey suiting with a light blue tie.

Her face set, she walked towards him.

He turned, pivoting on one foot. 'Miss Lang. Good morning.' It was as if nothing had ever happened; he might have been greeting her after an absence of a day instead of all those years.

He turned to the elderly American by his side. 'Mr Elliott, this is Julia Lang, Publicity Director for the hotel.'

The American looked approvingly at Julia's shoulder-length blonde hair and deep-set grey eyes. In a lobby full of pale-faced people in heavy winter coats she stood out sharply in her forest-green velvet jacket and black skirt.

He smiled warmly. 'Glad to know you, Miss Lang. I was just telling Mr Moscato here how impressed we are with the Burlington.'

'Will you be staying in London long?'

'Just a week. Mrs Elliott wants to see a couple of shows. I want to get some shirts made. Turnbull and Asser – I like their shirts.'

Julia smiled politely. 'If there's anything I can do while you're here . . .'

'Thank you, Miss Lang. We're being looked after very well.'

Julia excused herself and walked back towards the executive offices. She realized with a pang of dismay that just being near Guido Moscato had made her feel soiled. She had not expected that. Well, she would have to come to terms with his presence. It was that or quit; those were her only choices. But she loved her job. And if she walked out with two years left of her contract, her chances of working for another London hotel were slim.

In her office at the end of the corridor, Emma Carswell, her secretary, was waiting with a sheaf of letters to sign. Seeing Julia's expression, she frowned.

'You're looking glum.'

'I just ran into Moscato,' Julia said.

Emma groaned. 'He's finally here, then.'

'Arrived yesterday.'

'Did he say anything?'

Julia shook her head. 'There was someone with him.'

'You're sure he recognized you?'

'Of course.'

Emma nibbled on her lower lip. 'Of all people for the Sultan to hire.'

'He must think Moscato is a good choice,' Julia said.

'How did he ever hear of him?'

'Everyone knows the Palace on Lake Como.'

Emma put the letters on her desk. 'I still think you should have told the Sultan what happened . . .'

'Emma, the Sultan runs this hotel as a business. People's personal lives don't come into it.'

She moved round to the other side of her desk and sat down in the swivel chair.

'Are you going home to change for the party?' Emma asked.

'I brought a dress with me.'

She had been looking forward to the cocktail party that

evening, planned months earlier to celebrate the fifth anniversary of the Burlington's reopening after its £40-million face-lift. All the hotel's guests had been invited, together with people from London's social and political circles. Julia had even bought herself a black cocktail dress from Louis Féraud, an extravagance she excused by convincing herself it would be useful for other occasions. But with Moscato's arrival at the hotel much of her earlier enthusiasm had waned.

Emma paused before returning to her own office. 'Maybe it won't be so bad,' she said, her face rather implying the opposite.

Julia mustered a faint smile and reached for her pen.

By 7.30 p.m. the Terrace Room was crowded. Guido Moscato stood just inside the wide mirrored doors greeting guests.

Inside the huge room, bars had been set up at either end. In the centre a buffet table was laden with delicacies prepared by the Burlington's chef, Gustave Plesset. In a far corner a willowy young man was playing forties melodies on the piano. Blue-jacketed waiters moved among the guests offering canapés and drinks. The buzz of conversation was very loud.

'Don't just stand there. Mingle.'

Julia turned. Bryan Penrose, the hotel's Director of Sales and Marketing, was standing beside her. She smiled. She and Penrose were friends.

'You're looking spectacular,' he said. 'New dress?'

She nodded.

'I never want to see you in anything else,' he said.

He winked at Julia and moved away. Left alone, Julia scanned the room for familiar faces. Someone waved to her from the bar by the window. She recognized Bobby Koenig, an American screenwriter and frequent visitor to the hotel. He was standing talking to an impressive-looking man with grey hair. Julia moved towards him, nodding to people she knew.

'Julia.' Koenig grasped her hand warmly. 'You know this gentleman, of course. He's paying a fortune for the privilege of staying here. Julia Lang ... Robert Brand.'

She was faintly surprised to see Brand there. Although he was not registered under his own name and had requested no publicity, word had soon filtered down through the hotel grapevine that the secretive American billionaire had checked into the Empire Suite.

'Julia is Publicity Director for the hotel,' Koenig said. 'And one of the most eligible women in London.' He retrieved his champagne glass. 'She's single, she speaks fluent Italian and she once got a love letter from Marcello Mastroianni.' He turned to Julia. 'Am I right?'

'You're impossible,' Julia laughed. 'Revealing all my secrets. Anyway, it was Alain Delon.'

'Close enough,' Koenig said. 'Both actors.'

During this banter Brand had not taken his eyes from her. She felt vaguely disturbed by the intensity of his gaze. His eyes, she decided, were the darkest she had ever seen. He was an impressive figure in his beautifully cut dark suit. Impressive and handsome.

'Bobby tells me you have a new manager,' Brand said.

'That's right.'

'What happened to the last one?'

'He died. He was the one who brought me here. Andrew Lattimer. A lovely man.'

'Where were you before?'

'The Ambassador Royal.'

Was he really interested, Julia wondered, or just making a polite conversation.

'Miss Lang ...'

She turned. Freddy, one of the barmen, was holding out a glass of champagne.

She shook her head. 'No thanks.'

'Oh go on,' Koenig said. 'It's good stuff. Must be costing the hotel a fortune. Mind you, with what Robert's paying for his suite they can afford it.'

It occurred to Julia that Brand probably had no idea

what the suite cost. Such petty details were no doubt handled by his staff. She could not imagine him standing by the cashier's window filling out traveller's cheques.

Julia took the glass and put it down at the edge of the bar.

'You may not know it,' Koenig said, 'but Robert owns two of the best hotels in New York – the Raleigh and the Carlton House. He's always trying to recruit new talent for them. So watch yourself.'

'Tim Perrin's at the Raleigh?' Julia asked.

'He is,' Brand said. 'And doing a fine job. You know him?'

'He was assistant manager here.'

'We're very pleased with him. You must come and see us when you're next in New York.' Brand glanced around the room. 'You put all this together?'

'Most of it.'

'You got a great turnout.'

'Free drink,' Koenig said drily. 'Never fails. Anyway, Julia has magic powers.'

'I believe it,' Brand said. He had hardly taken his eyes from her. How old was he, she wondered. Early sixties? It was hard to tell, he exuded such energy. 'I suppose everyone tells you you could be Grace Kelly's kid sister?'

Julia, never comfortable with compliments, flushed slightly. 'Not everyone,' she said.

'I knew her years ago,' Brand said. 'Wonderful woman. Before Rainier came along, of course. I couldn't compete with a prince.' He looked at Julia intently. 'Any princes in your life, Miss Lang?'

'Mine's on the way, according to my horoscope,' she said, laughing.

'You know what the French say?' Brand chuckled. 'Every woman waits for the right man to come along. In the meantime she gets married.'

'You're sure that's what the French say?' Julia said.

'Positive.'

Was he flirting with her? She hoped so.

28

She needed a morale boost after her encounter with Moscato. And Robert Brand was one of the most charismatic men she had ever met. She felt a surge of attraction towards him and was disconcerted. This was a cocktail party for the hotel. He was a guest; she an employee. She must not forget it.

'If the peasants could see us now,' Koenig said, surveying the room, 'they'd be lining up the tumbrels outside.'

'We don't do this very often,' Julia said.

'Well you should,' Koenig replied. 'Give me the excuse to come here more often. I love this town.'

'Can't think why,' Brand laughed. 'It's freezing cold and it rains all the time.'

'What a masterly summing up of one of the world's great cities,' Koenig said, deadpan.

'Well, it's true,' Brand insisted.

'It's the last truly civilized city on earth,' Koenig said. 'A cornucopia of pleasures. New York is violent and vicious ... Paris is too desperately chic ... Rome is bedlam –'

'So is London,' Brand said. 'I don't understand what you see in the place.'

'I told you. It's civilized.' Julia watched Koenig, amused, as he got into his stride. 'Remember Sam Danovich, the producer? The great Sam? He brought me here thirty years ago to do a rewrite on a script. He loved it here. He said, "There's no other city in the world for the cultivated man." By the time I'd finished the film I agreed with him.'

'On the basis of what?'

'The conversation, for one thing. People here talk about ideas.'

'Give me an example,' Brand said.

'Well, just last night at dinner the woman next to me asked if I thought it was mere coincidence that none of the great philosophers – Spinoza, Kant, Schopenhauer, Nietzsche – was married –'

'You are too easily impressed, my friend,' Brand said.

29

'A little *Reader's Digest* trivia can hardly be categorized as good conversation.'

'Sneer all you like,' Koenig said. 'All I know is that back home in Los Angeles we'd have been asking people which dermatologist they used and how much the new addition to their house cost.'

'Both subjects of considerable interest,' Brand chuckled. 'Particularly if you live in a tiny house and have spots all over your face.'

'I'm being serious,' Koenig protested.

'So am I,' Brand replied. 'I promise you there are plenty of idiots here too.'

'Agreed,' Koenig said. 'But there's one other great thing about London: you don't need an Uzi by your bedside to feel secure.'

Brand turned to Julia. 'Our friend tends to exaggerate, as you've noticed. But then he's a writer.'

'Sorry, Mr Brand. I agree with Bobby. I love London too.'

'New York is much more exciting.'

'A morally bankrupt city,' Koenig said. 'With a social world made up of fools who consider it desirable to associate with people simply because they are rich.'

'Are you suggesting they don't do that in Los Angeles?'

'Only morons,' Koenig said easily. 'Morons and movie stars.'

Brand glanced round the room. 'Good God!' he said. 'Look who's over there. Jack Blacklock. Black Jack himself. We must go and say hello.' He turned to Julia. 'I enjoyed talking with you, Miss Lang. Perhaps we'll meet again.'

'I hope so,' Julia said.

Koenig smiled and squeezed her arm. Watching them leave, Julia felt curiously deflated. Brand had such a powerful presence it was as if she had been left in a vacuum.

Looking round she saw Moscato approaching. She felt a sense of dread.

'I saw you talking with Mr Brand,' he said. 'Does he seem happy with the hotel?'

'Perfectly.' She turned abruptly. 'If you'll excuse me, I have to talk to the reporters outside. They'll need some details of the party.'

She wove her way through the crowded room towards the door, taking a last glance at Brand and Koenig, who were deep in conversation with a tall, flamboyant-looking man wearing an eye-patch. They did not look her way.

The rain had eased as Julia left the hotel. Only a few reporters still stood around, hunched in their raincoats. Two of them nodded to her.

As she walked down the steps, she called goodnight to Henry Wilson, the uniformed night doorman.

'Good night, Miss Lang.'

Henry liked Julia. She always had a cheery word for him – unlike some of the other hotel executives. After six years he knew quite a lot about Julia Lang. He knew she was thirty-three and unmarried. He knew how conscientious she was; how late she often worked. He liked the way she held herself, the way she dressed. She was, in his book, a very stylish lady. He had even met her boyfriend, Michael Chadwick. Nice enough, but not good enough for her.

Tonight she seemed preoccupied. Working too hard, he decided, stepping forward to open the taxi door for a late arrival.

At 11 p.m. on Friday in Geneva, Paul Eberhardt picked up the telephone in his study and dialled the number of Georges di Marco.

'Georges, I'm sorry to worry you so late but there are a couple of papers here that require your signature.'

'My signature?' The old man's voice was vague. He sounded as if he'd been dozing. 'Surely it can wait until Monday?'

'I'm afraid not. I must express them to New York tomorrow. Don't distress yourself. I'll send someone round with them.'

'It's very late, Paul. I was about to retire . . .'

'I realize that, but this is really urgent. I wouldn't dream of bothering you otherwise. I'd bring them round myself but I am still at the office.'

'What papers are they, Paul? I don't recall – '

'The de Boissy estate.'

'I thought that was all settled.'

'There are a couple of loose ends.'

'Very well. Send them round.'

'The messenger will wait and bring them back.' Eberhardt paused. 'You haven't had second thoughts, I suppose?'

'Second thoughts?'

'Our discussion the other morning.'

'No, Paul. No second thoughts.'

'Then you must do what you think is right, Georges. We must all do what we think is right.'

When the buzzer sounded di Marco pressed the button to open the street entrance and unlocked the door of his apartment. He went into the bedroom to remove his comfortable slippers and put on more formal black shoes.

When he returned to the living room he was surprised to find the messenger standing by the open door with a large envelope in his hand.

'I did knock,' the man said.

'That's all right. Come in, come in. I just have to sign a couple of papers.'

He took the envelope from the messenger, a burly young man, and went over to the desk by the window. Inside the envelope were two blank sheets of paper. He turned, bewildered.

'There's nothing – '

Before he could finish his arms were pinioned behind

him and tape was wrapped around his wrists. He let out a whimper of fear.

'What are you doing?'

Before he could say more another tape was pasted over his mouth.

Eyes wide with fright, the old man was hustled out of his apartment. The door slammed behind him.

The morning following the cocktail party Julia had arranged to have breakfast with an American travel writer and take him on a tour of the hotel. When she finally got to her office Emma was waiting for her.

'I hear it was a great success,' she said. 'Everyone was there.'

'Not everyone,' Julia said. 'The Foreign Secretary didn't make it.'

'Oh pooh,' Emma sniffed. 'Who cares about him? Robert Brand was there, wasn't he? Imagine him turning up.'

'Life is full of surprises.'

There was a pile of messages on Julia's desk, together with that morning's mail.

'Anything important?' She flicked through the notes.

Emma held up a letter. 'There's an invitation to speak on public relations at the annual conference of the International Travel and Tourism Research Association in Acapulco. Expenses paid.'

'Acapulco,' Julia sighed. 'Wouldn't I just love to do that. But how can I get away now?'

'Tell Moscato to get stuffed and go.'

'Don't tempt me.'

Emma chuckled. 'So what shall I tell them?'

'When is the conference?'

Emma consulted the letter. 'A couple of months' time.'

'Don't reply just yet. Who knows what's going to happen?'

Emma turned to go. 'Oh, I almost forgot. There's a

bottle of champagne in your bottom drawer. Came an hour ago.'

After Emma returned to her own office Julia opened the drawer. Wrapped in Cellophane was a bottle of Krug '81. *Thank you for inviting me*, the card read. It was signed: *Robert Brand.*

Chapter 5

Julia Lang stood by the bedroom window of her flat, sipping a glass of white wine, looking out over the darkened town. It was a cold, wet night, the sky a seemingly endless panoply of grey. The lights of the pub on the corner were hazy in the light mist. Across the street she could see directly into another flat. In one brightly lit room a man and a woman were sitting in armchairs, reading. They looked comfortable, settled, at ease. She felt a momentary pang of envy. She was, she knew, ambivalent about marriage. Did she really want it? Would she trade her independence for a shared life with a man? When she had first come to London from Birmingham her one aim had been to have a career of her own. To abandon that plan now, to marry and have children – was she ready for that?

She knew she really liked Michael Chadwick, the man with whom she had been involved for a year. He was a design artist of great flair, who had already won most of the prestigious prizes available for his work. He was bright and cheerful and witty. She liked him a lot. She just didn't know if she wanted to marry him. He had already asked her twice.

She had many friends and was much in demand socially, but she did need a man in her life. Someone to wake up with, to touch during the dark hours, to watch shaving in the morning, to share breakfast with. Someone to talk to. Particularly at a time like this.

The re-emergence of Guido Moscato into her life had shocked her. She had known for only a month that he was coming. The Sultan of Malacca, who owned the hotel, had kept the news quiet until negotiations were complete. During those four weeks she had been plagued by indecision. Should she stay or should she go? And, if she walked out on her contract, should she give the Sultan, whom she liked, her reasons?

Sixteen years earlier, when she had staggered up from the Italian lakeside, bruised and battered, almost unable to see, she had vowed that one day she would settle the score with Moscato. Picked up by two English tourists, she had been taken to the small hospital at Bellagio where a doctor operated to save her right eye. Ten days later she had flown to London. Over the years the hatred she had developed for the man who had raped her had gradually abated. The idea that she might one day see him again had never occurred to her.

Now here he was, the new Managing Director of the Burlington. All her loathing for the man had come back. And, to her surprise, her resolve to somehow get even.

At the hotel only Emma Carswell knew what Moscato had done to her. Emma had become a friend and confidante as well as an efficient colleague. When Julia had arrived at the Burlington six years earlier she had been utterly dismayed at the sight of the secretary she had inherited from the previous Publicity Director. A large, raw-boned woman in her mid-fifties with grey hair and a rock-like jaw, Emma Carswell looked formidable indeed. But within a month she had proved invaluable. She did everything – kept Julia's appointment book, dealt with the mail, told white lies on the telephone when necessary, remembered birthdays, made endless cups of tea and quietly handled all the innumerable office tasks that bored Julia to distraction. Over the years they had developed a deep affection for each other and it was to Emma that Julia had confided her fears when she learned of Moscato's appointment.

Emma had been outraged. 'You poor dear,' she said, hugging Julia. 'What a contemptible bastard. Why didn't you report it?'

'It was different then,' Julia said. 'Attitudes have

36

changed a lot, thank God. Anyway, I doubt the Italian police would have taken the word of an English visitor against that of a respected hotelier. I just wanted to get out of there; to forget about it.'

'You think he knows you're here?'

Julia was sure. From the day he signed the contract Moscato would have had a complete list of Burlington Hotel employees before him. Discovering that Julia Lang was there apparently had not worried him. Perhaps he had reasoned he could get rid of her easily enough. A publicity director, however good, did not rate highly in the scheme of things. He would not know that she had a contract guaranteed by the Sultan himself with whom she had a warm and friendly relationship.

She loved the hotel and had made it her life. But her work would bring her into contact with Moscato on an almost daily basis. Could she stomach that? Should she?

Finishing her wine she got into bed. The sheets were cold through the satin of her nightdress. Rosie, her cleaning lady, had changed them that day. Shivering a little she curled up, trying to keep warm. Just before she fell asleep she thought about Robert Brand.

Chapter 6

Every Wednesday for almost twenty years Paul
Eberhardt had lunched with his lawyer, Maître Claude
Bertrand, at the Club des Terrasses, the private Geneva
club belonging to the *Groupement*.

Over their favourite dish, *friture de perchettes* – fried
fillets of small lake perch – and with a bottle of wine
between them, they would bring each other up to date
with events. Eberhardt considered Bertrand his best
friend as well as his trusted lawyer. On this occasion, he
decided, it would be prudent to bring up the subject of
di Marco.

'I am concerned about him,' he said. 'He's disappeared.
He has not been at the bank this week.'

'He may be ill. You've called his home?'

'Of course. He's gone.'

Bertrand frowned. 'Gone where?'

'I don't know. He called me last Friday night, late.
Something about a family emergency . . .'

'I didn't know he had a family.'

'A sister. In Zurich. I've called there. She hasn't seen
him in months.'

'How very odd.'

'Do you think I should report it to the police?'

Bertrand reached for another roll. 'I should wait until
the end of the week. You don't want to look foolish, Paul.
He's probably just taken a few days off.'

'Without telling me?'

'Old men do strange things.' Bertrand chuckled. 'Perhaps he's gone off with some woman?'

'Be serious, Claude. He's seventy-nine years old.'

'What of it? You're seventy-seven and still quite

38

vigorous.' Bertrand smiled slyly. 'How are things at Madame Valdoni's, by the way?'

Eberhardt glanced around the club. 'Keep your voice down, for God's sake.'

Bertrand poured them both another glass of wine. 'Take my advice. Wait until Friday.'

'If you think so,' Eberhardt said.

Around 8 a.m. on a chill Monday morning, a small boy throwing stones at what he took to be a log floating in Lake Geneva was horrified to discover that it was a man's body. When the police arrived from nearby Montreux they found sodden cards on the corpse identifying him as Georges di Marco, Vice President of the Banque Eberhardt in Geneva.

Contacted by the police, Paul Eberhardt drove immediately to the morgue at Montreux to identify the banker whose body lay on a gurney between two other cadavers. Eberhardt appeared stricken at the sight and for a moment it was thought he might break down. After a brandy in the police lieutenant's office he recovered. Could he think of any reason why di Marco should have drowned himself, he was asked. He could not. Di Marco had been due to retire shortly and was looking forward to it. When last seen at the bank he had been in good spirits.

'We were great friends,' Eberhardt added. 'He was with me almost from the beginning. I cannot imagine what drove him to do this terrible thing.'

The lieutenant nodded understandingly. You could never know, he reassured Eberhardt, what went on in people's minds.

At the funeral in Geneva two days later, attended by both Eberhardt and Claude Bertrand, there was only one relative of di Marco's present among the mourners – his distraught elderly sister. Eberhardt, his arm around her frail shoulders, told her he had arranged for her to stay on for a few days at the Richemond Hotel. All the bills were to go to him.

Chapter 7

Julia had just finished work on the hotel's weekly newsletter when Emma buzzed her.

'There's a Jill Bannister on the line,' she said. 'Says she's Robert Brand's personal assistant. That's a secretary who earns more money than I do.'

Surprised, Julia hesitated before replying. 'Put her through.'

'Miss Lang?' Jill Bannister's voice was English upper class but friendly. 'Mr Brand was wondering if you were free at lunchtime today?'

Julia felt a small rush of anticipation. 'I could possibly be.'

'Good. Can you meet him at the Delevingne Gallery in Duke Street, St James's? Say around noon?'

'I could make it by 12.30,' Julia said.

'That will be fine.'

Julia hung up. She was puzzled. Was he inviting her to an art show or lunch? For a moment she toyed with the fantasy that he wanted to buy the Burlington and was seeking her advice. She knew the first thing she would tell him: get rid of Guido Moscato.

She got up and went to the mirror and inspected herself. Not bad, she decided, glad she had opted that morning for her plum-coloured Escada jacket with the big gilt buttons and a black skirt. With her black boots it was an attractive outfit.

She went back to her desk and buzzed Emma. 'I'm going to look at some art with Robert Brand,' she said. 'Impressed?'

Emma chuckled. 'I'm trying not to be,' she said. 'But yes, I am. Very.'

* * *

The Delevingne Gallery was halfway down Duke Street next to a wine bar. When Julia arrived Brand was standing in front of an ornately framed painting of Venice's Grand Canal, talking to a young man in a dark business suit. He broke off as she came through the door, greeting her quite formally. 'Ah,' he said, 'here you are. Miss Lang, this is Nigel Burley.'

The young man extended a limp hand.

'Well, what do you think?' Brand demanded, nodding towards the painting.

'Stunning,' Julia said. 'Canaletto – right?'

'So Mr Burley believes,' Brand said.

Julia peered more closely at the canvas. 'It's not signed.'

Burley cleared his throat. 'Many of his works are not.'

Julia studied the painting again.

'There's been a lot of interest,' the dealer said. 'It's a beautiful work.'

'But not Canaletto, I think,' Brand said. 'More likely one of his imitators.'

'Imitators?' Julia said. 'How many did he have?'

'Many.' Brand stood back from the painting. 'He was widely imitated both in Venice and during his stay here. He was in Britain for almost ten years, you know, painting country houses, London views. People like Michael Marieschi, Antonio Visentini, Antonio Joli – their work often passes under Canaletto's name. I fancy this is Marieschi.'

'How do people know?' Julia was intrigued.

'They don't,' Brand said. 'Unless they are well informed.' He turned to Nigel Burley, who was impassively fingering the carnation in his buttonhole. 'How much are you asking?'

'Two million.'

'Pounds?'

'Yes.'

'A lot of money.'

'Worth it, we feel.'

'Bring it down a little,' Brand said. 'I might be interested. Though I doubt it's Canaletto.'

'I'll have to talk to Mr Delevingne,' the young man said. 'He's in France at the moment.'

'Do that,' Brand said. He took a card from his wallet. 'You can reach me at the Burlington for the next few days. After that at my New York office.'

'I'll let you know by Friday,' Burley said, accompanying them to the door.

Brand and Julia walked slowly up the street, stopping now and again to look at paintings in other galleries before turning into Jermyn Street.

'I trust you're hungry?' Brand asked. 'Best fish in London right here.' Without waiting for a reply he took her arm and steered her through the door of one of London's most expensive restaurants. The staff seemed to know him. The manager made a great deal of fuss, ushering them to a booth in one corner. As soon as the menus were brought, Brand put on spectacles. They seemed, if anything, to enhance his attractiveness. They ordered – grilled sole for Brand; fried plaice for Julia, with chablis to accompany the meal.

Brand sat forward, his hands together. 'You like that Canaletto?'

'But you said – '

'It's a Canaletto all right. Does no harm to throw people like Delevingne off balance, though. They think they know everything.'

Julia laughed. 'Shame on you.'

Brand laughed too.

'That other artist . . .'

'Marieschi? He's real enough. Imitated Canaletto a lot. But Canaletto was a superb draughtsman. His work stands out from the others.'

'You seem to know a lot about him?'

'I bought my first Canaletto when I was thirty. Began reading up on him – ' He broke off. 'This is a private conversation, you understand.'

'Of course.'

'It's just ... well, I realize you deal with the press a lot.'

'Only in matters relating to the hotel.' She smiled. 'Don't concern yourself.'

'Good. I won't.'

Brand seemed to relax when the waiter brought the wine. He sampled it and nodded. The waiter filled their glasses and departed. Brand shrugged. 'The truth is I don't like talking about my collection. Even if you love art, which I do, there's no way you can say: I have a Renoir, a Picasso and a Gauguin, without sounding crass.'

Julia nodded.

'I have one Rembrandt. I think it's genuine. One of my friends swears it's a Fabritius.'

'I don't know him.'

'One of Rembrandt's pupils. Rembrandt sometimes signed his students' paintings to get a better price for them.'

'Then you can't tell?'

'It's difficult. The Rembrandt Research Group, subsidized by the Dutch Government, examined ninety of his works and claimed that half were not genuine. Which means a lot of galleries are out millions of dollars.'

Julia, who had never spent more than £100 on a painting in her life and considered that extravagant, shook her head. 'So there are no real experts?'

'No.'

The fish arrived. Brand turned to her. 'When was your mother born?'

'In 1920.'

'Then your grandmother was probably born before the turn of the century. Do you realize if she'd had a little money to spend how many great artists were alive at that time? Cézanne, Monet, Renoir. Utrillo was still alive in the 1950s. Of course people here weren't even aware

43

of avant-garde French paintings until about 1910. Until then English taste rarely went further than paintings of Highland stags.'

'I should have had a wealthy grandmother,' Julia said.

Brand busied himself dissecting his fish. 'They're still alive, your parents?'

'They were killed in an air crash six years ago.'

'Ah.' She waited for the usual solicitous remark. He didn't make it. 'You're not a Londoner?'

'I was born in Birmingham.'

'I've been there,' Brand said.

'It used to be a fine old Victorian town,' Julia said. 'Then the planners went to work. Now it's a mess.'

Brand picked up his wine glass and swirled the liquid around. He looked at her, his black eyes boring into hers. 'Is it true what Bobby Koenig said? Are you one of the most eligible women in London?'

'A slight exaggeration.'

'But you're not married?'

'No.'

'Involved, I'm sure?'

Uncomfortable at the questioning she hesitated before replying. 'I am involved,' she said, more sharply than she intended. She met his gaze challengingly. 'What about you? Where is your wife, Mr Brand?'

'Robert, please. My wife is in Mexico. We have a place there.'

'She doesn't travel with you?'

'Rarely. She dislikes hotels. She prefers to stay in Acapulco.'

'I've been invited to speak there. At a conference.'

'You've never been?'

'No.'

'You must go. It's quite spectacular.'

'But you prefer New York?'

'My company is headquartered in Manhattan. And I have a house there.'

'Where do you keep your art? In Acapulco?'

44

'Can't keep valuable paintings there. Too much heat and humidity.'

'It sounds as if you don't see much of your wife?'

'No,' Brand said. He seemed relieved when the waiter came to take their plates.

Over coffee they talked about London.

'I don't really dislike it as much as I make out,' Brand said. 'I just like to provoke Bobby Koenig. He gets so mad at me.' He chuckled. 'Actually I think it's a fine city.'

'Does Bobby always take the bait?'

'Swallows it whole,' Brand smiled.

'I love this city,' Julia said, 'always have.'

'You live in town?'

'Near Regent's Park,' she said. 'One of those old mansion flats.'

'I know the area,' he said. 'Last year I rented a house overlooking the park.'

'Then you must know London well?'

'Fairly well. I'm here a lot.'

'Then I hope we'll see you back at the Burlington.'

'Have no doubts about that, Julia,' Brand said.

She held his gaze for a moment, then glanced at her watch.

'Ye gods,' she said. 'Look at the time. I've got to be getting back.' She jumped to her feet.

'That's too bad,' Brand said. 'I was enjoying myself.'

'So was I,' Julia said. 'And I learned a lot about Canaletto.'

He stood up. 'I think I'll stay for a second cup. Will you be all right?'

'Of course.'

As she walked along Jermyn Street to look for a taxi Julia's thoughts were jumbled. Clearly the conversation in the gallery had been designed to impress her. He was showing off. Though she had to admit that listening to a man contemplating buying a work of art for two million pounds was a lot more fascinating than seeing someone dithering over a twenty-pound sweater at Marks and Spencer.

But what was the point? Was he hoping to recruit her for one of his New York hotels? If so it was an odd way to go about it. If he was interested in her personally – and when a man wanted to know if you were involved he was usually asking: How about me? – then he was out of luck. She had no intention of getting involved with a married man, even an attractive one like Robert Brand. She had to admit he was charismatic. He positively exuded sex appeal. Dammit, she thought, why are those sort of men always married?

She looked at her watch again. It was a quarter past three. She was very late. She stood in the centre of St James's Street on a traffic island, praying for a taxi.

It was 3.45 by the time Julia got back to the hotel. As she walked into her office a woman rose to greet her.

'Good afternoon, Miss Lang. I'm Chantal Ricci.'

'Yes?' Julia was annoyed. Visitors were never allowed into her office without an appointment, but Emma was not at her desk. 'What can I do for you?'

Dark-haired and quite astonishingly pretty, Chantal Ricci was wearing a fitted double-breasted blue jacket and straight navy skirt. She looked chic and elegant.

'I just wanted to introduce myself.' She had a very slight accent. 'I'm starting work on the new magazine for the Burlington.'

'What magazine?'

'Mr Moscato didn't tell you?'

'I know nothing about it.'

'I believe the final decision was only made this week. The Sultan is excited at the idea.'

'Is he now?' Julia tried to cover her irritation by glancing through the pile of messages on her desk.

'I'm surprised we haven't met before,' Chantal said. 'I was deputy editor of *Trends* for three years.'

'What will you be doing on the magazine?'

46

'Editing it.' Chantal got to her feet. 'Anyway, I just wanted to say hello. I'm sure we'll be seeing a lot of each other. I have an office here in the executive corridor.'

'I didn't know one was free.'

'I believe it belonged to the Director of Sales and Marketing.'

Julia frowned. 'Bryan Penrose?'

'He's moved down the corridor. It's more convenient, apparently.'

Julia stared at the young woman standing before her. Twenty-five, tops, she decided. Stunning-looking. Obviously very sure of herself. You didn't need great talent or ability to produce a hotel magazine – many hotels, particularly those in Italy and Asia, had them – but you needed some. She felt vaguely upset. Producing a magazine for the Burlington would not necessarily have come under her aegis but she felt she should have been consulted.

'How often is this magazine to be produced?'

'Twice a year.'

'That won't keep you very busy.'

'Mr Moscato has other things for me to do as well,' she said. 'He feels there are several areas where I can be of help.'

'You're Italian?'

'Milanese.'

'Chantal is not an Italian name?'

'My mother was French; my father Italian.'

'I see.' You, Julia decided, are someone I must watch out for.

'Well.' Chantal flashed Julia a brilliant smile. She had a wide mouth; her teeth were regular and perfect. 'It was nice meeting you.'

After she'd gone Emma came in with a cup of tea.

'I'm sorry,' she said. 'She was in your office when I got back. She said it would be all right.'

Julia nodded. 'Her name's Chantal Ricci. She's going to bring out a magazine for us.'

47

'Whose idea was that?'

'Moscato's, I suppose. I knew nothing about it.'

Emma put down the cup. 'And how was the art show?'

'Interesting.'

'You should get out of the office more,' Emma said meaningfully. 'Puts a bit of colour in your cheeks.'

The nightmare recurred ...

'I would like you to consider staying on with us,' Moscato said. 'You're the best receptionist we've ever had.'

'But the other girl? I'm only a temporary replacement.'

'We'll find another spot for her.'

Julia had never felt happier. She loved Bellagio, the town on Lake Como where Franz Liszt had once spent a year, which had once played host to Stendhal and Mark Twain. And she loved the Palace Hotel. People there had been so kind she had now decided to make hotels her career. But she had promised her parents to go back to England after six months. And already she was a little homesick. Two weeks after their talk, when Moscato suggested dinner with his wife at *Il Cielo* on the lakeside, she was flattered and excited. Here was a sophisticated Italian hotel manager taking a personal interest in her. What luck!

That night she put on her prettiest dress and shoes. Flushed and excited she arrived at the restaurant early. Moscato was already there – alone. His wife, he explained, was not feeling well. The dinner was a great success, with Moscato being attentive and encouraging. Afterwards they walked back along the lakeside, admiring the full moon shimmering on the water.

At one point she stumbled and Moscato took her arm. And then it began. Turning, he kissed her so hard he bruised her lips. Startled, she pulled away. 'Signor Moscato, please don't.'

Then Moscato pushed her roughly to the ground, ripping off her dress, tearing at her pants. She screamed

48

but the scream stifled in her throat and a great stab of pain consumed her body as he thrust into her. 'Please,' she begged. 'Please. No.' She clawed at his face as he pounded into her but it was useless. The more she fought the more excited he became.

Then he began hitting her, slamming his right fist into her face, grunting like an animal as each blow went home. She felt blood in her eye and a tear in her cheek, and the taste of blood in her mouth.

Finally it was over and Moscato staggered to his feet. 'You asked for it,' he panted. 'Leading me on like that. You asked for it.' He stood looking down at her, breathing hard. 'Go and clean yourself up,' he said. With a final glance at her he turned and headed back towards the hotel leaving her lying there, bleeding and bruised, whimpering softly, almost senseless . . .

Chapter 8

Hunched over a cup of coffee, Albert-Jean Cristiani sat by the window of a small bar in the rue du Rhône watching passers-by as they walked along the fashionable Geneva shopping street. He was feeling despondent. It had been a difficult week so far. He had a deep-seated suspicion it was not going to get any better.

He sighed and raised his hand to order another cup. It was after 11 a.m. but he saw no point in hurrying. The investigation on which he was engaged was going nowhere. He might as well enjoy a few more minutes of people-watching. And contemplate his forthcoming retirement at the age of fifty-five. Just that week he had picked out a small office for himself on the corner of the Quai Wilson where he planned to set up as a private investigator.

For twenty years Cristiani, a short, stocky man with thinning hair, had been one of four special investigators for the Swiss Federal Banking Commission. When he had first joined the Commission it had been a puny thing with a staff of five. Now it was fully staffed with bright young lawyers and accountants eager to gain a few years' Government experience before branching out on their own. And it had clout. It was now a criminal offence to mislead or lie to the Commission. At the slightest hint of impropriety it invoked the clause in the 1971 Banking Law, which stated that the director of a bank must behave 'irreproachably'. Failure to do so could result in the Commission withdrawing a bank's licence.

Cristiani's main function was to monitor 'irregularities' in the bank system and report them back to his head office in Bern. Since he joined the Commission, there had been plenty of 'irregularities'. So many, in fact, that Cristiani had not been surprised when his irate boss finally called him in for a meeting.

'I've just had a call from the Director,' Commissioner Pierre Bonnet said grimly. 'He is incensed. The world now sees us as a place where any Mafia boss or drug dealer can hide his money. We've got to put a stop to it. We must restore Switzerland's reputation as a law-abiding country.'

Sitting opposite his portly boss, Cristiani had nodded dutifully. Was the Commissioner kidding himself? A law-abiding country? Bonnet knew as well as he did that for years the Bern Government had engaged in secret surveillance and eavesdropping on its own citizens. And that somewhere in the capital there were almost 600,000 dossiers on Swiss citizens tucked away.

But this was serious. This was about *banks*. The life-blood of Switzerland. He had not been surprised when, next day, Bonnet issued a strongly worded statement to every bank in Switzerland. It said, in effect: *No more scandals*.

He knew the edict would be ignored. It would have no more effect than the booklet the Big Three banks had issued some years before. In *The Truth About Swiss Banking*, they stated: 'The purpose of Swiss banking secrecy is to protect the innocent, not shield the guilty.' He was told the booklet produced guffaws of laughter in Washington where officials knew there wasn't a bank in Switzerland that would turn away a man with a suitcase stuffed with $100 bills.

Sometimes Cristiani wondered where all the cash came from. Drug money, of course, made up much of it. That, and money skimmed from the casino tables of Las Vegas and Atlantic City. But it was surprising to him just how many ordinary people now passed through Geneva's Cointrin Airport with tote bags stuffed with notes.

But it was not another money scandal that occupied Cristiani's thoughts as he sipped his second cup of coffee.

51

It was the death of Georges di Marco. There was something suspicious about it.

Despite his age, the man had been in apparent good health. He held an important position in one of Geneva's most respected banks. He was popular with his peers and friends. He had a pleasant apartment off the rue des Granges. He seemed financially well off. Why, then, would he have decided to end his life? It made no sense.

The question of the coat bothered Cristiani. When found, di Marco had been wearing only a suit. Cristiani could not imagine the elderly banker walking a mile to the lakeside on a freezing winter's night without an overcoat.

There was something else. He had no key in his pocket. Had he just walked out without locking the door? That, too, seemed unlikely.

Inspector Thibault, the police officer investigating the banker's death, had dismissed any suggestion of foul play by pointing out that there were no signs of a struggle. Cristiani had been astonished at such naivety. Only two years before there had been a report of a drowning in Lake Garda, ostensibly due to suicide. Later a man had confessed to the murder. The victim's hands and legs had been bound with tape, he explained, before being lowered over the side of a boat with a rope around his waist. When he was dead the man's body had been pulled back to the surface and the tapes and rope removed. No signs of struggle. An apparent suicide.

Cristiani had met di Marco several times, most recently when they had dined at the same restaurant. They had talked briefly and di Marco had asked to see him again. He had seemed agitated. Cristiani told him to call. A few days later, sounding nervous, di Marco had telephoned to set up a dinner appointment. Before they could meet again he was found dead.

When Cristiani telephoned Paul Eberhardt to discuss di Marco's death and voice his concern about the coat and the key, the banker had seemed equally baffled.

'I've thought about that myself,' Eberhardt said. 'I simply don't understand it. It's a complete mystery. Why did he do this terrible thing?'

Cristiani listened politely. Although he knew Eberhardt only slightly, the elderly banker had intrigued him ever since a rumour had surfaced a few years earlier that he was being blackmailed. The rumour stemmed from the fact that he had continued paying a former officer of his bank, a man named André Leber, 10,000 francs a month even though he had left the bank several years earlier. Cristiani's enquiries had come to nothing and in the end he had concluded that if the banker wanted to support a former colleague that was his affair. Leber had later died in a car accident.

Frustrated, Cristiani made his way homeward, holding his umbrella with both hands against the gusting rain. Perhaps the death of di Marco had been a genuine suicide, he decided. That was what the police and the coroner had determined. But if it wasn't, was it something to do with Paul Eberhardt?

Paul Eberhardt had spent an anxious morning. The phone call from Cristiani had worried him. Inspector Thibault was the man handling the di Marco investigation – yet it was Cristiani who was asking all these questions: What had di Marco's mood been when he left the bank that night? Was he depressed? How long was it before he was due to retire? Had anything happened at the bank to upset him?

Eberhardt felt he had answered the questions well, but he could tell Cristiani was not satisfied. He had brought up the question of di Marco's overcoat and the fact that he had left his apartment unlocked.

Eberhardt had confessed himself baffled.

What had surprised him was to learn that di Marco had invited Cristiani to dinner in Lausanne – far enough away to ensure privacy. So di Marco was going to tell his story just as he had threatened. And to an investigator of the Federal Banking Commission. Thank God he had acted in time to stop that.

He reached for his coffee. It had grown cold. He rang for Marte to bring him a fresh cup. He was safe. He was convinced of that. There was nothing to worry about. Nothing at all.

Chapter 9

Michael Chadwick had booked a table at the Connaught Grill, a place he often entertained clients and where, Julia knew, he would charge their dinner to expenses. He was in a buoyant mood.

'So how's the new manager?' he asked after they had ordered.

'I've hardly seen him,' Julia said. 'He's been locked away in his office.' When the news of Moscato's appointment to the Burlington had first broken she had considered telling Michael about what had happened in Italy. In the end she had said nothing.

'It won't affect you, will it?'

'I hope not.'

He turned to her, a smile on his face.

'If it does I've got the solution.'

'What's that?'

'Come with me to Australia. We'll get married there.'

'*What?*'

'I've been offered a job with Myers-Barswell.'

Julia took his hand. 'Michael, that's wonderful.' Myers-Barswell, she knew, was one of the top advertising agencies in Australia. It was the kind of firm Michael had dreamed of joining. 'When did all this happen?'

'Yesterday. I had a long talk with them. They know my work well. And it's big money. So this is a celebration.'

Julia leaned over and kissed him on the cheek. 'I'm thrilled for you,' she said. She felt like a hypocrite as she said it. Their relationship had dragged on because she had not had the heart to end it. Now, out of nowhere, the opportunity had presented itself.

'So what do you think?'

'It's wonderful news . . .'

'I mean, shall we do it?'

'Michael.' She laughed nervously. 'I can't just walk out on my contract.'

'Why not?'

'They'd sue me.'

'Come on, Julia. The Sultan adores you. Tell him what's happened. He'll understand.'

'You know how I feel about you,' she said. It sounded weak and she knew it. 'It's just – '

'You don't want to marry me,' he said flatly.

'It's not that. It's just – well, marriage scares me. Not marriage to you; marriage to anyone.'

'So how long are you going to wait?' he demanded. 'You're thirty-three years old. You say you'd like a child. You can't put it off forever.'

'Please, Michael, let's not argue.' She tried to inject a little enthusiasm into her voice. 'Everyone says Sydney is terrific. You'll have a wonderful time . . .'

'Don't push so hard,' Michael said. 'I get the message.' He looked up sharply as the wine waiter came over with a bottle of champagne in an ice bucket. 'That's not for us.'

'Compliments of the gentleman over there.' The wine waiter inclined his head and proceeded to uncork the bottle. Both of them looked across the crowded Grill. In the far window alcove Robert Brand was sitting with a handsome, well-dressed woman who looked to be in her early forties. Brand raised his glass to them.

'Who's that?' Michael demanded stiffly.

Julia felt her face flush. She felt suddenly embarrassed. Why? She had nothing to feel guilty about.

'Robert Brand,' she said. As the waiter poured the champagne she raised her glass. 'Go on,' she muttered. Michael raised his glass with a bleak smile.

'How do you know him?' he asked.

'He's at the hotel. I met him at the cocktail party the other night.'

'Who's the woman with him?'

'No idea.'

'You must have made quite an impression,' Michael said. 'This is good champagne.' He picked up the bottle from the ice bucket and inspected it.

'For God's sake,' Julia said.

'Cristal. You *did* make an impression.' He let the bottle slide noisily back into the ice bucket.

Julia realized Brand must have been sitting there for some time. She felt oddly discomfited. They ate their food in silence. Every time she looked up she was conscious of Brand's eyes.

'Look,' she said finally, 'I have a bit of a headache. Do you mind if we have an early evening? I've got a heavy day tomorrow.'

'Fine with me,' Michael said grimly. He raised his hand for the bill.

On the way out they stopped by Brand's table to thank him.

'This is Jill Bannister, my personal assistant,' he said. 'I believe you've talked.' The good-looking woman nodded. Brand looked at Julia. 'Should you be here at the Connaught? Won't that be construed as consorting with the enemy?'

'I didn't expect to be spotted,' Julia said. 'Anyway, it's a good idea to check out the opposition.' She smiled faintly, aware of Michael sulking by her side. She tried to bring him into the conversation. 'This is a favourite place of Michael's.'

'Well, I trust your dinner was as good as ours,' Brand said.

'It was.' Michael's tone was stony.

They talked for a moment longer and then went out into Carlos Place. In silence Michael drove Julia back to her flat. At the door he turned to her. 'You met him just once?'

'I told you. At the hotel.'

'He's interested in you,' Michael said. 'Doesn't try to hide it, either.'

He gave her a brief peck on the cheek before driving off.

When she stepped out of the lift she saw the white box propped against her front door. Inside were two dozen long-stemmed red roses. The card read: *Long-stemmed roses for a long-legged lady. R. B.*

Julia took them into the kitchen, put them in a vase and placed them on the hall table. If Michael had come up with me he'd have seen the box, she thought. That's all the evening needed.

But how had Robert Brand found out her address? Careful, Julia, she told herself. Careful . . .

Two days later Emma walked into Julia's office with an early edition of the *Evening Standard*.

'There'll be hell to pay over this,' she said.

'What are you talking about?'

'The Palace requested no publicity when the Queen lunched here yesterday.'

'That's normal.'

'There's a picture here on page three.'

'*What?*'

'Look for yourself.'

Emma put the paper in front of Julia, open at a picture of the Queen and a man identified in the caption as Sir Miles Cartland leaving the hotel. In the background stood Moscato. The headline ran: *Cosy lunch for two at the Burlington.* The story accompanying the picture listed what the Queen had eaten for lunch and noted: *Afterwards Her Majesty sent her compliments to the chef, Gustave Plesset.*

Julia groaned. 'How did they get this? Moscato must have seen the photographer.'

'Of course.'

'You think *he* did this?'

'Or his protegée, Miss Ricci?'

'Whoever it was is a damn fool,' Julia said. 'The Queen won't come here again.'

'Maybe Mr Moscato thinks it was worth it,' Emma said. 'Something for his scrapbook.'

While Emma went out to get sandwiches Julia tried to concentrate on a profile she was updating about the Sultan. Her thoughts kept wandering. She found it hard to believe that Moscato would have been so stupid as to ignore the Palace ruling that the Queen's private lunches were to be treated as exactly that – private. And yet . . .

At that moment the phone rang.

'Hello again, Miss Lang.' It was Jill Bannister on the line. 'Mr Brand was wondering if you would care to see the new Pinter play, which opens tonight? He has two tickets.'

Julia hesitated. Clearly someone else had let Brand down. 'I realize it's short notice,' Jill Bannister continued, 'but Mr Brand only returned from Rome an hour ago. I was able to get two cancellations.'

'He gets around, your boss,' Julia said.

'Yes, he does.'

Julia had not spoken to Michael since their disastrous dinner and was in no mood to spend the evening alone. 'I'd be delighted,' she said.

'He'll pick you up at 7.30 for the eight o'clock curtain.'

'I'm at 208 – ' Julia began.

'We have the address,' Jill Bannister said. 'Enjoy your evening.'

Chapter 10

As they entered the theatre lobby, crowded with people, some elegantly dressed, some in jeans and sweaters, Brand appeared tense. When a dark-haired young man nodded to him and said, 'Good evening, Mr Brand,' he affected not to notice. Then, as they walked towards the stalls entrance, a photographer who had overheard the exchange approached. 'This way, Mr Brand,' he called, raising his camera.

Brand quickly turned his back, steering Julia past the usher taking the tickets. She saw the photographer frown – hadn't she seen him somewhere? – before turning his attention elsewhere.

'I'm sorry,' Brand said, as they made their way to their seats. 'I don't like to be photographed.'

Julia said nothing. It was not, she guessed, that he minded being photographed. He didn't want to be photographed with her! In case his wife saw the picture? What was wrong with taking a friend to a first night? It wasn't as if they were seen entering a backstreet hotel.

At the interval, a champagne cocktail and a tonic water awaited them at the bar – arranged beforehand, obviously.

'Enjoying it?' Brand asked, as they moved to a quiet corner.

'Very much,' she said, deciding to put the incident with the photographer from her mind. So he didn't want his picture taken? So what?

'Writes good dialogue, Pinter,' Brand said.

'So they say. I've never met anyone who actually talks like that.'

'The pauses, you mean? Most people don't pause when they're talking, do they? They shoot off at tangents. It's interesting replaying a conversation on tape, as I have to sometimes.'

When they left the theatre, Brand's Daimler was waiting outside with Parsons, his elderly driver, at the wheel. By the time they reached Mayfair, Brand and Julia were laughing together. The car pulled up in Berkeley Square beside a small canopy.

They descended the steep steps to Annabel's. Brand seemed to be well known there, and nods and smiles greeted them as they proceeded along the hall towards the restaurant. The maitre d' welcomed them effusively before leading them to a table against the wall. It was still fairly early. The club was not even half full. Brand ordered drinks. 'I'm sorry the evening got off to a bad start,' he said.

Julia shrugged. 'I understand. You're a married man.'

'That's not it.' Brand seemed surprised that she had stated it so bluntly. 'My wife knows I have a social life here. It's just ... well, I have a great antipathy towards the Press. Photographers in particular.'

'They're just doing their job,' Julia said.

'They must do it without my help.' Their drinks arrived. Brand held up his glass and touched it lightly against hers. 'Look,' he said, turning to face her, 'you don't understand and I can't expect you to. It isn't that I didn't want to be photographed with you. Dammit, you're a beautiful woman, Julia; there isn't a man on this planet who wouldn't want to be pictured beside you. I just don't want to be photographed, period.' He looked into his drink. 'I'm known to be a wealthy man. And the only way I can have any kind of a private life is for people not to know what I look like. Then I can't be pestered. As it is, we get a hundred begging letters a week. Everyone wants something from me.'

'I'm sorry,' she said. 'I took it personally.'

'You shouldn't,' he said. 'It has absolutely nothing to do with you.'

Julia shook her head. 'We've already had several enquiries about you from newspapers.'

'Were you able to stall them?'

'I said you weren't registered, which is true.'

'If you have any problems refer them to my office in Grosvenor Square.' He shrugged. 'You know what they want? To sit down with me and waste hours of my time asking what it feels like to be wealthy. Either that or it's financial editors wanting me to forecast the market. I haven't got time for any of that nonsense. I work a long day. For me time is money.'

The club was beginning to fill up. When the waiter came over with the menus they both ordered the rack of lamb. From the wine list Brand selected a bottle of '66 Mouton-Rothschild.

Julia was still puzzled. 'If you never give interviews and don't have your picture taken, how did that photographer know who you were?'

'He didn't until that fellow called out to me.'

'There must be some photos of you about?'

'Not many. *Paris-Match* once staked me out in New York and Acapulco. Acapulco was no problem. I use a helicopter when I'm there; land right on the roof of my house. In New York I leave through the underground garage.'

'They never got the picture?'

'All they got was a picture of the car leaving the garage.'

'It doesn't sound too much fun, being you.'

'It has its moments.'

Julia glanced around the room. In one corner an elderly Englishman was pressing champagne on a young, heavily made-up woman, who was giggling. Suddenly Julia remembered. 'I forgot to thank you for the roses and the champagne you sent after the party.'

'I hope you've drunk it already?'

62

'I'm saving it for a special occasion.'

'You must drink it immediately. One thing I learned from my father was to live for today.'

'What did he do – your father?'

Brand looked at her for a moment as if trying to decide whether to confide in her or not. 'He was a financier. When he was quite young he set about making money.'

'Just like that.'

'All you need is the confidence to take risks.'

'I've met a few wealthy men at the hotel,' Julia said. 'None of them seemed particularly happy.'

'Did you ask them?'

'Of course not.'

'Why did you assume they weren't happy? Because they didn't go around smiling?'

'I suppose so.'

'Making money is a serious business,' Brand said. 'Anyway, you shouldn't trust people who go around smiling.'

The food arrived and they ate contentedly for a while, listening to the music coming from the dance floor. Julia had to remind herself to take it easy when the wine waiter approached to refill her glass. It wasn't every night she got to sample '66 Mouton-Rothschild.

'Your father must have been proud of you,' she said.

Brand shook his head. 'He died before I really got started. When I was twenty-one he gave me a large sum of money. I had a penthouse on Park Avenue, a butler, a chauffeur-driven car. And I was desperately unhappy.' He paused. 'Then I got a real kick in the stomach. My best friend killed himself with a shotgun. You know why? He was bored with life. He was twenty-five years old and he was bored with life. That jolted me to my senses. I decided to try my hand at business. Then my father died and left me his fortune. I used it well.'

'You make it sound so easy.'

'It is easy – if you have some capital and are prepared

to take chances. Most people don't try to *make* money with all the risks that entails; they just want to *have* money. I take risks all the time; speculate in currencies. Ten years ago I bought heavily into Deutschmarks. A month later the Deutschmark rose five per cent in one day against the dollar. I made $50 million overnight.'

'*Fifty* million?'

'Thereabouts,' Brand said. He smiled at her astonishment. 'I don't say that to brag. Just to make the point about taking chances.' He picked up his wine glass and then, having second thoughts, put it down again. 'Incidentally, I bought the Canaletto.'

'You did?'

'A million and a half,' Brand said. 'A steal. That man Delevingne doesn't know as much about art as he thinks.'

'From what you told me,' Julia said, 'nobody does.'

Brand turned to her. 'What painters do you like, Julia?'

'Oh, Utrillo, I suppose. Cézanne. Monet.'

'You've been to Giverny?'

'A long time ago.'

'When I was very young my father wanted me to be a painter,' Brand said. 'I had a tutor to teach me the basics but I had no eye for perspective; no talent at all. I went to Giverny too, and sat in that garden of Monet's, looking at the water lilies, trying to absorb something of what he must have felt. When I got home I painted a couple of water lilies. They looked exactly like fried eggs. I gave up.'

'So now you collect. The next best thing.'

'I suppose so. I get a lot of pleasure from my collection. When you come to New York you'll see it.'

'*When* I come . . . ?'

He leaned forward. 'I want you to join my team at the Raleigh.'

She laughed. 'You know nothing about me. How do you know I'm any good?'

'I know.'

'Anyway,' she said, 'I can't do that. I have a contract.'

'I'm sure if I talk to George we can work something out.'

'George?'

'The Sultan of Malacca.'

'His name isn't George.'

'We call him that. Nobody can pronounce his real name. We do business together.'

She looked around the dark, elegant room, listening to the murmur of voices from other tables. Incredible, she thought. A job interview in Annabel's.

'Well?' Brand was looking at her intently. She felt suddenly adrift; unsure of herself. Life had always seemed to her just moving from one set of problems to another, never getting ahead, never actually arriving at the point where she could say: I'm ready to start living. Was Brand offering her the chance?

'What exactly would joining your team entail?'

'You'd be doing just what you do now.'

'Tim Perrin would have something to say about that.'

'Julia,' Brand sounded exasperated, 'I own the damn hotel.'

'I understand that. But I know Tim and I like him. I won't be forced on him.'

'What on earth are you talking about?'

'If Tim wants me he must ask for me. It shouldn't come from you.'

Brand looked at her hard. 'But it was George Malacca who arranged your contract.'

'That's true. But it was Andrew Lattimer who hired me. The Sultan arranged my contract only because he wanted me to work for the Royal Malaysian in Kuala Lumpur, which he'd bought at the same time.'

'You didn't like the idea?'

'Not just then.'

The music from the dance floor at the far end of the room was getting louder. Julia wondered if he would ask her to dance.

'Will you think about it?' he asked.

'Of course.'

'You'd be such an asset,' Brand said. 'Bobby Koenig says you speak Italian. Was that from school?'

'I spent six months in Italy when I was seventeen. My mother's idea.'

'Rome?'

'With a family. Then I took a summer job at a hotel on Como.'

She noticed that some of the juice from her rack of lamb had spilled onto the tablecloth. Glancing at Brand's still almost full plate she felt guilty that she had enjoyed her meal so much.

Brand held up his hand and ordered coffees. 'I have to fly to Scotland tomorrow,' he said. 'Something's come up. You know where Silicon Glen is?'

'Somewhere near Edinburgh?'

'Biggest concentration of electronic manufacturing plants in Europe. We have a factory there making microprocessors.'

The idea that this hugely wealthy man should actually be visiting one of his factories astonished her. Surely he had people to do that sort of thing? 'Will you be there long?'

'A few days.'

'Do you need help at Heathrow? We have someone on duty . . .'

'Thanks,' Brand said. 'I'm leaving from Luton. The plane's there.'

Of course. He didn't fly like other people. There would be no lining up for him, no search of hand baggage. He would drive straight out to his private plane, climb aboard and be airborne.

'A real luxury,' she said. 'A private plane . . .'

Brand nodded. 'It makes life easier when you move around a lot.'

'You have a yacht too?'

He glanced at her, amused. 'You're interviewing me?'

66

'I'm sorry. I'm just interested. I don't usually meet people with private planes and yachts.'

'I'm sure that's your choice,' Brand said. 'An attractive woman like you . . .'

The insinuation annoyed her. 'Some women do use their looks to meet wealthy men,' she said. 'I'm not one of them.'

Brand leaned forward. 'Forgive me,' he said. 'I put that badly.' He laid his hand briefly on hers, then withdrew it. 'May I call you when I return from Scotland?'

'I won't walk out on the Burlington.'

'Don't be too sure.'

He finished his wine and glanced towards the dance floor. 'I have a mediocre sense of rhythm,' he said, 'but perhaps I can persuade you to take a whirl around the floor with me?'

Julia smiled. 'I'd love to.'

He held her close, in the old-fashioned way, so that their bodies locked together and she could react to the slightest pressure from him. He was not a great dancer but he was more than competent. As they moved around the edge of the floor he executed a few elaborate dance steps that she did her best to follow.

'Well,' she said when they returned to the table, 'that was something.'

'A pitiful attempt to convince you I'm more lively than I look,' he said.

'You're a much better dancer than you admit.'

'But no Baryshnikov.'

'Few men are.' She sipped her coffee. 'May I ask a personal question?'

'Of course.'

'What's she like, your wife?'

'Ah yes,' he said, 'back to reality. Well, you're probably right. Mustn't get carried away.' He paused, almost as if he had not been asked the question before and was unsure how to reply. 'She's very attractive,' he said at last. 'In my estimation, at least. She is not what you might call, well, affectionate, but perhaps that is my fault. She has not been entirely well for some time, unfortunately.'

'I'm sorry.'

Remembering a friend's claim that all married men, intent on seduction, had stories ready about their wives – how unkind they were, how lacking in understanding, how frigid – Julia was relieved that Brand, at least, did not fit the pattern.

'How long have you been married?'

'Thirty-five years. We met when I was just starting out. I was not a sophisticated young man. Grace was a photographer for *National Geographic* at that time, widely travelled. She had been down the Yangtze, gone overland to Lhasa in Tibet, driven through the Khyber Pass from Afghanistan to Pakistan. I had done nothing but spend money. It was she who gave me ambition.'

'You have no children?'

'We decided against it. We were both wrapped up in our careers. And, indeed, in each other. A mistake, perhaps.'

'You said she spends most of her time in Acapulco?'

'She likes it there. She has many friends.'

'And you?'

'There are a couple whose company I enjoy. One is a fisherman; the other a Polish sculptor, a great bear of a man: Voytek Konopka. He's quite well known there. You'd like him, I sense. When is that conference in Acapulco? The one you're invited to?'

'The end of next month.'

'I might arrange to be there. Show you around. What's the organization called?'

'The International Travel and Tourism Research Association.'

'Let me see what I can do.'

'I'm still not sure I can leave things here.'

'I'll pencil it in anyway.'

Taking a slim memo pad from his pocket he scribbled

something on it and handed the note to Julia. 'That's Jill Bannister's address and phone number. If you ever want to get in touch with me you can do it through her.'

'She sounds very efficient, your Miss Bannister.'

'She is. I'm lucky to have her.'

By the time they had finished their second cups of coffee it was after midnight, the club was crowded and the dance floor was packed. Brand called for the bill, signed it and, taking Julia's arm, led her out to the waiting car.

As he dropped her off at her home he said, 'I'll tell Tim Perrin to expect you sometime soon.'

'You can't do that,' she said, laughing.

'That's where you're wrong,' Brand said. He closed the door and the car slid away down the street.

The phone was picked up on the third ring.

'Hello?'

'It's me.'

'Well.' Grace Brand's voice was heavy with sarcasm. 'We haven't heard from you in a while.'

'There was nothing new to report.'

Grace Brand paused. 'And now?'

'There's a new face on the horizon. I think your friend may be about to stray again.'

'Who is it this time?'

'Her name is Julia Lang. She works at the Burlington Hotel.'

'What is she – a maid?' There was a sneer in Grace Brand's voice.

'She's the hotel's Publicity Director.'

'He's been seeing her?'

'A couple of times. Lunch. The theatre.'

'I see.' She paused. 'Keep me informed of developments.'

'Of course.'

Chapter 11

There was one person, Julia felt sure, who could tell her about Robert Brand, who now intrigued her greatly. What was his story? Bobby Koenig would know, but he had now checked out of the hotel. That left Lisa Faraday.

Since working with her during her brief stint as a model when she first arrived in London, Julia had remained close friends with Lisa. A bubbly and attractive redhead in her early forties, she was a former small-time actress who had hoped for a film career in the long ago days when it seemed Britain might actually have a film industry of its own. She had tried various jobs after that, including working as a secretary at an embassy in Bryanston Square and serving as a receptionist for a specialist in Harley Street. None of the jobs lasted. Lisa had one great trouble: she could not resist men. She slept with both the ambassador and the specialist. She had a list of former lovers that astonished Julia.

Her name began cropping up in divorce cases. Then she was offered a trip to Syria by a businessman she met at Regine's in Paris. He took her first to Damascus, then all over the Middle East, ending up in Cairo. There she was introduced to one of the young Saudi princes. Within a week she had moved in with him and left the business-man. Six months later she was pregnant.

As a result of the romance she was faintly notorious and decidedly newsworthy. She was also the recipient of a pension from the Prince, which allowed her to live, if not in luxury, at least in comfort in a five-room apartment in St John's Wood. And to educate the child of the liaison, a dark-eyed four-year-old named Deena.

Julia liked Lisa, for she was good-hearted and excellent

company. And, despite everything, undefeated. And it was to Lisa that she brought up Brand's name when they met for lunch at a restaurant round the corner from the hotel.

'Brand?' Lisa echoed, stopping with her fork halfway to her mouth. 'Robert Brand? You actually *met* him?'

'At the hotel. The cocktail party.'

'He was there? Incredible. What's he like? All those stories . . .'

'What stories?'

'You can't have forgotten. Jane Summerwood. The woman in the park . . .'

Julia frowned. 'I don't know what you're talking about.'

'It was in all the papers. She was beaten to death . . .'

'So?'

'You're unbelievable,' Lisa said. 'Brand was her lover. She was three months pregnant.'

'What?' Julia stared at her.

'He was supposed to be getting a divorce. It was a big scandal.'

Julia sat back, stunned. 'How could I have missed that?'

'It was last year. Perhaps you were away,' Lisa said. 'They never found out who did it. Brand was in New York at the time. There were rumours he had a heart attack afterwards.'

Julia, shaken by what she had just learned, was silent for a moment. Poor devil, she thought. What a ghastly thing to have happened. But it was curious. He had talked about his wife as though they had an amicable, if not close, relationship. Yet only a year ago he had been planning to leave her and marry this Jane Summerwood.

Lisa pushed aside her plate. 'Be honest. What did you think of him?'

Julia told her about the visit to the gallery, the subsequent lunch and their evening at the theatre.

Lisa's eyes widened. 'Perhaps he's interested in you? Jesus, Julia, be careful. He's not your league at all. The

71

Brand Corporation. Oil, ships, hotels, munitions. You know they've got an office in Grosvenor Square?'

'He told me.'

'A big place. I went to a party there once.'

'I don't even know if I'll see him again,' Julia said.

'Do you want to?'

'He's very good for morale. He wants me to join one of his hotels in New York.'

'That might be fun. But what about Michael?'

'He's been offered a job in Australia.'

'Is he going to take it?'

'I'm not sure.'

'Encourage him. You two aren't going anywhere.'

'I know it. The trouble is he doesn't.'

Lisa finished her coffee. 'Did Brand tell you he was still married?'

'Of course.'

'Her name's Grace. They've got this huge house in Acapulco. I've seen pictures of it in *Travel and Leisure*. They say it cost $30 million. Can you imagine?'

'No,' Julia said. 'I can't.'

They parted outside the hotel.

'You be careful,' Lisa said, looking concerned.

Julia nodded, her mind in a whirl. So Robert Brand had been going to marry another woman. She had been killed. It had been in all the newspapers. Had he assumed she did not know? Was that why he had taken a house in Regent's Park? To be with this woman?

She walked back to the executive corridor deep in thought.

When Julia arrived back at her office she found Emma had placed a copy of *Trends* on her desk, a page marked with a paperclip.

It was a full-length interview with Guido Moscato written by Chantal Ricci. The tone of the piece was adulatory. Moscato was called one of the world's great hoteliers, ranking alongside Jean-Claude Irondelle of the

Hôtel du Cap at Antibes and Kurt Wachtveitl of the Oriental in Bangkok.

'When Signor Moscato arrived in London he realized that the British capital had no hotels of the first rank,' she had written. Julia read this with growing astonishment.

> The Savoy had become like an old woman who has had too many face lifts by mediocre surgeons; the Ritz a pale shadow of its elegant older sister in Paris. Signor Moscato took a look at them and knew that London was crying out for a first-class hotel.

This is incredible, Julia thought. The article continued.

> Signor Moscato has entertained the Queen in the hotel's magnificent restaurant. The rich and famous from all over the world can be spotted rubbing shoulders in the lobby or sitting over drinks at the bar. The staff is the envy of every hotelier in London. Their loyalty to him is unquestioned. He makes every one of them feel that it is his or her contribution that makes the hotel great ...

And so it went on.

Julia reached for her buzzer. 'Have you read this?' she asked when Emma appeared.

'Can't you tell by my face?' Emma replied. 'I almost threw up.'

'He must be crazy,' Julia said. 'So must she. When the newspapers find out she's also working here they'll have a field day at our expense. I can't let those two get away with this sort of thing.'

Brandishing the magazine she stormed off to see Moscato.

73

'Why wasn't this cleared with me?' she asked angrily, confronting him in his luxurious office.

Moscato looked up at her. 'First, Miss Lang, I'd appreciate it if you would not take that tone with me. Secondly, there was no reason why you should know about it. Miss Ricci suggested the idea. I agreed. That's all there is to it.'

'Don't you realize how ridiculous this makes us look?' Julia snapped. 'Some columnist is bound to discover this woman is employed here.'

Moscato sat back. 'I am anxious to let people know what I am doing at the Burlington,' he said. 'You have suggested nothing – '

Julia gaped at him. 'You've only been here a couple of weeks . . .'

'Miss Ricci saw no need to wait.'

Julia stood quite still, trying to control her temper. 'Signor Moscato, this is not going to work unless we get something straight right now. I am the Publicity Director for the Burlington. Stories about the hotel go through me. All of them. I take responsibility for them. And never would I have allowed this to go through. It's rubbish.'

Moscato's face flushed. 'You are being impertinent, Miss Lang. I suggest – '

'I am always open to suggestions,' Julia said sharply. 'But any more wonderful publicity ideas – such as this piece of self-promotion, or advertising the Queen's visit here – will come to me for approval. I hope that's understood. I have a contract with the Sultan and as long as he feels I am doing a good job for the hotel this is where I stay. Good afternoon.'

Sitting at her desk, still fuming over her clash with Moscato, Julia remembered Lisa's remarks about Brand's house in Mexico. She buzzed for Emma.

'We keep *Travel and Leisure*, don't we?'

'Since they did that piece on us.'

'Could you get me the file, please, Emma?'

'Can I find something for you?'

'I just want to flick through it.'

Julia glanced at a dozen copies of the glossy travel magazine before she found it. After Brand's claim to abhor publicity she was surprised to find six whole pages devoted to Casa Shalimar, the opulent Brand house built on three levels above Acapulco Bay. There were fountains and waterfalls on every level and it was hard to see where the vast swimming pool ended and the sea began, so cleverly was the house designed.

This is truly paradise, ran the caption under one of the pictures, showing half a dozen guest suites, each with its own pool. There were no pictures of Brand, but several of Grace, one taken of her standing at the water's edge, silhouetted against the sunset. She looked elegant and serene. Julia examined it closely. Grace was a tall, slim woman, deeply tanned, wearing a flowing white caftan. Julia looked at her for a long time before putting down the file.

Why am I doing this? she thought. None of this has anything to do with me.

'Do you realize what you're suggesting?' Commissioner Bonnet glanced sharply at the investigator sitting on the other side of his cluttered desk.

'I've thought about it a lot,' Albert-Jean Cristiani said. 'Di Marco's suicide makes no sense.'

Bonnet grunted. 'He was an old man. He had nothing to look forward to.'

Cristiani moved his chair slightly to get the winter sun out of his eyes. 'I saw him not long ago,' he said. 'A restaurant in Geneva. He was concerned about something; wanted to talk. I told him to call.'

'You knew him well?'

'We'd run into each other now and again.' Cristiani moved his chair even further from the desk.

'Shall I draw the blind?' Bonnet asked.

75

'It's all right now.' Cristiani reached for his coffee. 'He called me to set up a meeting. He loved to eat, you know; he suggested we dine at Girardet's. He even made a booking for the following week.'

'Did he, indeed?'

'He even ordered the food in advance. A few days later they found him in the lake.'

'A sudden fit of depression?' Bonnet ventured.

Cristiani shook his head. 'Does a man go to the trouble of ordering dinner at the finest restaurant in Switzerland and then walk into Lake Geneva?'

'It's possible,' Bonnet said.

'But not probable?'

'No,' Bonnet agreed. 'Not probable.'

'And what about the overcoat?'

'What overcoat?'

'He wasn't wearing one. But it was bitterly cold that week. I cannot believe di Marco left his apartment and walked down to one of the bridges without a coat.'

Bonnet frowned. 'Perhaps he removed it; put it down. Someone could have taken it.'

'No. I talked to his sister last night. She collected his things before returning to Zurich. She says di Marco had a favourite coat – a black one with a fur collar. He wore it all the time.'

'So?'

'It was still in his closet.'

'Who knows how a man thinks when he's going to kill himself? Perhaps he couldn't bear to ruin it.'

'But he wore an expensive suit. From Busatti in Bern. I checked.'

Bonnet leaned forward. 'Perhaps you should tell the police? That young inspector in Montreux – what's his name?'

'Thibault.'

'Tell him your suspicions.'

'He considers the case closed.'

'Then that's it.' Bonnet sighed. 'Maybe when you set

up as an investigator you should make this your first case. Beats tracking down runaway kids.'

Cristiani ignored this. He got to his feet. 'If di Marco didn't drown himself,' he said, 'that leaves only two possibilities.'

'He fell. Or he was pushed.'

'I think he was pushed,' Cristiani said.

Chapter 12

For two days some of Julia's time had been devoted to compiling a list of people to be invited to a series of private dinners that the Burlington's chef, Gustave Plesset, was planning to give in his private quarters in the kitchens. There were to be four dinners with six guests at each. Gustave would host all of them and Julia had been asked to submit a list of possible guests. Final approval would lie with Moscato.

Among those on Julia's list were two Fleet Street editors, a well-known novelist, a Mayfair restaurateur and a handful of personalities she knew would spread the word about Gustave's cooking. The idea of dining in the chef's own quarters, she felt sure, would appeal to all of them.

The day after completing her list she was sent for by Moscato. She had not seen him since their row over the *Trends* interview and she was dreading another encounter.

When she walked in Moscato waved her to a chair. She remained standing, conscious that her heartbeat had increased markedly. She tried not to look at him directly.

'I spoke with the Sultan yesterday,' Moscato said. 'He informed me that your contract has another two years to run.' He leaned forward and adjusted the position of his desk calendar. 'Clearly it is in both our interests to get along during that time.'

He looked up at Julia. She said nothing.

'That said, I am far from happy with your choice of names for the private dinners,' Moscato went on. 'In France Gustave Plesset was a three-star chef. He is our

Maître Chef des Cuisines. As such, an invitation to dine in his quarters is something to be prized.' He opened the centre drawer of his desk and drew out Julia's list. 'Most of these people strike me as nobodies.'

Julia took a deep breath. 'I am well aware of Gustave's credentials. They've been included in many of my stories – '

'Then why have you not included the French Ambassador? Some Members of Parliament? Perhaps one of the Royals ... Princess Margaret?'

Julia stared at him, incredulous. 'Do you really imagine Princess Margaret would sit down at a table for six in our kitchens?'

Moscato's eyes narrowed. 'I want them invited,' he said. 'And except for these two – ' he ringed in red the names of the editors – 'you can forget the rest.'

Julia stood quite still. 'Three of the names on that list that you dismiss as nobodies are people who have done a great deal for this hotel – holding charity affairs here, giving dinner parties. Judith Cameron is the one who ran our etiquette course for youngsters – Mr Lattimer's idea. It was a great success – '

Moscato held up a hand. 'I am sure Mr Lattimer had numerous attributes,' he said. 'But he is no longer with us. I am now Managing Director of this hotel. Make sure the people I have mentioned receive invitations.'

Julia picked up the list from his desk. 'I will send out invitations to the Ambassador, Princess Margaret and a couple of Members of Parliament. That's four people. We need twenty-four for the four dinners. Who else do you propose to invite?'

Moscato took off his spectacles and polished them carefully. 'I am sure you will be able to come up with some other names,' he said.

'No,' Julia said firmly. 'I don't believe I will. In my opinion the names on my list are just fine. Since you disagree it would obviously be best if you decided on the others.' She turned and walked out.

'Well,' Emma said, as Julia strode into her office, 'did he like the list?'

'Loved it. He deleted all the names except the two editors.'

'What?' Emma stared at her in disbelief. 'Who does he want? The Duke of Edinburgh?'

'That would absolutely make his day.' Julia picked up her briefcase. 'I'm going home,' she said. 'We'll send out some invitations tomorrow. He wants Princess Margaret, no less. The French Ambassador. Some Members of Parliament.'

'He might get a couple of those,' Emma said morosely. 'Some of them will go miles for a free meal.'

Chapter 13

Since her first meeting with him when she had signed her contract, Julia had enjoyed good relations with the Sultan of Malacca, the small, balding Malaysian billionaire who owned the Burlington.

When he came to London they occasionally dined together, though never at the hotel, and she had always found him an amusing companion, full of good stories about his native land. The British-educated Sultan was ambitious. His aim was to own the finest hotel in the world. To that end he had lavished millions upon the Burlington. And each year he flew to London to check up on his prize, arriving unexpectedly and booking one of the four penthouse suites under another name.

When the news spread that 'Mr Thomas' had checked into the Regent Suite the night before, Julia cheerfully awaited his call. It was two days coming, and arrived in the form of a message asking her to join him in the suite at 4 p.m. This was unusual – always before he had called her himself – but Julia thought nothing of it. Right on time she presented herself at the door to be ushered into the sitting room by his secretary, a pleasant-faced young Malay. A moment later in came the Sultan.

'Julia, how nice to see you.'

Expecting the usual embrace Julia moved towards him. Instead he shook hands with her, rather formally, and indicated one of the sofas on either side of the coffee table. 'Sit. Let us be at ease.' He fidgeted around to make himself comfortable and clapped his hands. A moment later a full tea was served, the same as guests were having in the lounge downstairs – Earl Grey, finger sandwiches, warm scones with jam and Devon cream.

With a wave of his hand the Sultan dismissed the floor waiter. 'I've introduced these same teas at the Royal Malaysian,' he said. 'People told me it was a bad idea. Now the lounge is so crowded it's hard to get a table.' He poured tea for them both. 'Tell me, how are things with you?'

'Just fine, sir.'

'You are doing a wonderful job, Julia. All those stories you've managed to get in the American travel magazines.'

'We have had good coverage in America,' Julia agreed.

'And I'm delighted; delighted. However, I do know Moscato is anxious to increase our European coverage. He feels we must keep a balance with our guests. Americans don't want to come all this way to see a lot of other Americans. And there is always the danger that with another recession they will stay away.'

'That's true of European visitors too,' Julia said.

'Of course it is; of course it is. But when I arrived last night I did notice we don't have more than a dozen French and Italian guests. Perhaps you should be doing a little more promotion on the Continent? You can go whenever you like, you know – Paris, Rome, Berlin.'

'Thank you,' she said, pleased.

'Moscato tells me other hotels like the San Pietro in Positano and the Voile d'Or at St Jean-Cap Ferrat are faced with the same problem: too many Americans. It's risky, Julia; risky. You know that Americans tend to stay home whenever there's trouble. We don't want to find the Burlington deserted next time a bomb goes off somewhere. We must widen our net, Julia; widen our net.'

He held out the plate of scones. She shook her head.

'Please. I intend to have one.'

Reluctantly Julia took a scone and added jam and cream.

The Sultan leaned forward. 'How are you getting on with Moscato?'

Julia hesitated. She had anticipated the question on her way up to the suite and had determined not to fall into the trap of criticizing the Sultan's choice of Managing Director.

'Well, sir, I haven't really had much to do with him. We've had a couple of meetings. The last one over the dinners that Gustave Plesset is planning to have in his kitchen.'

'A good idea of Moscato's, that. Don't you agree?'

'Well . . . yes . . .'

'You seem unsure.'

'It's just . . . well, I thought it was Gustave's idea.'

'The original suggestion was Moscato's, I assure you. He put it to me weeks ago when we were discussing ideas for the hotel.'

'I didn't know.'

'I can see that.' He added sugar to his tea. 'You still haven't answered my question.'

'I have no professional problems at all with Mr Moscato.'

The Sultan looked at her over the rim of his cup. 'He seems to have some with you.'

'Oh?'

'He feels you resent his appointment here. And the appointment of Miss Ricci to edit the magazine, which, I might add, I approved.'

'That's absolute nonsense. I have nothing against Miss Ricci.'

'Moscato says you complained to him about the piece she wrote in *Trends*.'

'Rightly, I think. It was not cleared through me. It was a stupid thing to have done.'

'Tell me why.'

'She works here. Yet it was written as though it were an objective piece of reporting. If the newspapers pick up on that we shall look ridiculous.'

The Sultan nodded. 'I agree with you. It was self-serving.'

'There's something else. Publicizing the Queen's private lunch here was an outrageous breach of etiquette. She will not return. It had to come from him. Or Miss Ricci.'

'That, too, was ill-advised.' He paused. 'Does that explain the animus which exists between the two of you?'

'No, sir. It's personal. There is a good reason for it. I'm not prepared to go further.'

The Sultan looked at her searchingly. 'You put me in a difficult position, Julia. I brought Moscato to this hotel. I believe him to be a first-class hotelier.'

Julia said nothing.

'Clearly you don't agree?'

Julia remained silent.

'I want you to understand one thing clearly,' the Sultan went on. 'The Burlington is very important to me. I want it to be well run, and for it to be well run it has to be a happy place. For the good of the hotel you must settle your differences. Otherwise you would be wise to consider a move. That position at the Royal Malaysian is open again.'

Julia was surprised. 'I thought you hired Jenny Owen.'

'She has been first class. But she is leaving to have a baby.'

Julia put down her cup. 'I'm happy for her and sorry for you, sir. I know how good Jenny is.'

'You're still not interested?'

'I'm afraid not.'

The Sultan leaned forward, studying Julia's face intently. 'Moscato has made it clear to me that, but for your contract with me, he would have dismissed you by now.'

Julia felt herself flush.

The Sultan looked exasperated. 'I cannot imagine what can have taken place between you that has produced such dislike. You're sure you can't tell me?'

'I'm afraid not.'

'Moscato says your paths have crossed before.'

'When he was Managing Director at the Palace on Lake Como I was a replacement receptionist one summer.'

'So whatever took place between you happened there?'

'You'll have to ask him, sir.'

'I intend to. I want to get to the bottom of this.' The Sultan sat forward on the sofa. 'Look, Julia, let me be frank with you. The Burlington is not doing as well as I'd hoped. I have invested millions in it; it is, you might say, my folly. I came into the hotel business too late – I know that now – when the cost of rooms was going up and business was going down. There are just too many hotels.

'My financial advisers want me to sell the Burlington to one of the big groups. I am reluctant to do that. So Moscato is my last hope. He made a great success of the Palace on Como; I intend to give him the chance to do the same thing here. If he fails the hotel will go on the block. It's as simple as that.' He sat back. 'That's confidential, of course.'

She nodded. 'I'm sorry to hear all that, sir. This is a fine hotel.'

'But it's losing money. I am a businessman, not a philanthropist.' He got to his feet. Julia rose too. 'I have high hopes for Moscato,' he said, walking with her to the door of the suite. 'That is why I want you to settle your differences. Will you try?'

Settle her differences. Her *differences*? Why didn't she come right out with it and tell him the truth? *The man you've hired to run this hotel raped me when I was just seventeen years old. And you expect me to forget about it? Not a chance.*

She took a deep breath. She could not tell him. He was her employer. This was too personal.

'Of course.'

'Goodbye to you.'

Chapter 14

Julia had agreed to have a drink after work with Bryan Penrose, who was soon to marry Pam Helmore, the Burlington's chief cashier. She did not get home until nine o'clock. She was deeply discouraged. Any hopes that she would be able to work alongside Guido Moscato, despite her loathing for him, had been dashed by her meeting with the Sultan. Moscato would go on complaining about her and eventually the Sultan would pay off her contract. She would be out. The thought depressed her. The Burlington had been her home and her pride for so long she could not envisage working anywhere else. Now she had to face the fact that her days there were numbered.

Even if she went back to see the Sultan and told him what had happened on Como, what good would that do? He was not about to remove Moscato. He would once again offer her the job at the Royal Malaysian. If she turned it down, that would be the end of it. Perhaps, she thought, she should seriously think about Robert Brand's offer to go to New York. At least she'd be working for a friend.

After taking a hot shower she considered getting straight into her robe. But it was too early to wind down, she knew, so instead she put on her tracksuit and running shoes and, feeling virtuous, set off for the streets around nearby Regent's Park. On the way home she stopped at the deli at the top of the road to pick up a pasta salad.

The red light on her answering machine was steady when she returned but she pushed the playback button just in case. No messages. She had not heard a word from Michael since their dinner at the Connaught. And she had not called him. Sitting in the kitchen, eating her salad, she wondered how Robert Brand was getting on in Scotland.

Just then the telephone rang. It was Brand, calling from the plane.

She felt a rush of excitement. 'How was Scotland?'

'Wet.' He sounded so chipper she found herself smiling for the first time that day.

'You know what someone called Scotland?' she said. 'A 400-mile car wash.'

She heard Brand's throaty laugh at the end of the line.

'I had a thought,' he said. 'I have to fly to the South of France this weekend for a business meeting. I wondered if you'd care to come down, see the yacht. We could talk more about your move to New York.'

Out of the blue – literally – there it was. Just what she needed. A couple of days out of wintry London. Two days not to think about her rows with Moscato or her problems with Michael. Two days to forget about her cool meeting with the Sultan.

'Sounds wonderful,' she said. 'When would we leave?'

'Tomorrow around 10 a.m. That'll get us there in time for lunch. Back sometime Monday.'

'I'll be ready,' she said.

'We'll pick you up at nine.'

Julia called Emma to say she was feeling unwell and might not be in on Monday. Then she did a little dance around her bedroom. Amazing, she thought. I've had a hell of a day. Yet all it needs is one phone call and I'm glowing.

The Gulfstream IV, its gleaming white fuselage broken by a dark blue streak down each side, was parked in the private section of Luton Airport. Two pilots, both wearing neat blue uniforms, stood at the bottom of the steps waiting for them.

There were no formalities. Parsons drove the Daimler straight out to the plane, the luggage was loaded and they went aboard. The steward, a tousle-haired young man, also in uniform, collected their passports and showed them to an Immigration officer who had sauntered out to the plane. He merely glanced at them and waved.

The interior of the plane was comfortable but not particularly opulent. There were no regular airline seats. Instead, two large swivelling armchairs, in blue and gold, were placed on either side of the aisle. Behind one of them were two chairs on either side of a small conference table. At the rear was a banquette capable of seating three people or turning into a bed. Behind that were the galley and toilet.

'I'll show you the flight deck later,' Brand said. 'We can travel 5,000 miles nonstop. It's so computerized it can be programmed to take off and fly automatically from one runway to another.'

Determined not to appear too impressed, Julia nodded gravely. He was like a small boy, she thought, showing off his most expensive toy.

As the plane made an effortless climb to 40,000 feet above the wintry English countryside, Julia closed her eyes and sat back. She felt spoiled and cosseted. Once, she reflected, crossing by ferry from New Haven to Dieppe for a week at a small Left Bank hotel in Paris had been her idea of a great adventure. Now here she was flying in a multimillion-dollar jet. Would this trip be any more memorable than those long ago jaunts to the French capital when, carefree and happy, she had walked the boulevards with boyfriends and lingered over coffee at pavement cafés? Well, she thought, I'll soon find out.

Even in France, it seemed, Brand's name carried weight. They landed at Nice at midday and were escorted through Immigration by a courteous official who, bypassing Customs, led them straight to a waiting car.

Julia had been to the South of France with Michael, staying in the mountain village of Eze, but she knew little of the history of the region. Brand, on the other hand, seemed to possess a detailed knowledge. After lunch, as they drove along the Promenade des Anglais, he kept pointing out places of interest.

'That's the Regina; once the grandest hotel in all Europe. Now it's a condominium. Matisse stayed here. So did Queen Victoria. She used to ride her donkey, Jaquot, up and down this street with footmen walking ahead calling out: *"La Reine passe!"* Hard to imagine, isn't it?'

On the drive along the seashore, past the restaurants and beach pavilions now shut for the winter, Julia determined that, however spectacular Brand's yacht proved to be, she would act like a sophisticated woman. But when she saw the all-white yacht in Monte Carlo harbour her resolve to behave like a *femme du monde* crumbled. To her *The White Dolphin* looked enormous. She had no way of comparing it to other famous boats she had read about, but the size and opulence of Brand's yacht astonished her. Brand had explained that he rarely used it more than once or twice a year. She found this extraordinary. The idea that he should maintain a hugely expensive yacht for the infrequent visit, much as a Londoner might keep a Rolls-Royce in his garage on the off chance of needing it for the occasional weekend in the country, seemed to her preposterous.

After boarding, while Brand went to his study to make some phone calls, the captain, a ruddy-faced former Royal Navy man named Alistair Buchanan, took her on a tour. She learned there was a crew of thirty, including valets, a masseur and two chefs. There was a small cinema, a swimming pool and gymnasium.

Her own stateroom was carpeted in white, with a king-size bed facing a large picture window. On its elaborately decorated headboard a panel of buttons controlled the curtains and lights. One entire side was composed of wardrobes. When the maid allotted to her, Sylvie, explained how everything worked – at the touch of a button the outer wall lowered hydraulically, forming a platform from which she could dive straight into the sea when they were at anchor – she gave up all pretence of being unimpressed.

After Sylvie had unpacked and put her things away, Julia went around inspecting everything. Until that moment, she realized, she had not really faced the truth about Robert Brand. He was a titan. He owned this sea-going palace. It gave her the uneasy feeling of being a trespasser. This was Grace Brand territory. It went hand in hand with great wealth, private planes, armies of servants and opulent villas. It had absolutely nothing to do with her.

Yet here she was.

She changed into a white off-the-shoulder dress and put on rope sandals. She was about to leave the suite when Brand came to get her. He was wearing white cotton trousers and espadrilles and a French matelot's jersey that left his tanned, muscular arms bare. He looked considerably younger than his years.

'Got everything you need?' he asked.

She nodded.

'What do you think of her?'

'Extraordinary.'

'She's an ostentatious old tub. She was Grace's idea; not mine. Grace never cared for Ari Onassis and wanted to cap his yacht, the *Christina*. So we got *The White Dolphin*, fifteen feet longer than Ari's yacht. Silly, really. I use her mostly for business meetings; makes the tax man look more kindly on us.' He took her arm. 'Let's go up and have our welcome drink.'

They took the lift to the deck bar where a steward was waiting with a flute of champagne and a glass of orange juice. Brand took the flute and handed it to Julia. 'Well,' he said, 'we've got two and a half days. Where would you like to go?'

'You decide.'

'What about Corsica? You know the island?'

Julia shook her head, instantly excited. It seemed anything was possible with this extraordinary man.

'Then Corsica it is.'

'What about your business meeting?'

'I'll wrap that up this afternoon.'

Around 2.30 p.m. a heavy-set man in a grey business suit came aboard. While he and Brand had their meeting, Julia went up on deck for a swim in the heated pool. Afterwards she set out to explore the yacht properly. Brand, she found, was still in his study, talking. The door was open. She peeked in.

Brand looked up and smiled. 'Ah, Julia, come in. We have just finished. Let me introduce you. This is Hans Siebel of the Deutsche Bank.' He turned to the man and introduced Julia in fluent German.

The German bowed. '*Angenehm,*' he said, beaming.

He and Brand wound up their conversation in German and then Herr Siebel shook hands with them both.

After he'd gone Brand ordered tea.

'I didn't know you spoke German,' Julia said.

Brand shrugged. 'A smattering. It helps in business.'

Julia, who had attended a summer course in Heidelberg after she left school, wondered why he was being modest. His German accent was faultless and he was clearly fluent in the language. She had heard enough to know that. She was puzzled for a moment. Then, excited by the prospect of the cruise, she quickly put it from her mind.

While Brand finished a report Julia returned to her stateroom and took a nap. She awoke to the sound of mooring lines being brought aboard as the yacht was prepared for sea.

Rousing herself, she went into the bathroom and drew a bath. The bathroom was as opulent as the rest of the suite with heavy Turkish towels, expensive-smelling soaps and cosmetics of every make. Robes embroidered with the logo of the yacht, a leaping white dolphin on a blue background, hung behind the door. As she lay in the tub, soaping herself, for a fleeting moment she wished the people at the Burlington could see her. She dismissed the thought as unworthy, an adolescent desire to show off, but it remained at the back of her mind.

At seven o'clock there was a knock on the door. It was Sylvie. 'Madame would like me to help her dress?'

'What? Oh . . . no.' Julia felt embarrassed. 'I'm fine, thank you.'

This is the way to live, she thought, as the maid made a small curtsey and withdrew. No more problems. No more doing dishes. No more waiting for taxis. No more Moscatos. She smiled to herself and started to dress for dinner.

After a cocktail in Brand's study, they adjourned to the dining room, waited upon by white-jacketed stewards. The meal – cold salmon and asparagus, with strawberries and cream for dessert – seemed to Julia just perfect. After the stewards had cleared away, she and Brand took their coffees to the aft deck and, wrapped up in blankets, lay side by side on the chaises longues.

Lying under a sky studded with bright stars Julia felt deeply content. When I am old, she thought, I will remember this night. She tested herself for guilt and felt none. Cold wintry London, with all its problems, seemed to belong to another life. This man beside her, like some Oriental magician, had transported her to a different world.

'You could sail round the world in this,' she said.

'You could,' Brand agreed.

'Do you fancy the idea?'

'By myself? I'd be bored stiff.'

'Then make up a group. A few friends.'

'I did that last year. Spent a month cruising the Mediterranean. By the time the cruise was over we were at each other's throats.'

Julia raised herself up on her elbow. 'May I ask you a personal question?'

'Not too personal, I hope.'

'It's about . . . well, what happened a year ago.'

He hesitated. 'You mean Jane Summerwood?'

'You never mention her.'

He looked at her levelly. 'It's a very unhappy subject.'

'You'd rather not talk about it?'

'No. No. It's not that. It's . . . well, for a long time I couldn't . . . I couldn't bring myself to even mention her name. Now it's easier.' He finished his coffee and put the cup down on the deck. 'Look, I'll be perfectly honest with you, Julia. My marriage is a sham. But for many reasons I won't bore you with, our lives are intertwined. My wife has warned me repeatedly that she could – and would – do me untold harm if I ever try to leave her.'

Julia frowned. 'What could she do?'

'I can't go into details, Julia. But believe me, she could do me great damage.'

'But she couldn't stop you divorcing her, not if you want to. Surely it's just a question of money?'

He shook his head. 'It goes far deeper than that, Julia. It's very complex.' He was silent for a moment, looking out across the moonlit water. 'But you asked about Jane. I was very much in love with her. When she found she was pregnant I went to talk to Grace. I hoped, I suppose, that she might be sympathetic. Instead she went berserk.' He shook his head. 'Well, you know what happened. Jane was murdered in London. It destroyed me. It seemed my last chance of finding happiness had been taken away.'

'I gather they never found who did it.'

'No. I made my own enquiries. They came to nothing.'

'How awful for you.'

'I lost interest in everything for a while. Then I had a heart attack. My doctor told me to ease up but I found that impossible. I took the cruise I told you about and went right back to work.' He paused. 'A sad little saga.'

He looked at her and rose. 'I won't be a moment. Can I get you anything?'

'No thanks.'

When he returned five minutes later he was carrying a small, slim case. He sat on the edge of the chaise longue. 'Now may I ask you something, Julia?'

'Of course.'

'When we had that lunch in London I asked if you were involved with anyone. You said you were. But here you are on the yacht with me. Is your involvement not serious?'

Julia hesitated before replying. Since their dinner at the Connaught, she realized with a pang, she had not even thought about Michael. 'I'm very fond of the person,' she said. 'But, no, it's not serious.'

'Was he the man I saw you with at the Connaught?'

She nodded. 'Michael Chadwick. He's a graphic designer. A wonderful one. He's going to work in Australia.'

'I'm delighted to hear that,' Brand said. 'Soon, I hope.'

Julia smiled. 'Quite soon.'

Brand finished his coffee. 'I have to take a long trip myself after this weekend. I have meetings in Buenos Aires and Lima.'

'Will you be away long?'

'God, I hope not,' Brand said. 'I want to keep pressing you to come to work for me.' He handed her the slim case. 'Anyway, I got you something to remember me by.'

'What is it?' Julia felt suddenly nervous.

'Open it and find out.'

Inside the case a jewelled necklace sparkled against its black velvet base. She stared at it, dumbstruck.

She met Brand's gaze. 'These are diamonds.'

'I hope so.'

'I can't take this.'

'Why not?'

'Well . . .' Julia floundered for words. 'It's much too

expensive. And . . .' For a moment she was unable to put her thoughts together. 'You don't . . . I mean – This is the sort of gift you give a woman . . . you know . . .'

'Exactly.'

Julia looked again at the glittering stones.

'Van Cleef and Arpels will exchange it if you don't like it,' Brand said. 'Mr Duvall is the man there.'

'How could I explain this?'

'To whom?' Brand chuckled. 'Don't. Wear it only when you're with me.'

'But that's such a waste.'

'It depends how much time you spend with me.' Brand took the necklace from the case and slipped it around Julia's neck, fastening the clasp at the back. 'It looks wonderful on you.' He stood suddenly. 'Ready to turn in?'

'Reluctantly,' she said.

Outside her stateroom Brand put a hand on her arm. 'I am years older than you,' he said. 'I am married. I live on the other side of the Atlantic. I have all those counts against me. But I am deeply attracted to you and trust you have some feeling for me. I can either say goodnight to you now or come in and try to persuade you we can be most happy lovers.' He took a long breath. 'Forgive me. I am not putting this well. I have no verbal skills as a romancer.'

'Your skills are better than you suppose,' Julia said. 'But I think we should say goodnight here.'

She kissed him on the cheek, putting her hand over his.

Suddenly he had his arms around her and was kissing her passionately, his tongue probing the inside of her mouth, producing in her a whole range of tastes and urges. She felt as if she were being consumed. They broke apart, breathing hard. She looked at him for a few seconds as if trying to make up her mind. Then she led him by the hand into her stateroom, unfastening the necklace, stepping out of her dress and underwear, leaving them in a rumpled pile. Falling back on the bed she watched nervously as he undressed. She waited to see what he would do with his clothes. He left them on the floor. Michael always hung his up. Dammit, she thought, why think of Michael now?

Then they were together on the bed, clutching each other fiercely, his mouth on hers, her arms round him, their limbs moving together in the familiar rhythm.

Finally it was over and they lay together in the dark, exhausted, not moving, not speaking, listening to the sound of the engines as the yacht moved swiftly through the moonlit sea.

Chapter 15

When Julia awoke next morning she was surprised to find Brand was gone. She slid from the bed naked and padded across to the window to part the curtains. The yacht was at anchor in a small bay dwarfed on both sides by towering cliffs. A dramatic range of mountains loomed in the distance, topped by scudding clouds.

She looked at her watch. It was after nine. She had slept deeply and well. Donning a swimsuit she went up on deck. To the right of the bay was an old Genoese watchtower. Beside it a series of steep steps, cut out of the limestone cliff, led to a small restaurant high above, its table umbrellas providing a splash of colour against the cliff face.

'Come on in. It's freezing.'

Brand, a hundred yards away, swimming back towards the yacht, waved to her.

'Not a chance,' she called, smiling.

A few moments later he clambered back on board. 'Sleep well?' he asked.

'Wonderfully.'

'So did I. We must be doing something right.'

Julia gave him a long look. 'I'm not so sure about that.'

He laughed. 'Come, coffee awaits.'

They breakfasted on the aft deck; fresh orange juice, fruit and coffee. Sitting back, with the sun on her face, Julia told herself she should have no guilt. So she was having a fling, Lisa Faraday style. Why not? He was a wonderful lover and an attractive man. And although everything about Brand suggested a man of wide sexual experience he had managed to make her feel that for him, as for her, all of it was special.

'Well,' she said, sighing contentedly. 'If this isn't paradise it'll do for the moment.'

'One of my favourite islands, Corsica,' Brand said. 'And two of my favourite people are here.'

'Tell me.'

'You see that restaurant?' Brand pointed to the coloured umbrellas.

'I was just looking at it.'

'Chez Jean Louis. Terrific spot. We're lunching there.'

'With your friends?'

'They run it.'

Julia looked back at the steep cliff. 'I'll never make it up those steps.'

'The climb is worth it, I promise you. Now come on. Time for another dip.'

They spent the morning in and out of the pool, relaxing and reading. Around noon the motor boat was lowered into the water and they set off for the shore. As they approached, Julia saw just how high up the restaurant was.

'I'm surprised they get anyone up there,' she said.

'When you try the lobster,' Brand said, 'you'll see why they do.'

They began the climb, Brand leading the way. Halfway up Julia was alarmed to see him stagger and lean against the cliff face. She leaped to his side. 'Are you all right?' She grasped his arm.

'Fine.' He looked at her, breathing heavily. 'Stupid of me. I should have taken it more slowly.'

Julia held him tightly until his breathing returned to normal. 'You sure you want to continue? Maybe we should go back.'

'Nonsense. I'll be fine.' He reached into his pocket, took a pill from a silver case and popped it into his mouth. A moment later his colour returned. 'On we go.'

Moving slowly they finished the climb. Julia held his hand anxiously, but was relieved that the pill seemed to have restored him. At the top was a wooden platform jutting out from the cliff with four tables set for lunch, each covered with a red tablecloth and decorated with wild flowers. As they arrived an old man and a woman hurried from the small lean-to building at the rear. Both were beaming.

'Monsieur Brand, what a pleasure! When we saw the yacht this morning we hugged each other. It was like old times.'

Brand, out of breath, managed a smile. 'Jean Louis. Nicole. I must be getting old. Or those steps of yours are getting steeper.'

He introduced Julia to them and while the old man fussed over them, placing chairs at the edge of the terrace, Julia glanced down. A sudden attack of vertigo made her sway. She clutched the rail.

'*Attention, madame.*' Jean Louis grasped her arm firmly. 'Do not look down again.' He helped her to one of the chairs and then went to fetch champagne at Brand's request.

'*Maintenant,*' Nicole said. 'What shall it be? We have some wonderful lobster.'

'Say no more,' Brand said. He looked at Julia. 'Okay with you?'

'Perfect,' she said.

When the drinks came they sat side by side, looking out at the sea. The smell of wild flowers was everywhere. From where they sat *The White Dolphin* looked very small.

'You had me worried for a moment,' Julia said. 'You sure you're feeling all right?'

'Absolutely.' Brand squeezed her hand. 'I should have paced myself better, that's all.' He smiled at her. 'Well. What do you think of the place?'

'It's wonderful,' Julia said. 'So peaceful.'

'Don't be deceived,' Brand said. 'Actually, this is a violent island. Those mountains behind us are full of bandits and rebels. But here we're fine. Jean Louis and Nicole built this themselves.'

'Tell me about them.'

'He was a barman at the Georges V in Paris; she had a bistro on the Left Bank. They always dreamed of having their own place so fifteen years ago they came here.'

'You knew them in Paris?'

'I knew Jean Louis. When he moved here I looked him up.' He glanced down at the surging sea below, pounding on the rocks. 'Sometimes I envy him.'

'I can understand that.'

The lobsters were wonderful. And watching him eat with such enjoyment Julia was touched that this man, who could buy almost anything he wanted, whose yacht rode at anchor in the bay below, should be getting such pleasure out of this meal at his old friend's restaurant. She was glad when, after they had eaten, Brand insisted that Jean Louis and Nicole join them for coffee.

'Now you look better,' Jean Louis said. 'A good lunch, some wine, good air . . .'

'It was those steps,' Brand said. 'I'd forgotten what a climb it is.'

'You know the trouble with this man?' Jean Louis said, turning to Julia. 'He cannot believe he's getting old like the rest of us. He insists on acting as if he were still twenty-five.'

Finally it was time to go. Brand slipped some notes under the plate. Both Jean Louis and Nicole embraced him, then turned to Julia to shake hands. Ignoring their formal gesture she kissed them both on the cheeks.

Cautiously, holding each other's hands, Brand and Julia made their way down the steps to the jetty where the motor boat awaited them. Far above them, on the terrace, they could see the two tiny figures waving to them. They waved back.

When Julia arrived at her office on Tuesday morning Emma was waiting with a pile of letters.

'How're you feeling?' she asked. She looked concerned.

'Terrific. Why?'

'You said you were feeling sick when you called.'

'Oh, that.' Julia felt a twinge of guilt as she sat down; she'd forgotten about the lie. 'Just a stomach upset.'

Emma dumped the letters on her desk. 'These won't make you feel any better,' she said.

'What are they?'

'Regrets for Gustave's dinners.'

'How many?'

'All of them.'

Emma flicked through them. 'Princess Margaret regrets . . . The French Ambassador regrets . . . All five MPs regret . . . We've got a lot of regretful people here.'

Julia was torn between feeling smug that she had been right and concern for Gustave Plesset, whom she liked and admired.

'We're in trouble,' she said. 'That first dinner is set for next week.' She thought for a moment. 'Send a list of regrets to Moscato this afternoon, and I'll tell Gustave myself.'

After lunch Julia went to the kitchen to break the news to him. 'I'm sorry, Gustave. I told Moscato this would happen. I warned him the people he wanted wouldn't come. He wouldn't listen.'

Gustave looked morose. 'I have done this before, you know. In Paris. Everyone came. Journalists, writers, artists. They were a great success. Here they do not want to know.'

Julia put her hand on his arm. 'It's not that, Gustave. It's because Moscato invited the wrong people.'

Gustave frowned. 'He said the people on your list were of no importance.'

He shrugged and walked off to his own small office. The list of regrets went to Moscato's office around four o'clock. He did not acknowledge it. Plans for the chef's dinners were promptly abandoned.

'Do you know how much this necklace is probably worth?'

Sprawled on Julia's sofa, Lisa Faraday examined the

diamonds with a professional eye, her face incredulous.

'I don't want to know.'

'One hundred thousand pounds. At least. He must be crazy about you. When are you seeing him again?'

'Not for a while. The plane refuelled at Luton and took straight off for New York. He's going to South America.' She put the box back in her wardrobe. 'I still can't believe he gave it to me.'

Lisa was silent for a moment. 'You know what this means, don't you?' she said quietly. 'You are in line to become Robert Brand's next mistress.'

That night, lying awake in bed, Julia thought about what Lisa had said. The idea of a full-blown affair with Robert Brand both excited and terrified her. He attracted her more than any man she had ever met. She wanted to continue what they had started, but she knew there was no future there. Brand had spelled it out for her. He was married, and he had made it clear that for some reason divorce was out of the question. The best she could hope for was that most unattractive of roles, the mistress in waiting.

Was that enough for her?

Her thoughts turned to Michael Chadwick. She still had not seen or heard from him since their disastrous dinner at the Connaught. In a few weeks he would be leaving for Australia. She might not see him again. She reached over and dialled his number.

Chapter 16

'Well?' Commissioner Bonnet looked up warily as Cristiani walked into his office. 'What is it this time?'

'I want a tap on Paul Eberhardt's phones,' Cristiani said.

'You *what*?' Bonnet looked incredulous. He gripped the sides of his chair as if in need of support. 'Have you gone mad? Wire taps come under Justice – '

'They'll grant it.'

'On what grounds? Because you ask nicely? You idiot. Paul Eberhardt is one of this country's most distinguished bankers and you want to tap his phones? Why not tap the Prime Minister's at the same time?'

Cristiani ignored the taunt. 'It's Eberhardt I'm interested in.'

'Give me one reason Justice will say yes.'

Cristiani took a chair. 'Because of something you said a while back: "No more bank scandals".'

'What are you talking about?'

'There's one brewing at the Banque Eberhardt. I know it.'

Bonnet gave a weary sigh. 'You're not still on about that old fart's suicide?'

'That and the earlier murder. Yes.'

'What earlier murder?'

'André Leber. Killed in Zurich last year.'

'For Christ's sake, that was a hit-and-run accident.'

'I don't think so.' Cristiani sat forward. 'Think about it. Leber leaves the bank and Eberhardt keeps paying him – 10,000 francs a month, mind you – for five years. Then he's run down.'

'You're suggesting he was murdered?'

'I am.'

'By Eberhardt?'

'Probably.'

Bonnet gave an exasperated sigh. 'Why wait five years to do it? If this fellow posed some sort of threat, why didn't Eberhardt get rid of him right away?'

'I can't answer that. Perhaps he lacked the nerve at first.'

Bonnet shook his head. 'I can't believe I'm hearing this.'

'Then comes di Marco,' Cristiani continued. 'We know he was concerned about something. He wanted to talk to me. He's found floating in the lake one morning.'

'Look, are you seriously suggesting that Eberhardt dragged that old fool down to the lake and pushed him in? Be sensible.'

'He could have hired someone to do it.'

'You've got to stop reading those murder mysteries,' Bonnet said impatiently. 'You're getting carried away.'

'You don't think it odd, then? Two of his top men dead within a year?'

'I consider it a coincidence,' Bonnet said. 'Nothing more. If you think that's grounds for a murder charge then men in white coats will turn up one morning and take you away.'

Cristiani got to his feet. 'I'm going for a phone tap,' he said.

'You'll never get it.'

'I have a friend at Justice,' Cristiani replied. 'I'll convince him there's another bank scandal brewing.'

Bonnet glared at him. 'Thank God you've only got a few more weeks here.'

'I know I'm right,' Cristiani said doggedly. 'You want to bet 100 francs on it?'

'I would,' Bonnet said. 'But when you lose you'll put it down on your expenses somehow. And I'll have to sign the damn thing. So forget it.'

* * *

'He did *what*?' The voice at the other end of the line was slurred. Had she been drinking again?

'He took her on the yacht for a short cruise.'

'Where's he now?'

'On his way to South America.'

'With her?'

'No. She's here in London.'

There was a long pause. 'Maybe it's just a flirtation?'

'He bought her a diamond necklace.'

'The bastard.'

'I'll keep you informed. And thanks for the cheque . . .'

The Devonshire Arms was crowded when Julia walked in. Michael was sitting in one corner with two glasses of wine on the table. The fact that he had already ordered her usual drink irritated her. She tried not to show it.

'Been here long?'

'A few minutes.'

The wine will be warm, she thought. She picked up her glass and sampled it. It was warm.

'I'm glad you called,' Michael said. He seemed nervous. 'Haven't seen you for a while.'

'I've been busy,' she said lamely.

'How're things at the hotel?'

'Grim. You saw the *Standard* ran a picture of the Queen leaving the hotel after a private lunch?'

'So what?'

'The Palace requested no publicity. Now she won't come back.'

'Who cares?' Michael said.

'Be sensible, Michael. You know how important that sort of thing is.'

'Well, it bloody well shouldn't be,' Michael said. 'I can't stand all that toadying to the Royals.'

'Having the Queen lunching at your hotel can hardly be classed as toadying,' Julia said sharply.

Michael took a long swallow. 'It's him, isn't it?' he said.

'Who?' Julia felt her cheeks redden. 'What are you talking about?'

'Come off it. I knew as soon as I saw Brand in the Connaught that he was after you. You've been seeing him, haven't you?'

Julia said nothing.

'He's married. Did you know that?'

'I don't want to discuss it,' Julia said.

'You don't want to discuss it,' Michael mimicked. 'So what am I supposed to do while you're fawning over this man? Sit and wait for you to come home?'

'We're not married,' Julia flared.

'Nor are we likely to be,' he snapped. 'I'm not interested in picking up leftovers.'

'That's a shitty remark, Michael. You know me better than that.'

'Do I? Listen to me. I've dedicated a year of my life to you. I've been in love with you since I first met you. Stupidly I thought you felt the same way about me.'

Julia kept her eyes on the table. This was a terrible mistake, she thought; I should never have called. What did I hope for? An amicable farewell?

'I trusted you,' he went on. 'But the first fucking millionaire that comes along – off you go. Isn't that Lisa Faraday's turf? I thought she'd cornered the market in screwing rich men. Or are you going to divide it up between the two of you?'

People were glancing at them.

'Keep your voice down,' Julia said.

'You were with him last weekend, weren't you?'

'Yes,' Julia said quietly.

'I knew it.' His voice was thick. It was obvious he'd had several drinks already. 'Where did you go? Some intimate hotel in the country; somewhere we've been together? Or does he have his own favourite love nest?'

'We went to Corsica,' she said.

'Corsica!' He gave a hoot of bitter laughter. 'How

106

romantic. I suppose he wanted to be sure no one saw you.'

'It was a business trip for him.'

'What was it for you?'

'I wanted to see the island.'

'Interesting, was it? What you saw of it. Or did you never leave the hotel room?'

Julia knew she should get up and walk out. But she had instigated this meeting. She didn't want it to end on a bitter note. 'That isn't worthy of you, Michael.'

'Is what you're doing worthy of you, Julia? Are you going to sit there and tell me Brand didn't fuck you in Corsica?'

'If he had it would be none of your business,' she said.

He looked at her accusingly. 'God, how you must have laughed when I told you about going to Australia. "I'm thrilled for you." Isn't that what you said?'

'I was genuinely pleased.'

'So you'd be free to see your rich friend.'

'That's unfair, Michael.'

'Is it? Is it? How do you expect me to react when I find the woman I've spent a year of my life with is bedding another man? You think he's going to marry you, is that it? You think you're going to inherit the Brand millions? Forget it. Mistresses always get dumped in the end. Don't you read the papers?'

Julia started to rise.

'Sit down,' Michael snarled. He grabbed her arm fiercely. Looking at his handsome face, now twisted with anger, Julia was shaken. It was like seeing a stranger.

'Let me go.'

'First tell me this,' he said. 'What's he got that I haven't? Apart from a hundred million or so? What is it? A bigger cock? Or are you just turned on by his private plane?'

'I don't expect you to understand,' Julia said quietly. 'I don't understand it myself. I certainly never intended to hurt you – '

'You didn't intend me to find out, you mean.'

'There was nothing to find out. I had dinner with him once. I went to Corsica with him for the weekend. That's all.'

Michael closed his eyes. Julia saw that he was close to tears. She reached out and touched his arm.

'Don't,' he said, pulling away. 'You want me to be stiff-upper-lipped about the whole thing – right? May the best man win. The British tradition.'

'Look,' she said, 'I don't know what's going to happen. Maybe nothing.'

He covered his eyes with his hand. She felt anguished for him; angry with herself. He had every right to be furious. She felt a sudden need to make up for the hurt she had caused him.

'I'm so sorry,' she said.

'Oh go to hell.'

Julia got up and pushed her way out of the pub. She half expected him to follow her. But when she turned, the street was empty.

Well, she thought, that's the end of that.

'You can't wait any longer,' Emma said. 'You've got to make a decision about that conference in Mexico.'

Julia had not slept well after her meeting with Michael. She felt tired and dispirited.

'Remind me.'

'They want you to speak on public relations and the hotel business.'

Julia glanced out of the window. It was a dull, grey day with rain threatening. 'Call them,' she said. 'Say I'll be delighted to participate.'

'I told you not to tell Michael,' Lisa said.

'I didn't. He knew.'

'He didn't know. How could he *know*? He was guessing and you fell for it.'

'He asked if I'd seen Robert. What was I supposed to do? Lie?'

'Of course.'

'I wouldn't do that. Not to Michael.'

'You're hopeless,' Lisa said. 'You don't deserve to succeed as a wanton woman.' She paused. 'Did he call you a rotten lying slut?'

'More or less.'

'Men always call you a rotten lying slut if you go off with someone else. Don't let it upset you.'

They had been to see a film in Leicester Square. Both had hated it. On the way home they had stopped in Piccadilly for a pizza.

'If you want my opinion – ' Lisa began.

'I'm not sure I do,' Julia said.

'You're getting it anyway. You shouldn't have called Michael. That's over. He'll go off to Australia and meet one of those bronzed bimbos. You're better off with Robert Brand.'

Chapter 17

'What the hell is going on at the bank? Why did that partner of Paul's commit suicide?'

Grace Brand glowered at her husband across the breakfast table. She was not a woman who liked surprises and his unexpected arrival in Acapulco the night before had put her in a foul mood. His explanation that he was on his way to South America and had decided to drop by to say hello had further irritated her. She knew him well enough to know he did not drop by anywhere unless there was a good reason.

Brand put down his newspaper, frowning. 'I don't know what you're talking about.'

'The *Herald Tribune* had the story. It was that older man, the one who's been with Paul from the beginning. He walked into the lake.'

Brand, shaken, stared at her. 'Di Marco? Was that the name?'

'Could have been.'

'Good God! How terrible.'

Grace looked at him suspiciously. 'You told me you'd just seen Paul. How is it you didn't know?'

'I saw him last month.' Brand shook his head. 'I can hardly believe it. Why would he have done such a thing?'

'Who knows? But I'm concerned. It draws attention to the bank.'

'Paul must be devastated.'

'Unless it was his fault,' Grace Brand said caustically. 'It probably was. I've never trusted that bastard. He's a devious son of a bitch.'

Brand passed his hand over his eyes. He felt a slight headache coming on. 'I'll call him when I get back to

London,' he said. 'See what I can find out.'

Grace rose, her caftan billowing behind her. 'I thought you were en route to South America?'

'Then I fly back to London.'

'You're spending a lot of time there these days,' she said. She made no attempt to hide the sarcasm in her voice. 'What's the attraction?'

'It's the base for our European operations,' Brand said.

'I'm sure it is,' she said. She paused by the door. 'I have some people coming to dinner tonight at nine. Will you be joining us?'

'If that's all right?'

'Please yourself,' she said.

People claimed that Acapulco had the most beautiful bay in the world; more spectacular, even, than Rio de Janeiro. Brand had never cared for the bay or the town. It might prove a welcome sight to sun-starved travellers arriving from wintry Europe or Canada, but the fierce sun and heat always drained him of energy. And the chasm between wealth and poverty depressed him. If you lived in the Las Brisas area it was easy to convince yourself that the place was as glamorous as the travel brochures proclaimed. A trip down the hill into the teeming town would quickly disabuse you.

It was twenty-five years since Brand and his wife had completed Casa Shalimar. It had six guest houses, each with a private swimming pool. The marble-floored living area was completely open on one side to the sea. There was a dining room seating sixty and a smaller eating area, down by the rocks, that boasted a giant aviary of exotic tropical birds. *House and Garden* had called it 'one of the most extraordinary houses in the world'. Brand, who had become a Mexican resident and built the house solely for tax purposes, now spent as little time as possible in the place. There was a good reason.

He could not bear to be near his wife.

* * *

Finishing his breakfast he retreated to his air-conditioned office to finish the newspaper. But he was preoccupied. Since flying down the night before he had found his thoughts turning more and more to Julia Lang. Only once in his thirty-five-year marriage had he attempted to make a break from his wife. Determined to marry Jane Summerwood, he had flown to Acapulco to plead with Grace. He had been utterly shocked by the fury she unleashed on him.

'You treacherous bastard!' she shrieked, striking him across the face, a blow that resulted in deep scratches down his cheek. 'You think you're going to walk out on me after all this time? Think again.'

'She's pregnant,' Brand said quietly.

For a moment he feared she would have a stroke. Her face went mottled; her eyes seemed to glaze over. 'After what you did to me, you dare tell me that?' she shouted. 'You *dare*? She can rot in hell as far as I'm concerned. She'll never have your name. *Never*.' Her eyes, flecked with red, filled with hate. 'Leave me, and your whole goddamn empire will crash down around your ears. You hear that?'

A month later, after Jane had been found murdered in London, Grace had called him in New York.

'There is a God,' she crowed. 'The whores of the world do get punished. Now what are you going to do?'

Repelled and nauseated, Brand had hung up on her.

Now here he was again. Trying for the second time. Since his trip to Corsica with Julia, he had determined to make one last effort to lead a normal life, to have a marriage, perhaps even a child, with a woman he cherished. He had intended to bring up the subject over breakfast. Grace's mood had made that impossible. And the news about di Marco's suicide had distressed him, for he had liked the old man.

He sighed, looking out of the window at the bay. The subject of divorce, he realized, would have to wait for another time. Meanwhile he was stuck in the house and

112

would have to endure another of his wife's dinner parties. He prayed they could get through this one without one of her drunken outbursts.

There were only six at dinner, for which Brand was thankful. He knew two of the guests: a Mexican politician of dubious morality and an Argentinian polo player who seemed to be a permanent house guest in Acapulco. Grace introduced the others, one of whom – a Canadian Member of Parliament turned novelist – seemed to have strong views on every subject that came up. Over the vichyssoise he pontificated about the failure of the United Nations. During the main course he informed everyone just where China was heading. Over dessert he bemoaned the abysmal state of education in the United States. Coffee found him arguing about the merits of various ski resorts.

Brand listened politely to it all, now and then interjecting a word or two, wondering bemusedly how Grace could stand this sort of thing night after night. It was no surprise that she drank so much, he reflected.

As soon as he could, Brand excused himself from the table and retired to his study to work. An hour later Grace joined him there.

'You were your usual gracious self tonight,' she said. 'I don't know why you bothered to show up.'

Brand put down the report he had been reading and removed his spectacles. 'I'm sorry if my social graces leave something to be desired,' he said. He got up and poured himself a brandy at the sideboard.

'I wish you wouldn't do that,' Grace said sharply. 'We do have servants, you know. Anyway, Dr Kiernan warned you about drinking after your heart attack.'

'For God's sake,' Brand said. 'All I'm having is one small glass of brandy.'

He returned to his chair and glanced out over the darkening bay. The sea, unruffled, looked like a sheet of black ice.

'You're not looking at all well,' Grace said. 'Señor Guerrero remarked upon it.'

'I've been under considerable pressure lately,' Brand said.

She looked at him mockingly. 'Really. I understood you found time to take a cruise.'

'I had a business meeting in the South of France,' Brand said, surprised that she knew. 'I took the *Dolphin* out for a couple of days.'

'I hope they were enjoyable ones,' she said.

Brand met her gaze. 'If you'll excuse me, Grace, I have to finish reading this report.'

'What time do you leave in the morning?'

'About ten.'

'I won't see you,' she said. 'I have a massage at that hour.' She moved towards the door. 'You came here for a reason. What is it?'

'I decided it was time we had another talk.'

'About what?'

'Our relationship.'

She wheeled on him, eyes glittering. 'You dignify what we have by calling it a relationship,' she hissed. 'You spend your time in London with your whores while I stay here alone. You call that a relationship?'

Brand held up a hand. 'Let's not go over all that again.'

She stood looking at him for a moment, then turned and swept out.

The talk was definitely postponed.

Chapter 18

Brand had been gone five weeks. His business meetings in Buenos Aires had taken longer than expected, he explained when he telephoned Julia, but he would be back in New York soon, then fly immediately to London. Hearing his voice she felt the familiar tingle of excitement. How meagre her own life seemed by comparison. She realized for the first time how easy it was to fall in love with someone's lifestyle. It was not just Brand who excited her; it was everything he did. Her own days at the Burlington now seemed almost intolerably pedestrian and monotonous. Sometimes, sitting at her desk, she found herself daydreaming, imagining herself accompanying Brand on these trips, meeting interesting people, sharing his glamorous life.

Her work at the Burlington continued to frustrate her. Since the decision not to go ahead with Gustave Plesset's private dinners she had seen Moscato only once. He had been icily polite. Meanwhile, word trickled down from the executive corridor that Chantal Ricci could do no wrong as far as he was concerned. She had been given a large expense account, was being allowed to eat regularly in the hotel restaurant – which Julia could do only when entertaining visitors – and had a contract giving her six weeks' annual vacation.

Julia felt angry and humiliated. Over lunch with Lisa she vented her feelings.

'Listen,' Lisa said. 'Don't let this Italian idiot get you down. So she's got all these perks? So she's editing the magazine? What do you care? It's less work for you.'

'If I had any pride I'd just walk out,' Julia said.

'Wrong. Make them buy out your contract. And walk

away with a fat cheque.' She scooped up the last of the spaghetti carbonara. 'Talking about money, what news from the Western front?'

'He called yesterday,' Julia said. 'He should be back in a week or two.'

'Thank God for that,' Lisa said. 'Now maybe we'll get a few smiles out of you.'

Paul Eberhardt was feeling uneasy. Talking with Grace Brand on the telephone always upset him. He knew she was unstable – Robert Brand had confessed that much – but her call to him that morning had been particularly unpleasant. After a brief reference to di Marco's death she came right to the point.

'My husband says he came to see you. What did he want?'

'Really, madame, you must ask him that. I am not at liberty – '

'Now you listen to me,' she said. 'When I ask you a question I expect an answer. Is that clear?'

She was talking to him as if he were some junior cashier. He was tempted to slam down the phone but dared not. He knew what a dangerous adversary this woman could be.

'We discussed the movement of certain monies,' he replied.

'Be specific.'

'I encouraged him to invest in Gulf Acquisitions,' Eberhardt said. 'The stock is healthy.'

'Never mind that. How much?'

'Ten million dollars.'

'Can he do that without my agreement?'

'Yes, madame, he can.'

'Has he done it?'

'The paperwork was completed last week.'

'From now on, Monsieur Eberhardt, you will advise me of all financial moves my husband makes. Is that quite clear?'

116

Eberhardt was shaken. 'Madame, I really feel that is something to be worked out between the two – '

'Did you hear what I said?'

'Yes, madame.'

'See that you do it.' The line went dead.

Chapter 19

Shielded from the fierce sun by a giant yellow umbrella Grace Stansfield Brand sat on the upper terrace of Casa Shalimar. She reached for the Tom Collins on the table by her chair and looked towards the bay where a large catamaran, crowded with holidaymakers, was passing below the house.

Faintly she could hear the guide explaining over the loudspeaker that this was the home of Grace and Robert Brand and one of the showplaces of Acapulco.

Everyone agreed on that.

Grace had adored the Mexican resort since flying there to do a photo spread on the place for the old *Life* magazine. Teddy Stauffer had been alive then, the former Swiss bandleader who had almost single-handedly put Acapulco on the map by inviting friends like Errol Flynn and Howard Hughes to visit the town. Now it was one of the most glamorous resorts in the world.

Normally Grace enjoyed her first drink of the day. But the phone call with Eberhardt had disturbed her.

Robert, she knew, would never have flown to Geneva merely to discuss investments with the banker; he would have done that over the telephone. There had to be a more important reason for his visit. Was he attempting, yet again, to separate their financial affairs? There could be only one reason for that; he was once more trying to break away from her.

That meant another woman.

Julia Lang.

Could Robert really be serious about her? Was the Jane Summerwood story to be played out all over again?

Twenty years earlier Grace Brand had sworn to herself

that Robert Brand would pay for what he had done to her. He had destroyed her life; it was only right that she should try to destroy his.

She finished her drink and went back into the house.

In his suite in Buenos Aires' Alvear Palace Hotel, Robert Brand was feeling exhausted. He had just completed weeks of intensive negotiations to build a giant industrial plant near the town of Azul. It would employ 3,000 people. The negotiations had gone well but they had been long and wearying. He felt he could sleep for a week.

He reached for his dry martini and, looking down at the traffic in the wide boulevard below, thought about Julia back in London. He realized he was finding it more and more difficult to get her out of his mind. The prospect of losing her appalled him. But he knew very well that to someone as straightforward as Julia, it was inexplicable that he could not just walk away from his marriage and pay his wife whatever she demanded.

When he had first met Grace Stansfield she had seemed to him one of the most interesting women in New York. They had made a good trade. She gave him the entrée to New York society; he gave her the money to achieve one of her cherished ambitions – to become a prominent hostess.

It had worked for a while; until that terrible day twenty years ago when he had made the mistake that had haunted him ever since. After that Grace had never been the same. Her breakdown had turned her from a sophisticated companion into a madwoman.

The doctors who attended her at the clinic had advised him to commit her. 'She will only get worse,' they told him. 'Your life together will become intolerable.'

Compassion had made him reject their advice; compassion and the knowledge that, crazed as she was, she still possessed the power to ruin him if he attempted to walk away.

Putting down his drink he went back to his desk to

pack up his papers. The rest of the Brand Corporation negotiators had gone back to New York that afternoon. The next day he was due to fly to Lima for two days of talks with Government ministers. Then he would be back in New York, en route to London.

And Julia.

Three times during the past week Paul Eberhardt had seen the same green Volkswagen parked on the opposite side of the street to the bank. A short stocky man had been sitting in the driving seat reading a newspaper. Each time Eberhardt drove away, the Volkswagen had pulled out and followed him.

There was something else. Several times during telephone conversations he had heard a click on the line. The Bern Government, he knew, had long engaged in secret surveillance of its citizens, but never in his most paranoid moments had he imagined he too might be suspected of wrongdoing.

But there was no doubt about it: he was being followed. His phone was tapped.

When he got home that night he decided he would arrange a meeting with Maître Bertrand. Bertrand had many friends in the Government. He would find out what was going on. Comforted by that thought Eberhardt opened the safe and took out the can of film. It was Thursday, his evening at Madame Valdoni's. He hoped the Oriental girl would be available again. She was really quite extraordinary.

Chapter 20

Six weeks after Brand had left for South America Bobby Koenig walked into Julia's office. 'Surprise,' he said, thrusting a bouquet of flowers at her.

Her face lit up. 'What are you doing here?'

'I've come to invite you to lunch. Can you get away?'

'You bet I can,' Julia said, exhilarated by the arrival of Brand's friend.

'The Greenhouse at one. Don't be late.'

Over lunch Koenig was in buoyant mood. He had, he told Julia, just raised the financing to shoot a movie in London. For the first time he was going to produce.

'You're the first person I've told,' he said. 'Even Robert doesn't know yet.' He chuckled. 'By the way, how is the old villain?'

Surprised at the question she looked at him. Did he know about them? 'He's fine, I think. He isn't here.'

'I know that.' Koenig laid a hand on her arm. 'Julia, Robert is my best friend. We have no secrets from each other. I know what's been going on.'

Julia felt a sudden rush of affection for this man who had introduced her to Brand. She leaned across the table and kissed him on the cheek.

'Is it serious?' he asked.

'Is what serious?'

'You're prevaricating, Julia.'

'I don't know how to answer your question.'

He smiled. 'You say yes or no.'

'I don't want to say anything.'

'But you like him?'

'What's not to like? He's a magician. He waves a wand and things happen. I've never known anyone like him.

But you shouldn't be asking these questions. Robert's married.' She nibbled at a piece of bread. 'What's his wife like?'

He thought for a moment. 'She's . . . well, she's not like him at all. She's volatile; full of verbal fireworks.'

'But it's not a happy marriage?'

'Who told you that?'

'He did.'

'He doesn't usually discuss his marriage.'

'He did with me.' Julia was pensive for a moment. 'You don't think they'll ever divorce?'

'I don't think they can.'

'That other woman, Jane Summerwood – I suppose you knew her too?'

'Yes.'

'Was she anything like me?'

Koenig chuckled. 'There's nobody like you, Julia.'

'So what have you found out from this expensive phone tap?' Commissioner Bonnet peered at Cristiani over the top of his half-moon spectacles.

'Eberhardt's had a couple of interesting phone calls from Brand's wife in Acapulco.'

Bonnet raised his eyebrows. 'Interesting. How?'

'She wants him to let her know every time Brand moves his money around.'

'Does she indeed?' Bonnet scowled. 'What did he say?'

'He told her no way – ' Cristiani began.

'Good for him. The nerve of the woman.'

'Then he backed off. Said he would. I think she's got something on him.'

'Like what?'

'That's what I'm trying to find out. Why would one of our most eminent bankers even listen to that kind of talk?'

'Perhaps because Grace Brand and her husband have millions stashed away in his bank.'

'Even so. It makes no sense.'

Bonnet leaned forward. 'You're a suspicious bastard,

Cristiani. That's why you're a good investigator. I'll be sorry to lose you . . .' He broke off as Cristiani pushed a paper across his desk. 'What's this?'

'Expenses.'

Bonnet picked up the sheet. 'Lunch with contact,' he growled. 'God in heaven, don't you ever eat on your own?'

'Not at the Lion d'Or,' Cristiani said.

When he returned home that night Cristiani was struck by a sudden thought. He picked up the phone and dialled the number of the *Journal de Genève*. He asked to be put through to Berthe Heydecker, their chief financial journalist and an old contact of his. In the past he had given Berthe some good stories. Maybe now she'd have some information he could use in return. He invited her to dinner.

Chapter 21

Julia had never been late in her life. Now her period was three weeks overdue. She tried not to worry; she'd been emotionally upset recently; perhaps that had done it. She checked her calendar again. Had she forgotten to take the pill? No, she was sure of that. Puzzled, she telephoned her doctor in Wimpole Street. She liked and trusted Dr Grierson; he would put her mind at ease. She arranged to see him the following Monday.

'It's not possible.'

'I'm afraid it is, Julia.'

Julia removed her heels from the stirrups and swung into a sitting position on the edge of the table. She stared at the young doctor, crisp and clean-looking in his white coat.

'But I'm on the pill.'

'It happens every now and again. No one knows why.'

I'm pregnant, Julia thought. She felt faintly sick.

Dr Grierson consulted her chart and asked a few general questions.

'Take plenty of exercise,' he said when he had finished. 'I see no reason why you shouldn't have a fine healthy baby.'

She left the doctor's office in a daze and walked home. How could it have happened? It was unbelievable. The reality of it totally unnerved her.

Back in the flat she stripped and examined herself in the bathroom mirror. Was it her imagination or were her normally pink nipples turning a light shade of brown? She splashed cold water in her face and put on her robe. She was pregnant with Robert Brand's child.

He was married and had no intention of getting a divorce.

Dear God, she thought, what am I going to do?

'What *are* you going to do?' Lisa sat in Julia's lounge studying her friend anxiously.

'I don't know yet.'

'There's only one thing you *can* do. I'll send you to my man.'

Julia stared at her. 'I won't have an abortion.'

'You're not going to have the child? That's crazy.'

'A lot of single women have children. Look at you.'

Lisa sighed. 'I had Deena because I wanted her. And the Prince looked after me. Even so it hasn't been easy. Not many men are willing to take on a woman with an illegitimate child.'

'I'm not interested in another man.'

'One day you may be.'

'I can't think about that,' Julia said.

Lisa was silent for a moment. 'When are you going to tell Robert?'

'As soon as he gets back.' She hesitated. 'I just hope he doesn't think I did this deliberately.'

'Of course he won't. It was just bad luck.' She paused. 'I still think you should get rid of it.'

'The idea makes me sick.'

'Maybe now. But just think about a few months down the line when it'll be too late to do anything. You'll have a stomach out to here – ' she stretched both hands in front of her – 'what are you going to do then?'

'He'll look after me.'

'Are you sure? You'd be surprised how many married men behave like shits when they find they've fathered an illegitimate child.'

'You don't know him,' Julia said.

'I'm sure it's the romance of the century, Julia. But what do you expect him to do? Marry you and make everything okay? You know he won't do that.'

'He may change his mind when he knows about the child.'

'Good. He'll qualify for *The Guinness Book of Records*.'

Julia realized she was feeling nauseous; whether from panic or the pregnancy she had no way of knowing. What if Brand did turn his back on her? How would she support herself? She had a few thousand in the bank but that would not go far. She could sell the diamond necklace. The thought gave her some comfort.

'You're sure he is coming back soon?' Lisa asked.

'He said so.'

'What if he doesn't?'

'What do you mean?'

Lisa sighed. 'Look, my naïve and trusting friend, men like Robert Brand don't always do what they say they'll do. How long has he been away already? Six weeks? He's hardly rushing back to you.'

'He's been busy.'

'Yeah. Sure. Take my advice. Go and see my man in Harley Street. You'll be in and out in no time. You don't even have to tell Robert.'

'I want to tell him,' Julia said doggedly. 'Don't you see that? He's never had a child. This might be his last chance.'

Lisa looked at her. 'I hope you're right,' she said.

At their weekly lunch Maître Claude Bertrand had news for Eberhardt. 'I have talked to people in Bern,' he said, putting down his wine glass. 'You were quite right. Your phone is tapped.'

Eberhardt's face registered consternation. 'But why?'

Bertrand looked gloomy. 'There's a fellow named Cristiani. Works for the Federal Banking Commission. Know him?'

'We've talked on the phone.'

'It seems he persuaded the people at the Justice Ministry to install the tap after di Marco's death. He doesn't believe it was suicide.'

'But that's absurd. The police closed the case – '

'I know that, Paul. But Cristiani thinks it's too much of a coincidence that the Leber fellow was run down and killed in Zurich last year and then di Marco was found drowned.' He looked hard at Eberhardt under his bushy eyebrows.

Eberhardt took a deep breath, letting it out slowly.

'The man must be mad. Is that who's been following me? The Volkswagen?'

'I don't know.'

'Why is this man hounding me?' Eberhardt tried to instil outrage into the question. 'He has no police powers.'

'I can't answer that question, Paul.' Bertrand broke open another roll. 'But if I were you I would be very discreet for a while.' He glanced enquiringly at his friend. 'There's nothing going on at the bank, is there? Nothing untoward?'

'Of course not.'

'Then you've got nothing to worry about.'

Chapter 22

Albert-Jean Cristiani had been married once, to a woman named Juliette, who had left him after five years for a Turkish diplomat. Since then Cristiani had sworn off women and kept his distance from Turkish diplomats. But tonight's dinner was not a date; it was work. Berthe Heydecker was the best financial journalist on the *Journal de Genève*. She had good contacts in banking circles and always seemed to know what was going on. The Geneva press in general was notoriously protective of Swiss institutions and rarely printed anything scandalous about its banks. But Cristiani knew that, although they refused to print scandals, they were sometimes prepared to discuss them over a glass or two of wine.

On the few occasions when Cristiani took a woman to dinner he liked her to be attractive, interesting, sexy and to smell good. Berthe Heydecker failed on all four counts. She was ugly, boring, unsexy and smelled slightly of sour milk.

He just hoped she was going to be able to help him. Particularly as the Lion d'Or was her choice. The famous restaurant boasted many great dishes, among them *loup à la vapeur au gingembre*. She was sure to have that, he thought. And Bonnet was sure to go through the roof when he saw the bill.

The restaurant was filled with good-looking women and well-dressed men. Cristiani had put on his best suit for the occasion, a silver-grey number he had bought during the last year of his marriage. Berthe Heydecker was wearing an unattractive brown woollen suit, which fitted her poorly.

After the maitre d' had placed them at one of the worst tables Berthe became animated.

'You know the dish I absolutely adore?' she said. *'Loup à la vapeur au gingembre.'*

'Really?' Cristiani said. In his mind's eye he could already see Bonnet scowling. 'I don't think I've ever had that.'

'It's absolutely wonderful,' she said. 'One of their specialities. I think I'll have that.'

'Why not?' Cristiani said with a suggestion of bonhomie he was far from feeling.

'What about you?' Berthe said.

'I'm not really very hungry,' Cristiani lied. 'I think I'll settle for something quite simple.' In the end he picked a plain lake fish and chose a decent wine, Aigle Les Muraille, to accompany it.

For several minutes they discussed the weather, the large number of Arabs in town and the high cost of living. Then Cristiani got to the point. Had Berthe heard any rumours about the Banque Eberhardt?

'Such as?'

'Anything at all,' he said.

'Since di Marco's suicide, you mean?'

'I don't think it was suicide,' he said.

She frowned. 'Oh come now, Albert-Jean. The police had no doubts.'

'I know that,' he said. 'Neither does Commissioner Bonnet. I'm not so sure.'

For the next five minutes he catalogued his suspicions for her.

'I'd forgotten about André Leber,' she said. 'I suppose that does make it a bit odd.'

'Two of his top men,' Cristiani said. 'Dead within a year.'

'In suspicious circumstances.'

'Di Marco was going to tell me something,' Cristiani said. 'He called to set up a dinner. Then he was found drowned.'

'What do you think he wanted to talk about?'

'No idea. Maybe the bank's in trouble?'

'Surely not? They're very solid. Some huge accounts there – Marie de Boissy ... Paul Hoffman ... Robert Brand. Brand was here, by the way, just the other day.'

'Doing what?'

'Seeing Eberhardt, I was told.'

'I wonder what brought him to Geneva?'

She tittered. 'Perhaps he wanted to be near his money.'

'I wouldn't mind being near it myself,' Cristiani said. 'I wonder what he's worth.'

'Billions,' Berthe said. 'Of course, the Brand Corporation uses Chase Manhattan in New York. It's Brand's personal fortune that's here with Eberhardt.'

'You ever meet Brand?'

She shook her head. 'He doesn't give interviews. At least I've never read one.'

Cristiani dissected his fish. 'Would you automatically hear if there was something brewing at the bank?'

'I imagine so. I know people there.'

'Alain Charrier?'

'No. He's very close-mouthed. Most of my information comes from people lower down the ladder.'

'Charrier's been there for some time?'

'Thirty years or so. Since he left Credit Suisse.'

'I'll say one thing for Eberhardt,' Cristiani said, 'the people around him are very loyal.'

'Very.'

Cristiani poured her another glass of wine. 'What about Eberhardt's start here? Know anything about that?'

'I think he opened the bank in the late thirties, just before the war.'

'Would there be anything in the *Journal*'s old files?'

'No idea.'

'Might be something. Give me a handle on all this.'

'I'll have a look,' she said.

She took the dessert menu from the hovering maitre

d' and consulted it. There goes another thirty francs, Cristiani thought sourly.

She turned to him. 'Are you going to have something?'

'Just coffee for me.'

'You don't mind if I do?'

'Of course not,' Cristiani said. 'Have anything you want.' She picked the apricot soufflé. Cristiani tried hard not to wince.

Chapter 23

Nervous and distracted, her mind so fragmented she found it hard to concentrate on work, Julia spent the next few days slipping in and out of deep depression. The knowledge that she had a child inside her totally unnerved her. She moved restlessly about her office, avoiding Emma as much as possible, working late into the evening. Since his last call from Buenos Aires she had heard nothing from Brand. This further depressed her.

Early one afternoon Chantal Ricci swept into her office. 'Hello,' she said. 'Haven't seen you for a while.'

'I've been here,' Julia said dully.

'Everything going well?'

'I think so.'

'I've seen several mentions of the Burlington in the papers. That your doing?'

'That's my job.'

'Terrific.' She gave Julia a bright smile. 'Listen, I need a favour. Have you got anything on the early history of the hotel? How it started; that sort of thing? It was a private mansion, I'm told.'

'It was.'

'There must be old photographs somewhere. Could you get that girl of yours to dig them out for me?'

'You mean Emma?'

'Whatever her name is. Signor Moscato has decided we should have some early pictures in the magazine. I think he's right.'

'It'll take some time,' Julia said.

'Get her on to it right away, will you? I need them by the day after tomorrow. Deadlines, you know.'

She smiled again and swept out of the room.

Smarting at the arrogance of the woman Julia got up and paced the office. Damn her, she thought. Patronizing bitch. So sleek and coiffed and sure of herself.

That afternoon and all the next day she and Emma went through the old files for stories of the Burlington's early days when it was first converted from a millionaire's townhouse into a fifteen-room hotel. Emma spent the following morning putting the photographs together and writing the captions.

Two days later came a handwritten note from Chantal: *Thank you for your assistance on this project. We really appreciate it.*

Was that the royal we, Julia speculated. Or did she mean: Your boss and I? She threw it in the waste basket.

When Julia got back from lunch the next day there was a note on her desk: *Jill Bannister called from New York.* Julia's spirits lifted. At last – news from Brand. She buzzed Emma. 'When did she call?'

'Half an hour ago, thereabouts. She sounded upset you weren't here. Said she'd call back later. Whenever later is.'

The afternoon dragged. There was no further call from New York. Julia spent the time revising her weekly newsletter. She now included potted biographies of the personalities staying at the hotel together with the reasons for their visits to London. Since developing this idea the hotel had been mentioned in several interviews.

She did not get back to the flat until late. She knew she should go for a walk round the park but she was afraid she would miss Jill's call. Just as she was stepping out of the shower the phone rang. Wrapping herself in her robe she rushed for the receiver.

'Hello.'

'Miss Lang? It's Jill. Jill Bannister. I called you earlier . . .'

'I know. I'm sorry I missed you.'

'It's about Mr Brand. He collapsed . . .'

'What?' Julia felt an inner flutter of fear.

'He's in the hospital in Peru. But he's all right. He wants you to know that.'

'When was this?'

'This morning our time. I just got a call from the doctor there. Mr Brand went to Machu Picchu with a couple of Government people. It's high, you know, twelve thousand feet. He was foolish; he set out to climb Huayna Picchu, which is even higher.'

Julia closed her eyes. Her hand gripping the receiver was damp. 'Where is he now?'

'He's in a place called Cuzco. His own doctor gets there tonight. They're flying him to New York tomorrow.'

'Can I talk with him?'

'I'm afraid not.'

Julia was filled with dread. 'What can I do?'

'There's nothing. Just sit tight. Try not to worry. I'll call you as soon as I can.'

She hung up. Julia sat on the edge of the bed, holding the receiver, feeling stricken. Robert would die without ever knowing she was having his child. She remembered the way he had faltered as they climbed the steep cliff in Corsica. He knew he had a bad heart yet he carried on as if he were perfectly fit. Now this. She must try to think positively, she told herself. Men had heart attacks all the time and recovered from them. She mustn't overreact. Perhaps this was not even a heart attack. He had 'collapsed', whatever that meant. Now he was in hospital. His doctor was flying down. He'd have the best possible care. Of course he'd be all right. Consoling herself with this thought she got into bed, eventually drifting into a troubled sleep.

The item was the third story in the gossip page of London's top-selling tabloid the next day.

> I hear all is not well at London's most
> distinguished hotel, the Burlington in

134

Knightsbridge. It appears that a new addition to the staff – shapely Italian Chantal Ricci – has been putting a few noses out of joint at the elegant hotel, a favourite hangout of the world's celebrities. Brought in to edit a forthcoming hotel magazine by Managing Director Guido Moscato – about whom she recently wrote a sycophantic puff piece in *Trends*, her old magazine – Ricci has managed to alienate so many of the staff with her arrogance that several are threatening to quit. Mary Merrill, housekeeper at the hotel for the past five years, has already handed in her notice. Moscato, it seems, is so impressed with his new find that he has given her a grand office next to his – demoting Bryan Penrose, the hotel's able Director of Sales and Marketing, to a burrow further down the hall. Does the fact that both Moscato and Ricci hail from Milan have anything to do with this? And does the Sultan of Malacca know? And would he approve if he did? As is widely known, he considers the Burlington the finest jewel in his colourful turban.

Julia, coming in late after a disturbed night, found the piece on her desk, ringed in red. An hour later Moscato called her in.

'You saw this?' he asked, holding up the paper.

'Of course.'

He searched her face with unemotional eyes. 'Who is this man?' He glanced at the top of the column. 'Jeremy Orde?'

'A gossip columnist.'

'You know him?'

'I've met him.'

Moscato put down the item. 'I want to know where this came from. Obviously someone on the staff passed it on. I want you to find out who.'

Tired and irritable, beset by worry, Julia looked at him contemptuously. 'What do you expect me to do? Line up the staff and question them? That's ridiculous. And it isn't my job.'

Moscato glared at her. 'I know that. What I want you to do is call this man Orde and find out who gave him the story.'

'You expect him to tell me? You don't know much about British newspapers. Anyway most of that story is common knowledge . . .'

'It is a cheap piece filled with innuendo,' Moscato said. 'I had hoped that during the time you have been here you had formed a better relationship with the press.'

Julia reddened. 'My relationship with the press is excellent. But a story is a story. I told you that piece in *Trends* would boomerang. You thought you knew better.'

'Your rudeness to me is quite unacceptable,' Moscato said angrily. 'I warn you I will not put up with it.'

'You're the one making this ridiculous request,' Julia said. 'Now if you'll excuse me . . .'

She left before he had a chance to reply.

Plenty of exercise, the doctor had said. Right, Julia decided, she would walk home. Well wrapped up against the chill of the evening she set off towards Hyde Park Corner. There she cut through the underpass, emerging in Park Lane where a short walk brought her to Grosvenor Square. She stood for a moment looking around. A few doors along from the Britannia Hotel she found the building that had drawn her towards the square, its small brass plate announcing The Brand

Corporation. Crossing the street she stood beside the memorial to the men of the American Eagle Squadron who had fought with the RAF in the Second World War. She looked back at the building. A few lights were still on downstairs, but most of the windows were dark.

Why was she doing this, she wondered. Why was she standing there on a winter night like some jealous mistress looking up at a lover's apartment? Was it a pathetic attempt to feel close to Robert, to stand where perhaps he had sometimes stood? She didn't know. All she knew was she had never felt so alone. Michael was no longer a part of her life. Robert was thousands of miles away, perhaps dying. Her days at the Burlington were numbered. And she was pregnant.

She felt numb with depression.

When she got home she went straight to the bedroom. The light on her answering machine was winking. It was Lisa seeking further news about Brand. Julia had told her about his collapse earlier. The message ended: 'I'm cooking tonight. Chicken piccata, your favourite. Come about eight.'

Pleased, Julia changed into her tracksuit and took a taxi to Lisa's flat north of the park.

'I can tell by your face,' Lisa said, 'you've heard nothing more.'

'Not a word.'

'That doesn't mean anything. Robert Brand is an important man. And a rich one. He'll have the best medical attention in the world. I'm sure he'll be all right. Maybe it was just a mild attack.'

'You think so?'

'You've got to be optimistic,' Lisa said. She took Julia's arm. 'Come and help me in the kitchen. Incidentally, we're invited to a dinner party next Saturday and I've accepted.'

'I'm not in the mood.'

'It's Simon Winnick. And you're coming. He likes

you and you like him and you've got to get out
among people instead of cooping yourself up in that flat.
Okay?'

'Okay,' she said. Lisa was right. She needed cheering
up.

Chapter 24

Simon Winnick's dinner parties were always elegant affairs and when the time came for her to get ready Julia was filled with misgivings. She had felt nauseous all day. Her instinct was to hide away in the flat, to see nobody. But she knew it was important that she pull herself out of her slump. Mingling with new people was a good way to do it. And there was one thing about Simon's dinners: the guest list was always interesting.

Julia had met him at a cocktail party at the hotel three years before and had liked him immediately. The Conservative politician was a man of wit and style, as good at listening to stories as telling them. She and Lisa had several times been invited to his house in Eaton Square and each time had stayed late, so good was the conversation. What made these affairs particularly enjoyable to both women was the fact that they were never invited as dates for people; they were there simply because Simon enjoyed their company.

Julia, whose pregnancy had still not started to show, had already decided on her all-purpose Louis Féraud black cocktail dress for the occasion. And she determined to wear Brand's diamonds. Guests at Simon's dinners were always elegantly dressed and she knew this might be one of the few occasions when she could actually wear the necklace. Taking it from its hiding place she went into the bathroom and put it on. It was the first time she had worn it since Brand had given it to her on the yacht and, standing before the mirror, she was captivated by its sparkling beauty. She was dressing up, she realized, for the first time in weeks. Not to impress any of the other guests but to make herself feel good, to temporarily banish gloom from her life.

When Lisa arrived in the taxi she took one look at Julia and her eyes widened. 'You look sensational. You'll knock them cold.'

Julia forced a smile. 'Who's them? Anyone I know?'

'A couple of politicians. Some business tycoons. An editor or two. Some authors. You know Simon. It'll be fun.'

Lisa's forecast proved accurate. When they walked into Winnick's house they found twenty people milling around in his ornate drawing room, sipping drinks and talking animatedly.

Julia recognized a couple of actresses, a well-known columnist, two Members of Parliament and a playwright. After introducing them Simon led them over to the small man standing with his back to the fire. With a rush of pleasure, Julia realized it was the Sultan of Malacca.

He took her hand. 'It's nice to see you again, Julia.'

She was surprised to see him there. She had supposed him long gone. 'I'm delighted to see you, sir.'

'Please,' the Sultan smiled, 'this is a social occasion. Call me George.'

Julia turned to Lisa. 'This is my friend Lisa Faraday. Lisa – the Sultan of Malacca.'

Lisa's reaction was entirely predictable. Her eyes widened. Her smile broadened. The volume of her body language increased markedly. 'Julia, why have you been keeping this lovely man to yourself? I've been waiting years to meet him.'

For the next ten minutes, as they stood talking, Lisa never took her eyes from the Sultan, being in turn coquettish, funny, charming and just plain sexy. Julia, who had seen her friend in action before, wondered if her goal was the Sultan's bed or just his admiration. Bed, she eventually decided, as Lisa continued to turn on the charm.

'You know something, your Highness?'

'George. Please.'

'You don't realize what a treasure you have in Julia.'

'Oh, but I do, I do,' the Sultan said.

'You couldn't. Because everything she does is dismissed by that man Moscato.'

Julia was horrified. 'Lisa. Stop that.'

'It's true,' Lisa persisted. 'She's absolutely wonderful at her job. The Burlington's had more pieces written about it than any hotel I know. That's her doing. But all Moscato does is criticize.'

Flushed with embarrassment, Julia wheeled on her friend. 'I forbid you to go on.'

The Sultan put his hand on her arm. 'Do not distress yourself, Julia. Clearly this is something about which your friend feels strongly. She is right to mention it.'

'Not here,' Julia said grimly. 'Not a dinner party.'

'It's quite all right,' the Sultan said. 'Really.'

Angrily Julia excused herself and walked over to join a couple she did not know. She was seething inwardly.

'You look like you're ready to blow up the place,' the man said. 'Who are you mad at?'

'Myself, actually.'

'That's a waste of time,' the man said. 'Far more rewarding to be mad at other people.'

The woman, who looked vaguely familiar, smiled. 'You're from the Burlington, aren't you?'

Julia nodded. 'Julia Lang.'

'I think you know my mother, Judith Cameron?'

'Of course.' Julia brightened. 'She ran our etiquette course for youngsters. She's a wonderful lady. And such fun.'

The woman swirled the ice in her glass. 'You heard what happened, I suppose?'

'No.'

'She's chairing this year's Primrose Ball. Because she'd had such a good relationship with all of you she wanted to hold it at the Burlington. But they turned it down.'

Julia stared at her, astonished. 'Who turned it down?'

'Some Italian woman. Ricci, is that her name? Mother was told she was in charge of those things now.'

Julia took a deep breath. 'I knew nothing about this,' she said quietly. 'Let me look into it.'

'It's too late for that. They're holding it at the Savoy.'

Julia felt a knot of anger forming in her stomach. She turned to look at the Sultan. He was still talking with Lisa. I ought to march right up and tell him about this, she thought; explain to him the importance of the Primrose Ball. It would have been a great coup for the Burlington. But she knew she would be wasting her time. He would take it as yet another criticism of Moscato and Chantal Ricci. And, after Lisa's outburst, he would almost certainly react badly.

At that moment dinner was announced, and everyone moved into the dining room. Julia found herself sitting between one of London's most influential publishers, Anton Lazlo, and Sir Francis Calder, a former Minister in the Hong Kong Government.

'This lady works at the Burlington Hotel,' Lazlo said to Calder. 'She'll be interested in what you've just been telling me.'

Calder put down his wine. 'I was just saying that unless we put some sort of cap on tourism we're in for terrible trouble. Britain has nineteen million tourists a year – far more than it can cope with. Everywhere you go people are tripping over themselves. What about a few years down the line when the Chinese and Russians have money and start travelling? You won't be able to get on a plane; you won't be able to get into a hotel. If you want to spend a week at the San Pietro in Positano they'll say: ' "We can give you two days in 1999. Nothing before that." Seeing Julia's smile he said sharply: 'I'm serious.'

'I know you are and you're quite right,' Julia said. 'But what's the answer?'

'Countries must put a ceiling on the number of tourists they'll accept in any year – just as they do with immigrants. They must stop this endless building of hotels. It's self-defeating.'

'Calder is right,' Lazlo said. 'China will be a capitalist society one day. What's their population? Over a billion. That means millions of Chinese businessmen fighting to get seats on the airlines.'

'It's an alarming thought,' Julia agreed.

As the evening wore on the discussion between the two men became more and more animated. Julia found herself becoming weary. She glanced at her watch and was astonished to see it was past midnight. Several people were on their second brandies. One or two had already left. She glanced down the table to catch Lisa's attention but saw she was deep in conversation with the Sultan.

'I'm afraid it's past my bedtime,' she told the two men. 'I must be off.'

'Tomorrow's Sunday,' Lazlo protested. 'You don't have to work.'

'I've a lot to do,' Julia said. She said goodnight and made her way to the other end of the table.

'You're leaving?' the Sultan said, rising. 'Lisa had just persuaded me to go to Annabel's for a nightcap. Though in my case it's soda water. You won't join us?'

'Another time, perhaps,' Julia said.

She said goodnight to Lisa, who gave her a cat-like smile, and went with Simon to the door. He stood with her until a taxi came by.

'You should come to all my dinner parties,' he said. 'You illuminate the room.'

Julia laughed. 'I think Lisa was doing the illuminating tonight.'

'She's certainly exuding fairly high wattage,' Simon said. 'She and the Sultan seem to have hit it off quite splendidly. It will be interesting to see how that develops. And, knowing Lisa, it will develop.' He looked carefully at her necklace. 'Nice bit of jewellery, that,' he said. 'A present?'

143

'A present,' Julia said.

'Not bad,' he said. He took her hand. 'Lisa tells me Michael's off to Australia.'

'He's been offered a great job there.'

'You'll miss him. You've been together some time.'

'Please, Simon, I don't want to talk about it.' She kissed him on both cheeks. 'You give wonderful dinner parties,' she said. 'Invite me again.'

'Count on it,' he said.

As the taxi turned round Hyde Park Corner and headed up Park Lane Julia sat back against the cold leather and thought about the evening. When she recalled what Lisa had told the Sultan about her relationship with Moscato she mentally cringed. How could she have been that crass? He might be 'George' at a dinner party but he would most certainly revert to being the Sultan of Malacca, all high owner of the Burlington, next morning. Oh well, she thought, what's done is done.

When she entered her bedroom the light on her answering machine was winking. She pressed the play-back button, half fearful of what she might hear, half hopeful.

It was Robert Brand.

'We've just left New York, Julia. I'll see you tomorrow.'

She slept badly, disturbed by fearful dreams. By six she was wide awake, standing in front of the window, watching dawn creeping over the rooftops.

At seven she called the hotel and spoke to the duty receptionist. 'Do we have a booking for Robert Brand today?'

'Came in last night. The Empire Suite. Same as last time.'

He's back, she thought. Incredible. He's back. But anticipation was tinged with dread. Had Lisa been right? Would he be horrified to find out she was pregnant?

Chapter 25

They had arranged to meet at the flat at four o'clock. Brand would stay only a short while, he said; he was tired and exhausted from the flight.

As the hour approached Julia became increasingly nervous. She paced the floor, checking her watch, adjusting her hair. At five to four she was standing by the window, searching for a glimpse of the Daimler. When it finally appeared she was trembling so much she went into the lounge and poured a brandy to calm her nerves.

The moment he walked in, her nervousness gave way to alarm. She stared at him, aghast. He seemed to have shrivelled. His gait was unsteady; his complexion cyanotic. He looked feeble and frail.

'Dear God,' he said, searching her face. 'Do I really look that bad?'

She laughed nervously, taking his hands in hers. 'If only you knew how good you look to me.' She led him into the lounge.

'I'm weak as a kitten,' he said. 'Embarrassing. Let me sit.'

She bunched some cushions behind his head. He took out a handkerchief and dabbed his forehead. Despite the cool of the afternoon he was sweating. He lay back, looking at her; no longer the thrusting tycoon but a sick, ageing man, seeking strength and reassurance from a young, vibrant woman.

'I've missed you,' he said.

She reached out and took his hand. 'I'd have come,' she said. 'I didn't know where you were.'

'It would have been too difficult,' he said. 'Grace

came up from Mexico. I was in intensive care for five days.' He smiled bleakly. 'They thought I wouldn't make it.'

She gripped his hand tightly. 'What do the doctors say?'

'I have to have a bypass immediately. Quintuple. Otherwise . . .' He broke off.

'But that's commonplace now, Robert. Lots of people have them. Everyone says how much better they feel afterwards. When . . . when would this happen?'

'Next week. I'm supposed to be resting at home right now. But the hell with that.'

'You took such a risk, coming here.'

He took a deep breath and let it out slowly. 'Jill Bannister told you what happened?'

'You went to climb a mountain . . .'

'I was such a damn fool. I'd been in Lima talking about building a resort down there. One of their ministers suggested a visit to Machu Picchu. Wasn't enough to see it, though. I had to show off.' He paused, breathing heavily.

She poured him some tea. His hand shook as he took the cup.

'My own doctor flew down from New York. He's booked me into Houston for the surgery. Best heart men there, he says.'

Julia took his hand again. 'You'll have the operation, Robert, and everything will be fine.'

'You think so?'

'I'm sure of it.'

'I wish my doctors were as certain. They say my ticker is a mess.'

He put down the cup and let his head fall back against the cushions. Staring up at the ceiling he was silent for several minutes.

'I did a lot of thinking, Julia. I've had two warnings; I won't get a third. If I want to go on living I have to slow down, go for walks in the woods, lie on the beach, forget

146

about business . . .' He gave her a weak smile. 'Did I ever tell you my father left me a lot of money?'

Julia nodded.

'All I had to do was leave it in the bank, let it grow. But no. I had to prove to myself I deserved to be wealthy. I spent the past forty years proving it; promoting the Protestant work ethic.' He breathed hard. 'Look where it got me – a gurney in a broken-down Peruvian hospital.'

'I'll go for walks in the woods with you,' Julia said quietly.

'I know you will.' It was a whisper, hardly audible. He dabbed his forehead again.

Julia leaned towards him. 'I'm pregnant, Robert.'

Brand seemed to stop breathing for a moment. He just stared at her, bewildered, a stricken expression on his face. Her heart sank. He doesn't want to know, she thought. He's sick and ill and he doesn't need this.

Then she saw his face change. He pulled himself up straight.

'Ours?' he asked.

'Ours.'

'Jesus,' he said. His voice cracked. He cleared his throat. 'How wonderful.'

She had guessed right. She felt as if a giant weight had been lifted from her shoulders. She reached for his hand again. He clasped it tightly.

'A baby,' he said. 'For God's sake. I think that's great.' He paused. 'You're sure?'

'Positive.' She smiled.

He shook his head. 'Incredible. Here I am at death's door and you've got new life inside you.'

'You're going to be fine, Robert.'

'Damn right. I'll get well. This calls for champagne. You still got that bottle?'

'I have, but that's for when you're well.'

'Then tomorrow. In the suite. We'll celebrate. I'll feel better then.'

There was a buzz from the street door. 'That'll be Parsons,' Brand said. 'Time for me to go back and rest.'

Julia helped him to his feet. 'How long can you stay in London?'

'I fly back Tuesday.'

'Shall I come with you?'

'Even if you came you couldn't see me,' Brand said. 'Grace will be there. But pack your bags. Afterwards I'll send the plane for you. We'll go some place warm. Fiji, maybe. In the sun. The two of us.'

She went down in the lift with him.

'Come round at eight tomorrow,' he said. 'We'll talk some more and have dinner.' He embraced her. 'It's great news. Such great news.'

Julia stood on the edge of the pavement as dusk settled over London, watching the big black car until it disappeared from sight.

The Empire Suite was the jewel in the Burlington's crown. With its canopied terraces, marble floor, Persian scatter rugs, blue and white curtains and antique furniture, it would, Julia thought, have delighted César Ritz himself, the man who first conceived the idea of a hotel as a palace. Everything about it was calculated to impress, from the original art on its walls to the valuable *objets d'art* in the display cabinet.

When Julia arrived via the service lift, she found Brand in a robe, finishing a telephone call. Some of his normal colour seemed to have returned. She was immediately encouraged. 'You look so much better,' she said.

'I do, don't I?' He looked at himself in the wall mirror. 'Nothing like fatherhood to restore one's sense of purpose.' He took her hands in his. 'How are *you* feeling?'

'Terrific,' she said. 'Now.'

'None of that sickness stuff?'

'Sometimes.'

Brand handed Julia a packet of slim books from his desk. She looked at the titles: *Childbirth Made Easy, Your*

First Child, Coping with Pregnancy. 'Had them sent over from Hatchards,' he said. He chuckled. 'I read most of them last night. The things we put you women through.'

Julia, touched by his gesture, kissed his cheek. 'You're going to make a great father,' she said.

'I hope so.' He glanced at her, looking, for one brief moment, almost boyish. 'Thought of any names yet?'

'It's a bit early for that.'

'Good to be prepared. How about Walter if it's a boy? My father's name.'

She tried it out. 'Walter Brand. That sounds nice. And a girl?'

'You choose. What was your mother's name?'

'Mary Elizabeth.'

'I like that. Mary Elizabeth Brand. Goes well, don't you think?'

Could she use the surname 'Brand' if they were not married? She started to say something, then changed her mind. 'Lang' was good too, she thought. Walter Lang. Mary Elizabeth Lang.

Brand relaxed into a corner of the long sofa and patted the cushions for her to sit next to him.

'Did I make any sense yesterday?' he asked. 'All that rambling. I was so jet lagged.'

'You made a lot of sense. It is time you slowed down.'

He nodded. 'Take time to smell the roses. Isn't that the expression? But you can't spend your whole day smelling roses. I'd still want to be involved with the company in some capacity. Advisory, probably. We'd have lots of time together.'

The question could no longer be avoided. 'What about your wife, Robert? Why won't she let you go if the marriage is over?'

'Because she's a sick, crazy woman. She can't be happy so she's determined I won't be either. That's why you must never, ever, tell anyone what I've just arranged for you. It might get back to her. She seems to know every damn thing I do. Frankly, she scares me.'

'What are you talking about?'

'I've just opened an account for you at my bank in Geneva.'

Julia was instantly embarrassed. She had never been at ease talking about money. Face to face with Brand made it even more difficult.

'You didn't have to do that. I have my own money.'

'I'm sure you do. But you won't be able to continue here much longer. And having a baby is expensive.' He gave her a small smile. 'I read those books, you see.'

An account in Geneva. The idea made her feel oddly sophisticated. She felt a wave of relief. Everything was going to be all right.

Brand patted her knee. A fatherly gesture. 'When can you leave here and come to New York?'

'A couple of months, probably. I have to be fair to the Sultan.'

'We'll find a nice apartment for you. One overlooking the park . . .' He broke off. 'What were we talking about?'

'Your wife. Saying nothing about the account.'

'Ah yes.' He turned to look at her. 'Julia, my wife is seriously disturbed. She had a breakdown twenty years ago and has never recovered. Unfortunately our funds are hopelessly intertwined. We own the Brand Corporation jointly.'

'A separation, then?'

'That's what we have now. I rarely see her. She spends most of the year in Acapulco.'

Julia suffered a moment's apprehension. 'You said a moment ago she seemed to know your movements. Does she know about me?'

'No. I've never mentioned your name. Never will.'

'What about Jane Summerwood?'

'I told her about Jane. I won't lie to you, Julia. I'd hoped to marry Jane even before I found she was pregnant. When I told my wife she went crazy. She was like a mad person. When Jane was killed she called to gloat.'

'That's sick.'

'That's the way she is.'

'But can nothing be done? Is there no treatment?'

'Nothing.'

'It's scary,' Julia said. 'If she knew about my baby – '

'She won't,' Brand said. 'She's never going to get near you. I promise you that.' He rose slowly, steadying himself on the arm of the sofa, and went across to the desk. He scribbled something on a scratch pad. 'Here's the bank,' he said, returning. 'The Banque Eberhardt. Call them tomorrow. Get the account number. Talk to Paul Eberhardt himself.'

'It might be easier if I transferred it to my bank here,' Julia said.

'Don't do that,' Brand said. 'Problems with tax. Leave it where it is for now.'

'I don't mind paying the tax,' Julia said.

'On $20 million?'

'*What?*' The word came out in a gasp. Julia felt her cheeks redden.

'Take Eberhardt's advice. He's an experienced banker.'

'Twenty million dollars?' Her mind simply refused to accept the figure. She swallowed. 'That's a fortune.'

'It's a lot of money,' Brand agreed. 'I don't want you or our child to have any worries.'

Julia felt slightly dizzy. 'I think I need a drink,' she said.

'Good idea.' Brand reached for the phone and dialled room service. 'Time we celebrated the good news.' He ordered a bottle of Dom Perignon. When the buzzer announced the arrival of the floor waiter Julia went into the bedroom.

Twenty million dollars! She repeated the figure to herself, trying to make it sound real. With one telephone call – or was it a note? – the man in the next room had removed all her worries. She sat on the edge of the bed, her thoughts in turmoil. Should she wait two months or should she just walk into Moscato's office and fling the contract in his face? Why should she care about the

Sultan's feelings? He had already made it clear she would be out if there were any more complaints from Moscato.

She heard the door shut as the waiter departed and a moment later Brand walked in holding two flutes of champagne. His step seemed almost sprightly. She started to rise. 'No,' Brand said. 'Stay right there.' He put the champagne flutes on a side table and sat beside her. 'You are the most wonderful thing that has ever happened to me,' he told her.

Before she could reply Brand took her in his arms and kissed her passionately, his tongue sliding between her lips. His robe fell open. She felt his arousal.

'Come,' he said. He tried to lift her dress.

She pulled away, petrified. 'Robert, we mustn't. You're still . . .'

He shrugged himself out of the robe. Naked he seemed unbelievably sexual to her. No longer the sick and feeble man, but alive and virile. He kissed her again.

'I need you,' he said hoarsely. 'Now.'

Overwhelmed, she put aside her anxieties, and undressed. Then he was all over her, kissing her neck, her breasts, her stomach. They fell back on the bed, Julia arching up as he thrust into her. He seemed, if anything, more passionate than in their previous encounter, almost oblivious to her as he strove to reach a shuddering climax. She held him then as he gradually quietened, feeling a great surge of emotion for this man whose wealth and power could do so little to help him achieve what he surely wanted: the chance to see his child grow up.

They lay quietly for a long time until Julia, feeling him grow heavy, said gently, 'Robert?'

There was no reply.

'Robert?' she said again, aware with growing alarm how heavy he had now become.

No reply.

As the truth slowly sank in she was paralysed with disbelief and panic. 'Robert!' She tried to shake him. 'You must wake up.' Pulling herself from under his inert body she sat up, rolling him over. His eyes were open, staring at the ceiling, his mouth fixed in a rictus halfway between a smile and a scowl. 'Oh, dear God,' she moaned. 'Dear God, help me now.'

She leaned over him, pressing her lips to his, breathing deeply. After a couple of minutes, two sweating, gasping minutes, as she felt his lips growing cold beneath her own, she knew it was hopeless. Brand lay dead. Her heart pounding in her chest, her face streaked with sweat, she reached down and tried to close his eyes. She could not.

He was dead. The thought unhinged her thinking. They were both naked in his suite. The buzzer might sound at any moment with the arrival of the night maid. She had to get dressed. She had to get out of there. She staggered to the bathroom and stared at her face in the mirror, her eyes wide with horror. Overcome with nausea she bent over the toilet and threw up. For a moment she sat on the bathroom floor, shivering, her mouth sour. Then, rising shakily, she wiped herself clean and rinsed her face in cold water. Retrieving his robe from the floor she covered him, trying not to look at the dead eyes, which seemed to be shrinking into their sockets.

Numb with shock, her mind refusing to function properly, she pulled on her dress, fumbling with the buttons. She stuffed her bra and panties into her bag, looking around, fearful she might have forgotten something. She looked a mess. There was no way she could use the lift. She would have to use the emergency exit. She looked around the room once more. Then, as if afraid she might awaken him, she tiptoed from the bedroom and let herself out of the suite.

Chapter 26

Julia lay on the bed in her darkened flat, curled in the foetal position, hands clasped together, unable to think or move. Robert was dead. She was pregnant. There was nowhere to go, no one to turn to.

Again and again she went over the events of the past two days, as if by reliving the hours she had spent with him she could find an explanation for the grief that now engulfed her.

What if he had not come to London? What if she had not made love with him? Would he still be alive now? Was guilt to be added to the nightmare?

The flat, which had always given her solace and comfort, now seemed an empty place, cold and unfriendly. She shivered. When the lift ground to a halt at her floor she sat up quickly, listening, trying to convince herself that it was Robert. There had been a terrible mistake; he was not dead; he had come to fetch her. Then she heard the door of the flat across the hall open and close and she lapsed back into despair, knowing the night would be long, knowing she would not sleep, knowing there was worse to come.

Brand's death was front-page news in the London papers next morning.

He had been discovered naked in his £1,200-a-day suite at the Burlington Hotel by the night maid. Suzy Miller, a young Irish girl Julia knew well, described how she had found him. 'He was lying on the edge of the bed,' she reported. 'There must have been someone with him when he died because a bathrobe had been draped completely over him.'

Millionaire's Death Mystery, was the *Daily Express* head-line. The *Daily Mirror* reported: *From the state in which Brand was found it is believed that he had been with a woman when he died. Burlington Hotel a Millionaire's Love Nest?* ran the headline. Both papers ran the same grainy picture of Brand taken some fifteen years earlier as he left his New York office. Some of the stories called him 'the richest man in the world'. Others settled for 'industrial giant' and 'art-loving tycoon'. The *Sun* attempted to contact Grace Brand in Mexico but was told she had collapsed.

The stories detailed Brand's enormous holdings in real estate, oil, radio stations, cattle ranches, tankers and hotels. There were pictures of *The White Dolphin*, the Gulfstream jet and the house in Acapulco, described as 'Xanadu by the sea'.

Most of the papers contacted Julia's office during the day. Discovering that she had called in sick with flu they telephoned Moscato direct. Next day he was reported to be outraged at the scandalous stories being printed about his wealthy guest. 'Clearly he felt unwell after taking a shower and lay down on the bed, pulling a robe over himself,' he said.

Although the Chelsea police, called in immediately, made it clear there was no suspicion of foul play, and the hotel doctor stated categorically that it was a straight-forward heart attack, stories about Brand continued to surface all week. A married multimillionaire found dead in an expensive London hotel suite with suggestions of a mystery woman – a tabloid news editor could not ask for more.

Parsons, tracked down by a group of photographers and reporters, threatened physical violence when he was accosted leaving the hotel. A picture of the old man, arm upraised, appeared in the *Evening Standard*. Then one of the papers got hold of a young steward from *The White Dolphin* who, baited with money, talked about Brand's cruise to Corsica with a young woman. 'They seemed very much in love,' the steward reported. 'They certainly slept together.' Next day several papers took up the hunt for the woman. A reporter, sneaking a look at the log of *The White Dolphin*, found out where it had gone in Corsica and confronted Jean Louis and Nicole. They sent him on his way. 'Mr Brand was a cherished friend of ours,' Jean Louis said angrily. 'We do not betray the friendship now that he is no longer here.'

Huddled in her flat Julia combed the papers each morning, fearful that her relationship with Brand was about to be exposed. As the days passed, and it was not, she felt ashamed at her concern. She ate nothing but dry toast and fruit. The thought of food nauseated her. When Lisa finally insisted on coming to see her she was shocked how gaunt and ill Julia looked.

'Look,' she said, 'you can't go on like this. Deena isn't due back from her father's till next month. I'm going to move in to look after you.'

'I'd rather be alone,' Julia said.

'He wouldn't have wanted this,' Lisa said. 'He'd have been horrified to see you like this.'

With fatigue and exhaustion battling despair for first place in her body Julia looked at her friend with hollow eyes. 'I loved him, Lisa. I loved him so much.' And then the tears came and racked her body as Lisa held her close.

It was a week before Julia returned to the hotel. To her relief she discovered that Moscato had gone to Rome on a two-week vacation. She still looked pale and sick, and Emma made no secret of her concern.

'You should still be in bed,' she said severely. 'You're not at all well. Please see the doctor.'

Julia looked at the grey-haired woman whose distress was so clearly genuine and squeezed her hand. 'Thanks, Emma. I'll be all right.'

She wished she could be certain this was true.

* * *

By this time Julia had missed Brand's funeral, which took place privately in New York. A service was held afterwards at St Patrick's Cathedral. *Black limousines stretched around the block,* reported the *Independent*'s correspondent in New York.

Elliott Hirsch, who for more than thirty years had acted as the Brand Corporation's general counsel, and who now took over as President, eulogized Brand as a brilliant man and a great philanthropist, who was always prepared to share his wealth with those less fortunate. So moving were some of the tributes that Grace Brand, who had flown in from Mexico, broke down during the service and had to be escorted out.

Reading this at her desk Julia felt an increased sense of isolation. Robert Brand had been her lover; he was the father of her unborn child. Now he was buried some 3,000 miles away, being praised by people of whom she had never heard.

She closed her eyes, fighting hard to keep the tears from coming again. God in heaven, she thought, will I never stop weeping?

As the days passed, stories about Brand disappeared from the news pages. Soon the press was taken up with a new sensation. And although at first the Burlington had buzzed with rumours about Brand's death – with Emma speculating endlessly whether any of them were true – soon they too ceased.

Julia rarely left the office before 7.30 p.m. Now that Lisa had moved in with her they usually ate at home, for Julia wanted to avoid seeing people she knew.

She did her best to follow the regimen set down by the doctor, drinking a lot of milk, eating well-balanced meals prepared by Lisa and taking plenty of exercise. Sometimes, when the nausea continued on and off throughout the day, she was wiped out by the time she reached home.

Again Lisa broached the subject of abortion. 'There's

just no way you can keep this child,' she said. 'You've got to make a decision.'

'I don't want to talk about it,' Julia said.

'You've *got* to talk about it. While Robert was alive it might just have worked. But now you're on your own. Soon you'll have to quit your job. You think that bastard Moscato will keep it open for you? No way. You'll have a child and no job. For God's sake be sensible. Don't fall into the trap of thinking what you're doing is courageous. It isn't.'

'I know that.'

She had already come to a decision. She would not have an abortion. With Robert gone that seemed the ultimate act of betrayal to his memory. And she wanted the child. She was not being courageous, or sentimental, or romantic. She wanted the child because it was his. And he had made it possible for her to have it and support it.

'There's something I haven't told you,' she said. 'Robert made sure I was taken care of. He made arrangements.'

Lisa, pouring herself a glass of wine, looked up. 'What sort of arrangements?'

'He opened a bank account for me.'

'Then you've got some money?'

'I think so.'

'What do you mean, you think so?'

'I haven't signed papers or anything. I was supposed to do that the next day. Then – '

'Where is this money?'

'In Switzerland.'

'Why there?'

'It's his bank.'

'Do you know how much?'

'Twenty million dollars.'

Lisa half rose from her chair, knocking over the red wine. It spilled across the white cloth and dripped down onto the floor. She jumped up to get a paper towel, looking at Julia with astonishment.

'Twenty million dollars?'

'Yes. He said he wanted us to be all right.'

Lisa tossed the wine-soaked paper into the waste bin. 'And I've been worried sick about you. Julia, you're rich. You've no more worries. You can keep the child; you can do anything you like.' She shook her head. 'Which bank is it?'

'I'll get the paper.'

She fetched the page.

'Banque Eberhardt,' Lisa read. *'Rue de Hesse. Geneva.'* She looked up. 'You must call them immediately. Ask what the next step is.'

'Isn't that a bit tasteless? So soon?'

'Julia, this is a bank we're talking about. Banks don't have souls. This is business. If Robert set up an account for you there the money belongs to you. Promise me you'll call tomorrow.'

'I promise.'

Paul Eberhardt slammed down the telephone, shaken by Grace Brand's drunken rage. The woman was out of her mind. She was asking him to do the unthinkable, to undo an account that had already been set up, confirmation of which was in his files and in the computer.

Did she really think he could suppress it? Pretend that the order for a £20 million transfer of funds had never taken place? The idea was insane.

Although the order to set up the new account had come through the day after Robert Brand died, instructions for it had gone into effect before his death. That made it legal and binding. That was Swiss law.

But if he ignored Grace Brand's shouted demands, what then? She was crazy enough to do anything.

And what about the Lang woman? What was he supposed to tell her when she called? *I'm sorry. There is no account.* How could he do that?

He cursed himself for calling Mexico. He had felt bound to offer sympathy to the widow and, since Brand was now dead, bring up the subject of the new account. He had not anticipated the stream of abuse which followed.

He buzzed his secretary. 'I need the last Brand file.'

A moment later she came in holding a folder. 'Will you need me further, Monsieur Eberhardt? It's past six.'

He glanced at his watch. 'So it is. No, Marte, you may go.'

'The file?'

'I'll replace it myself.'

He opened the file and flicked through the contents. There it was in Brand's own writing.

Following my phone call you are to set up an account for Julia Lang, Flat 5, 208 Great Portland Street, London W1, England, and transfer £20 million from account 0279270 held with you. Acknowledge. Brand.

Scribbled at the bottom was the word 'Acknowledged', followed by Eberhardt's initials.

It was the last message in the file. Attached to it was Brand's obituary clipped from the *Herald Tribune*.

Eberhardt picked up the phone and dialled the extension of his new partner, Alain Charrier.

'We have a slight problem . . .' he began.

When Julia tried to call the Banque Eberhardt, having got the number from directory enquiries, she was so nervous she twice misdialled the last digit of the code. Finally she got it right.

'Banque Eberhardt.'

'I'd like to speak to Monsieur Eberhardt.'

'Who's calling?'

'My name is Julia Lang.'

'One moment.'

One moment became two. Then three. Finally the voice came back: 'I regret, madame, that Monsieur Eberhardt is unavailable. Perhaps one of our officers could help you.'

160

'Thank you.'

A minute later a deep, heavily accented voice came on the line: 'This is Alain Charrier.'

'My name is Julia Lang, Monsieur Charrier. I'm calling with regard to an account set up for me by Mr Robert Brand.'

There was a long pause. 'Your name again?'

'Julia Lang. I live in London.'

'Who do you say set up an account?'

'Robert Brand.'

Another pause. 'Are you sure it was this bank?'

'The Banque Eberhardt. I'm positive. He wrote it down.'

'One moment.'

Finally the man came back. 'We seem to have no record of your name, Miss Lang.'

'Perhaps it was done directly with Monsieur Eberhardt?'

'Who set up this account?'

'I told you.' Julia realized her voice had risen slightly. 'Robert Brand. You are his bankers, aren't you?'

'We never discuss our clients, Miss Lang. In any event, as I say, I can find no trace of an account in your name.'

'There must be some mistake.'

'Perhaps you should write us a letter, Miss Lang, stating the facts. We will certainly look into it further.'

'Why can't you tell me now?'

'Good day, Miss Lang.'

That night over dinner Julia related the conversation to Lisa.

'Fly to Geneva,' Lisa said. 'See this man Eberhardt. Get it straightened out. You know banks. Someone probably lost the file.'

'They sounded as if they didn't believe me.'

'They're Swiss, Julia. They don't believe anybody where money is concerned.' She finished her dessert.

'You know Al Sherrill, the *Herald Tribune* Financial Editor?'

'No.'

'He lived in Geneva for a couple of years. He's sure to know someone you can talk to if you run into problems. I'll call him tonight.'

The following week, with Moscato still away, Julia took the Monday off and flew to Switzerland.

Chapter 27

Julia arrived at Cointrin Airport in drizzling rain and took a taxi into town. Geneva looked grey and grim; the skies were overcast; the magnificent mountains, which form such a dramatic backdrop to the ancient city, were shrouded in mist.

She had been there once before on holiday with her parents but that had been in summer when the waterfront was busy with steamers plying their way between Geneva and the lakeside towns. Now the pleasure boats bobbed at anchor in the harbour.

She checked into the Hôtel des Bergues and, after lunch in the restaurant and a glass of white wine to bolster her confidence, took a taxi to the rue de Hesse.

She was surprised when the cab drew up outside a grey building with nothing but a small brass plate to identify it. Only the heavy wrought-iron door suggested anything but an ordinary office building.

In the lobby a uniformed attendant sat behind a desk on which stood a couple of TV monitors.

'I wish to see Monsieur Eberhardt,' Julia said.

'You have an appointment?'

'He will know who I am.'

'Your name?'

'Julia Lang.'

'Please.' The attendant indicated a door to one side of the lobby. 'If you will wait in there.'

Julia went into a small anteroom that held nothing but a desk and two chairs. On the desk were that morning's editions of the *Wall Street Journal* and the *Financial Times*.

Two minutes passed.

A man, grey-suited and silver-haired, wearing

pince-nez, walked in. 'Miss Lang? I am Alain Charrier. We have already spoken on the telephone. How can I help you further?'

'I asked to see Monsieur Eberhardt,' Julia said.

'He is not here.'

'When will he be here?'

'I cannot say.'

Julia tried to keep her voice calm. 'Monsieur Charrier, there seems to be some confusion about an account opened here in my name by Robert Brand.'

'So you said.'

'Have you made further enquiries?'

'We can find no trace of the account.'

'But that's impossible. Mr Brand told me categorically that he had set up an account for me.'

'When was this?'

'Just before he died.'

'What is the number of this account?'

'I do not know.'

Charrier frowned. 'All accounts at this bank have a number, Miss Lang.'

'I was to get it the following day.'

'I see.' Charrier nodded. 'One moment.'

He was gone ten minutes. Julia grew increasingly restive. What was wrong? Why was he keeping her waiting like this? She felt panic setting in. Finally Charrier returned.

'Miss Lang, I have made the most careful enquiries. We have no record of any account.'

'Perhaps there is a code ... ?'

'We do not have codes here, Miss Lang, except internal ones. There must be some mistake. Another bank, perhaps?'

'It was this bank,' Julia said.

'I'm afraid not. Now, if you'll excuse me ...'

He stood by the door waiting for Julia to leave. Defeated, she went out into the lobby and down the steps to the street. It was raining hard and there were no taxis in sight. By the time she reached the corner where the rue de Hesse turns into the busy Boulevard Georges Favon she was soaked. There was a café on the corner. She went in and had a coffee, waiting to see if the rain would ease up. When it did not she stood patiently outside until a taxi came by. Back at the hotel, wet through, she took a hot bath and changed into dry clothes. Then she called the woman Al Sherrill had recommended that she contact – Berthe Heydecker of the *Journal de Genève*.

'I was wondering if you had time for a drink while I am here?' she asked, after introducing herself. 'I am in Geneva for one night only and need some advice.'

'I see.' There was a short pause. 'Do you know the Bar Anglais at the Bristol Hotel? In the rue de Mont-Blanc?'

'I can find it.'

'Why don't we meet there? Say about six. Ask the barman to point me out.'

'I'll be there,' Julia said.

There were only half a dozen people in the bar; a group of five solid-looking businessmen in one corner and a woman in her late fifties, hair cut in an old-fashioned pageboy style, wearing heavy rimmed spectacles, sitting alone at a table. She looked up as Julia walked in.

'Miss Lang? I'm Berthe Heydecker.' She raised a hand to summon the waiter. 'I've ordered a glass of white wine,' she said. 'What will you have?'

'A Perrier, please.'

'You're sure? This wine is really good.'

'I don't drink much.'

The drinks arrived with a dish of peanuts. Heydecker scooped up a handful and washed them down with wine.

'So. Al Sherrill is thriving?'

'Very much so,' Julia said, hoping she would not have to go into details about the health of the mysterious Mr Sherrill whom she had never met.

'I do some work for him occasionally,' Heydecker said.

'Research. Mostly he looks for bank scandals.' She smiled thinly.

Julia put down her glass. 'Miss Heydecker, I'm hoping you can tell me something about a banker here named Eberhardt?'

'Paul Eberhardt?'

'That's right.'

'What would you like to know?'

'Well . . .' Julia hesitated, unsure how to continue. 'I am having some problems with his bank. An account was set up for me there by a friend. The bank denies all knowledge of it.'

'And you have been to the bank?'

'This afternoon. They said they have no record of an account. They won't even admit that the man who arranged it is a customer.'

Heydecker made a dismissive gesture with her hand. 'Swiss banks never divulge the names of their customers.'

'Is this man Eberhardt totally honest?'

Heydecker smiled showing uneven teeth. 'Miss Lang, Paul Eberhardt is one of the most distinguished bankers in Europe. I think you could say he is honest.'

'When I went to the bank I was told that he was out of town,' Julia said, her hopes of getting any information from Berthe Heydecker beginning to wane.

'Perhaps he is. Whom did you see?'

'A man called Charrier.'

'Alain? I know him well.'

'He wasn't very helpful.'

'They're very discreet, Swiss banks.'

'The thing is, can you advise me what to do? How can I find out if an account was set up?'

'Miss Lang, the Banque Eberhardt is the third largest private bank in Switzerland. If they have no record of an account in your name then, believe me, there is no such account.'

'I believe that there is.'

166

Heydecker shrugged. 'Perhaps you should contact the person who set it up and have them call the bank.'

'That person is dead.'

'Ah. That does make it difficult.'

'Do you know Monsieur Eberhardt?'

'Yes, indeed.'

'I was wondering . . . could you possibly call and talk to him? Perhaps set up a meeting for me?'

Heydecker stared at her. 'That would be most improper, Miss Lang. This is not my affair. I cannot possibly intrude. In any event he would most certainly refuse.' She glanced at her watch and put some money down on the table. 'I'm afraid I must go. I'm sorry I cannot help you.' She got to her feet, smoothing down her rumpled skirt. 'Do give my best to Al when you see him.'

She shook Julia's hand, waved to the barman and clumped out. Julia remained seated for a moment, her depression mounting. She should never have come. The trip had been a complete waste of time. The nausea she had felt earlier that day was resurfacing. She picked up her coat and walked gloomily back to her hotel.

'You know what I think?' Lisa said. 'You should go back to Geneva and demand to see this man Eberhardt. Don't give up. Dammit, it's a fortune.'

'I know that,' Julia said. 'But I'm not putting myself through that humiliation again.'

Lisa looked exasperated. 'So you're going to throw up your hands?'

'Look,' Julia said, 'I have no proof of any of this. Robert said he'd opened an account for me. They say he didn't. Maybe there was some mix-up. Who knows? It's an important bank. Why would they lie to me?'

'That's a very good question,' Lisa said quietly. 'Try to figure out the answer.'

*   *   *

Two days later, as Albert-Jean Cristiani arrived home after a particularly depressing afternoon, the phone was ringing.

'I've got something to tell you,' Berthe Heydecker said. 'I met a woman called Julia Lang the other afternoon. She's English. She had come here to see the people at the Banque Eberhardt because she says someone arranged an account there for her. But when she made enquiries they denied it. I thought you might be interested.'

'I'm more than interested,' Cristiani said. 'Who did she see there?'

'Alain Charrier.'

'Not Eberhardt?'

'They told her he was out of town. It's true. He was in Zurich. I checked.'

'What sort of woman is she?'

'Attractive. Well dressed. I formed the opinion she might take matters further.'

'Why did she call you?'

'We have a mutual friend, Al Sherrill. Used to be here with the *Herald Tribune*. That's why I agreed to see her.'

Cristiani found himself smiling. Things were looking up. There *was* something going on at the Banque Eberhardt.

'Thanks, Berthe,' he said.

'Any time. Oh, I looked through our old files as you asked. There's nothing there. Just a couple of interviews with Eberhardt in which he talks about opening the bank in the thirties. Nothing helpful.'

'Thanks anyway. We'll dine again soon.'

'I hope so.'

But don't hold your breath, Cristiani thought as he hung up. My days of expense account dinners are coming to an end. Only a few more weeks and he would be on his own, without the backing of the Federal Banking Commission.

Chapter 28

The following Wednesday Paul Eberhardt confided his concern about Julia Lang to Maître Claude Bertrand.

The lawyer smiled sympathetically. 'You are having a difficult time, my friend. Phone taps, a car following you, now this.'

'I'm concerned about this Englishwoman,' Eberhardt said. 'Who knows what trouble she may cause?'

'She was Brand's mistress, you say?'

'According to his widow.'

'Tell me again when you received Brand's instructions about the account.'

'He phoned me the day before he died. His written note arrived a day later. I had already set up the account on his instructions. It was in the computer. When I telephoned his widow to convey my sympathies I had to mention it. She was most abusive. She ordered me to cancel the account.'

'A difficult lady, you told me.'

'Impossible. I believe her to be mentally unstable.'

'What proof does the Lang woman have of Robert Brand's intention?'

'None that I know of.'

Maître Bertrand carefully removed a speck of fish from his teeth and reached for his wine. 'There you are then, Paul. There is nothing she can do. And you cannot go against the widow's wishes. That would be most unwise.'

'I'm concerned that this Lang woman came here to the bank.'

Bertrand thought about this. 'Alain told her there was no such account?'

'That's right.'

'Then I see no cause for alarm, my dear Paul. I think you are worrying unnecessarily.'

They parted and Eberhardt walked back to his office. It was a bright, sharp, winter's afternoon with a light wind blowing off the lake; the kind of day when Geneva is at its best. Normally he would have enjoyed the walk but now he was beset by worry. It was all very well for Claude Bertrand to say there was no cause for alarm. There was plenty of cause for alarm. Who knew what Julia Lang would do? To her $20 million was undoubtedly a fortune; something worth fighting for. What if she went to the Federal Banking Commission?

'There's something troubling me,' Cristiani said. He sat back in his chair in Commissioner Bonnet's office, a tape recorder in his lap.

'I've a good idea what it is,' Bonnet said sourly. 'How you're going to exist without someone like me to sign your expense sheets.' He held up a form. 'Dinner with contact,' he read. 'Three hundred francs.' He glared at Cristiani. 'You had to take this contact to the Lion d'Or?'

'As good a place as any,' Cristiani said.

'I'm sure,' Bonnet said. 'Would I be right in assuming this contact was a woman?'

'Berthe Heydecker,' Cristiani said.

'*What?*' Bonnet was incensed. 'That old hag. What could she possibly tell you? The *Journal de Genève* should have fired her years ago.'

'She has good sources,' Cristiani said.

'And what did she tell you over this 300-franc dinner?' Bonnet asked sarcastically.

'Something very interesting. But first listen to this.' He switched on the tape recorder. 'This was a call Eberhardt placed to Grace Brand just after her husband died.'

Bonnet glared at him, then leaned back in his chair, his hands laced behind his head, gazing at the ceiling as the tape unwound. When it finished he sat forward, his expression changed.

'She's telling him to break the law.'

'What's more he's going to do it. Nice, huh?'.

'It's incredible.' Bonnet frowned. 'I can hardly believe it. Who is this woman, Julia Lang?'

'My guess is she was Brand's girlfriend. Must have been really something – $20 million! You don't get that for a one-night stand.'

'The way Grace Brand talked to Eberhardt . . .' Bonnet shook his head. 'Dammit, the man is next year's Chairman of the International Bankers' Conference in Vienna.'

'I keep telling you,' Cristiani said. 'She's got something on him.'

'What did Heydecker tell you?'

'Julia Lang went to the bank to ask about the account. They said it didn't exist. She then called Heydecker – they have a mutual friend, apparently – and asked for her help. Heydecker told her she could do nothing.'

'What did the Lang woman do?'

'Went home, apparently.'

'You think she'll leave it at that?'

'I hope not. I hope she comes to us with a complaint. Then we can take action.'

'Not so much of the "we",' Bonnet said heavily. 'You're out of here in a week or two.'

'*You* can take action.'

'It's a tricky situation,' Bonnet said. 'Eberhardt's an important man. It's a private bank.'

'He's breaking the law to please Brand's widow,' Cristiani said. 'There's got to be a very good reason.'

'Yes,' Bonnet replied. 'Money.'

'It's more than that,' Cristiani said. 'The Brand fortune is immense. Twenty million dollars is peanuts to Grace Brand.'

'Maybe.' Bonnet shook his head again. 'What in God's name can Paul Eberhardt be thinking of, doing this?'

'His skin,' Cristiani said.

*   *   *

171

At the end of that week the registration material and programme of events for the forthcoming Travel and Tourism Research Association conference finally arrived. Julia went through it carefully. She was scheduled to speak on the second day. She would be staying at Las Brisas.

The idea of getting out of London for a few days was appealing. She could forget about her problems for a while, soak up the sun and mix with some interesting people.

She called Lisa, who had now moved back to her own flat. 'I just got the papers for that conference in Acapulco I told you about. I'm off next week.'

'Lucky you,' Lisa said. 'It'll do you good. Just make sure you don't run across that crazy woman.'

'I won't,' Julia said. 'I have the advantage. I know about her but she doesn't know a damn thing about me.'

Chapter 29

The long flight from London left Julia exhausted and irritable. Tired and nervous, she stared out at the lush countryside as the taxi sped along the road towards Acapulco. But once over the mountain as the stunning half-moon bay came into view, her spirits rose. It was breathtaking. There were banks of cotton wool clouds above the mountains to the right. In the bay a Mexican destroyer lay at anchor. Beyond it in the harbour was a white cruise ship. Paragliders soared above the beach. A moment later the taxi swerved into the hillside entrance to Las Brisas Hotel. Julia was glad to discover she already knew some of the other people attending the conference. The time passed quickly. Her speech was judged a great success and she was invited to take part in several of the ensuing discussions. By the end of the second day she found she had made many new friends.

'We need people like you in this association,' one of the members, a cheery man named Alex Wintour, said. 'You really know what you're talking about, and have a real gift for putting it across.'

Julia, whose morale had been low for so many weeks, began to blossom. With part of the group she drove over to the lagoon half an hour away to lunch on one of the islands. She joined some of the others on a sunset cruise around the bay, then went to La Perla restaurant to watch the Mexican boys diving from the high rocks into the floodlit sea. And, with her new friends, she visited the market to buy Mexican plates and ornaments.

Julia began to feel invigorated. The sun, ever present, cheered her after the grey shroud that hung over London in wintertime; the friendliness of the Mexican people enchanted her and the professionalism of the TTRA members impressed her.

On the last day, when she came back from a final swim at La Concha, the hotel's beach club, she found a handwritten note awaiting her in her room.

She read it twice, incredulously.

> Mrs Grace Stansfield Brand requests the pleasure of the company of Miss Julia Lang this afternoon for tea. Four o'clock.

Julia spent the next half-hour in a state of shock. It was unbelievable. Grace Brand knew who she was. How could she? Who could possibly have told her? Even more mystifying, how had she known Julia was there at the hotel?

Baffled by the sense of unreality she now felt, she paced the room, her thoughts in turmoil. She felt unnerved and vulnerable, all the confidence generated by the past three days destroyed. *Grace Brand knew who she was.* Had Robert Brand told her? Impossible. She had asked him that. But who else knew of the relationship and, more to the point, knew she was in Acapulco at that moment? She had told only two people – Emma and Lisa – and neither of them would have said a word.

But as four o'clock approached she found herself becoming curious about the woman she had heard so much about. And wondering what possible reason Grace Brand could have for wanting to meet her. *Tea at four o'clock.* It was almost laughable in its old-fashioned formality.

Still deliberating, Julia sat out for another half-hour in the sun – it was the last time she would see it for many months, she knew – and then made up her mind. She had nothing to lose, she decided. She would go.

*　　*　　*

As the taxi turned down a rough side road and bumped and rattled along beside the sparkling bay, Julia found it hard to believe that this was the right way.

'You're sure?' she asked the driver, although it was already clear he spoke hardly any English.

'*Si, si. Casa Shalimar.*' He pointed ahead.

At length they turned into a wide square bounded on three sides by trees and flowering bushes and on the other by tall wrought-iron gates. In front loomed a white marble mansion so dramatically poised above the sea it might have been a movie set. Julia recognized it immediately from the magazine pictures she had looked at.

A white uniformed man emerged from a guard post behind the gates and looked questioningly at Julia. '*¿Si, señora?*'

'My name is Julia Lang. I am here to see Señora Brand.'

The guard consulted a list in his hand and said something to another man in the guardhouse. The huge gates swung open slowly. Julia entered.

'Please.' The guard motioned for her to follow him down a flight of steps lined on both sides with bougainvillaea bushes. He handed her over to a young Mexican man wearing a crisp white uniform, who ushered her into a small anteroom. Tall French windows let out to one of the terraces. A side table was laid for tea. Feeling increasingly nervous Julia took a seat on the edge of one of the white sofas. The Mexican stood almost at attention by the door.

A moment later Grace Brand walked in. She was taller than Julia had expected, a slim woman, deeply tanned, with high cheekbones, dark eyes and a thin mouth. She was wearing a white turban and an ornately patterned caftan. She looked to be in her early sixties but could have been older. She wore no jewellery, but about her was the gloss of money. She stared at Julia for a moment and then dismissed the young Mexican.

The moment he had gone she walked forward, arms outstretched in greeting. She grasped Julia's hand warmly. 'My dear Julia, I'm so glad you were able to come. I've been wanting to meet you for a long time.' She took one of the chairs and sat facing Julia, her back straight as a drill sergeant's.

'It's kind of you to invite me,' Julia said, bewildered by the greeting. 'This must be a difficult time for you.'

She shifted her position on the sofa. The seat was very soft and she found herself sitting several inches lower than Grace Brand. She tried to raise herself up a little.

'Now. First things first. How do you like your tea? Milk and sugar?'

'Please.'

Grace Brand poured the tea and handed her a cup. She smiled pleasantly. 'You seem a little nervous, my dear. Please don't be. I simply felt that as you were here in town it would be foolish not to meet. After all, we have Robert in common and I know you must have been as devastated as I was by his death.'

'I didn't realize – '

'That I knew about you and Robert? Come now, Julia; let's not be naïve. I am not exactly isolated here, you know.'

'I know that. It's just that – '

'I suppose I should resent you,' Grace Brand went on. 'But I don't. Though I am a trifle jealous that it was you and not I who was with him at the end.' She looked straight at Julia. 'You were with him, of course?'

Julia nodded.

'What exactly were the circumstances?'

'What do you mean?' Julia put down her cup.

'Well, Robert was naked in his suite when he died. Obviously you weren't discussing the relative merits of Keats and Shelley.'

Julia flushed. 'I don't think – '

'He was fucking you, wasn't he?'

Julia stiffened. 'Really, Mrs Brand – '

'Please, call me Grace. I do so much want us to be

176

friends. I get quite lonely down here. There are so few worthwhile people to talk to.' She smiled again.

Julia tried to sit up higher. 'Mrs Brand, I'd like to make something perfectly clear. I became involved with Robert only because I understood your marriage was over.'

'He told you that?'

'Yes.'

'I expect he also told you I'd had a breakdown and the doctors told him to lock me up?'

'He did say – '

'That was his usual line. He used it with all his mistresses. It must have been quite effective. It got them on their backs in no time – ' She broke off. 'Is the tea to your taste?'

'Mrs Brand – '

'Grace, please.'

'Are you saying Robert lied about your marriage?'

'Did I say that?'

'Not exactly.'

'Then I'll thank you not to put words in my mouth.'

Julia finished her tea. 'I don't blame you for feeling bitter about me, Mrs Brand. But why invite me – '

'Bitter? My dear Julia, I am not bitter at all. You are right about our marriage. Robert and I were about as far apart as it's possible to be while still maintaining a relationship.'

'Then I don't see – '

'What don't you see, Julia?'

'Why you didn't get a divorce? Robert told me you refused to consider it.'

'Oh come now.' Grace Brand gave a sardonic laugh.

'It's not true?'

'Of course not. Had he ever asked me for a divorce he could have had it at any time. I am financially secure. I have this house. Since he was never here what possible difference could it have made?'

'He told me your financial affairs were so inter-woven – '

'That at least was true. They were. But that could all have been sorted out by the lawyers. No, the truth is Robert remained married to me because it suited him to do so. That way he could never be trapped by his little whores. Clearly he told you a different story.'

'Completely.'

'You heard how I made his life hell. I'm sure you lapped it up. Why wouldn't you? You were so busy getting fucked you didn't want to feel any guilt.' She smiled. 'Am I right?'

Julia bristled. 'Are you telling me your husband was a liar?'

'My husband, Julia, and your lover. Yes, that's what I'm telling you. He was a bloody liar. His whole life was a lie.'

'It's hard to believe – '

'Is it? Surely you're not that goddamn stupid?'

Julia got to her feet. She wished she had never come. 'Mrs Brand, there seems little point in continuing this conversation.'

'Julia. Don't be so sensitive. We are both mature women. Sit down for heaven's sake.'

Reluctantly Julia sank back on the sofa. 'Mrs Brand, rightly or wrongly I had a relationship with your husband. I loved him very much.'

'Are we being totally frank with each other, Julia?'

'Of course.'

'Then why don't you admit that Robert told you I was crazy?'

'He never put it like that.'

'How did the bastard put it? Did he say I was schizophrenic?'

'He said you were a very unhappy woman who wanted to make him unhappy too.'

'He was such a liar.'

Julia's eyes narrowed. 'If you were so far apart, Mrs Brand, why wouldn't you give him his freedom to marry Jane Summerwood?'

178

Grace Brand's face seemed to contort. 'Now just a minute. Just one goddamn minute. You're not going to bring that whore's name up in this house. Understand? That I won't have. That cocksucking little bitch. He got her pregnant, did you know that? Then came whining to me for help. Robert Brand never knew the meaning of love. His idea of loving a woman was to give her some trinket from Cartier, screw her stupid and then, when things went too far, come to me. You know what he said? "The bitch is getting serious, Grace. I've got to get out of it." We were sitting in this very room; he was where you are now. So I got him out of it.'

A small nerve had begun to beat in Julia's throat. The room was absolutely still.

'Please, Mrs Brand, be serious – '

'I do wish you'd call me Grace.'

'This conversation is – '

'Is what, Julia?' Grace Brand leaned forward.

Julia realized the back of her dress was soaked in perspiration. 'You don't really expect me to believe you were responsible for Jane Summerwood's death?'

'You can believe any goddamn thing you like.' Grace Brand laughed. 'Who did you suppose killed the little bitch? Some tramp in the park? Robert wanted out of it. I got him out of it. What about some more tea?'

Julia shook her head, momentarily too numbed to speak. I've got to get out of here, she thought desperately. This woman is truly insane.

'Mrs Brand – Grace – what you've told me is all very interesting – '

'I'm glad. I didn't want you to leave Acapulco without hearing my point of view. Otherwise you might have spent the rest of your life pining for Robert and not realizing what a lying, blackhearted shit he really was.'

'I don't – '

'What did he give you from Cartier, Julia?'

She's crazy, Julia thought; crazy and dangerous. Yet so much of what she says is true.

'Nothing.'

'He gave you a trinket, surely? You can tell me. We're friends now, Julia. Where did it come from? Bulgari, Van Cleef?'

'He gave me a necklace.'

'Worth a lot, was it? He was always generous with his mistresses. Too well brought up to leave the money on the dressing-table after he'd fucked you.'

Julia got to her feet. 'I have to go now.'

'But you have not finished your tea,' Grace Brand said. 'And you haven't seen the house.' She rose.

Julia stood still. Her heart was beating wildly. 'Perhaps some of the things you have said about Robert are true,' she said. 'I have no way of knowing. But one thing I realize he did not lie about. He said you were not well. You don't have to be a psychiatrist to see that he was right.'

Grace Brand's eyes seemed to bulge. Julia brushed past her and ran out and up the steps to the waiting taxi. She was drenched in perspiration. The woman was truly mad. Everything Robert said about her was true. She was terrifying.

As the taxi rattled along the bumpy road she slumped against the worn, cracked seat feeling bruised and shaken. Never in her life had she been through anything like that. She realized her hands were shaking and she was terribly afraid. For herself; for her unborn child. What could that woman not do?

Julia took a mirror from her handbag and studied her face. She looked ghastly, pale and wild-eyed. She tried to calm herself, to tell herself that the next day she would be on her way to London and safety. But was there safety even there? What about Jane Summerwood? But Grace Brand's boast that she'd had her killed was surely nonsense, the ravings of an unstable woman. She might be vicious and vindictive but what could she do to someone 7,000 miles away? The idea was absurd, as absurd as her claim that Brand had never wanted a divorce. Julia *knew* that couldn't be true. She could not have been that wrong about Robert Brand. Would she ever know the truth about him? No, she thought; not now.

Then, as the taxi turned on to the main road and careered up the hill towards the hotel she remembered that long ago conversation with Brand when he had talked about Acapulco. *'There are a couple whose company I enjoy. One is a fisherman; the other a Polish sculptor ...'* What was the sculptor's name? She could not remember. But how many Polish sculptors could there be living in Acapulco?

'I need your help,' Julia said to the duty receptionist. 'There's a Polish sculptor living here ...'

'Voytek,' the receptionist said. 'Up the mountain. Voytek Konopka.'

'That's it. That's the name. How can I find him?'

'Everyone knows Voytek.' He picked up a telephone directory from the desk and leafed through it. 'You want me to call him?'

'Please.'

He dialled the number, yelled something in Spanish and handed Julia the receiver.

'Mr Konopka, please.'

'This is Voytek.'

The line was very faint. She raised her voice. 'My name is Julia Lang. I was a friend of Robert Brand.'

'Where are you?'

'Here in Acapulco. I was wondering if I might see you?'

'Come now. Tell the taxi driver my name. He will know how to find me.' He hung up.

Chapter 30

As the taxi breasted the top of the mountain it turned sharply up a rough road and came to a stop beside a long white wall. At the end was a small gate.

'Voytek,' the driver said pointing to the gate.

'Come back for me in one hour.' Julia pointed to the dial on her watch.

'*Si, si*. One hour.' The driver nodded. He was the same man who had taken her to the Brand house.

Julia opened the gate and made her way up a flight of stone steps leading to a studio perched atop the hill. On either side of the steps were metal designs and sculptures, some suspended on the wall, some lying on the ground. At the top was a carved wooden door set on wrought-iron hinges. It was half open. She hesitated a moment, wondering whether to enter.

'Come in. Come in.'

A moment later she was confronted by a giant of a man, heavily bearded, his grey hair tousled. He was wearing a smudged white shirt and torn jeans. He was barefoot.

'You are Julia. The friend of my friend.'

Julia smiled uncertainly. 'I'm not interrupting anything?'

'Some interruptions are welcome.' He beamed.

'It's just . . . I need to talk to you. I've just had the most terrible experience. I . . .'

He took her arm and led her through the cluttered studio to a wide terrace with a view of the whole sweep of Acapulco Bay. 'You see,' Voytek said. 'A room with a view.' He chuckled. 'You like red wine?'

She nodded.

'Good. We will relax and watch the sun go down.' He gestured towards an iron table on which stood two glasses and a bottle. 'I sit here every evening. After a long day in the studio and at the foundry it cleanses my soul.' He poured a generous glass for both of them. Sitting down heavily he turned to her. 'So,' he said, 'here you are. Robert's Julia . . .'

'You knew about me then?'

'Yes,' he said. 'I knew about you. Robert talked to me often.'

'That makes it easier,' Julia said. 'I wanted . . . I needed to talk to someone about him.'

The big Pole spread wide his hands. 'I have all evening. First, though, calm yourself. Take in this beauty. Enjoy your wine.'

Julia took a sip of wine. She looked down the mountain. 'It is lovely here,' she said.

'As long as you look at it from this height,' he said. 'Down there the bay is polluted. Your first trip?'

She nodded. 'A conference.' She told him about the TTRA meeting.

'Something happened at this conference to upset you?'

'No. It was something else.' She took another sip of wine. 'You know Grace Brand well?'

His mouth tightened perceptibly. 'I know her.'

'I have just come from the most awful meeting with her.'

Voytek frowned. 'You went to see Grace? Why would you do that?'

'She invited me. She sent a note to the hotel asking me to tea.'

He looked bewildered. 'I don't understand. How did she know about you?'

'I don't know. But she knew. And she knew where to find me.'

'It doesn't make sense.' He shook his head. 'Robert never mentioned your name to her.'

'She has a source somewhere,' Julia said.

Voytek grunted. 'You should have ignored the invitation.'

'I know that now. I was stupid to go.'

'What happened?'

Julia felt some of her earlier panic subsiding. She felt safe sitting with this man. Safe and, in a curious way, protected. 'It was what was said. It was frightening. She was terrible about Robert. She called him a wicked liar. She must have hated him.'

Voytek looked at her sympathetically. 'I know how she can be. Totally irrational. She is not well, you know?'

'I realize that.'

'Everything changed after her breakdown.'

'You knew her before, then?'

'From the time I first arrived here. Twenty-five years ago. She invited me to one of their dinner parties. It amused Robert that I turned up in my old clothes: I had been working late in the foundry downtown and had no time to come back here to change. The other guests were all in their finery: Italian slacks and shirts; Gucci loafers. Robert and I became immediate friends.'

'But not Grace?'

'I am not the kind of man she would bother cultivating.'

'She said some unbelievable things,' Julia went on. 'She told me Robert never really wanted a divorce; that he preferred to stay married to her.'

'That's ridiculous. Robert wanted desperately to be free of her but their finances were so entangled it was impossible.' He paused for a moment. 'There was something else . . .'

'Tell me.'

'I sensed – I know it sounds absurd – I sensed that in some way he was afraid of her. It was almost as if she knew something about him; some secret from his past.'

'You think that's possible?'

'How do I know? Robert never discussed the past with me. He was one of the most private men I've ever known. The thought of being in the public eye horrified him.'

'He told me that was the only way he could avoid being pestered,' Julia said.

'I have my own theory,' Voytek said. 'Robert liked to cultivate the myth that he was a self-made millionaire. The truth is he inherited a fortune from his father. I think he felt that detracted from his reputation as a great businessman. So he never talked about his early days.'

'He told me he'd inherited a fortune. But also that he'd multiplied it.'

'He did. He was incredible. He had a brilliant mind. I was with him once in Paris at an Industrial Conference. He walked into the room where some of Europe's most important industrialists were assembled; big men from Fiat and Siemens, Bayer and ICI. When Robert arrived they all fell silent and paid attention. They knew they had something to learn from him.'

The idea of this dishevelled giant sitting down with a group of immaculately dressed European industrialists made Julia smile. Voytek smiled too.

'I know what you're thinking,' he said. 'I sat at the back.' He chuckled. 'I used to tease Robert, you know; tell him he was a typical American barbarian only interested in making money. But the truth is he was a very cultivated man, knowledgeable about art.'

'I discovered that,' Julia said.

'And he'd read an extraordinary amount. He was an intellectual, really. He'd not only read Plato and Rousseau but could quote from them at will. Not too many American businessmen can do that. One of his chief criticisms of his own country was that there are no role models for the cultivated man; the only thing that counts in the US is celebrity – ' He broke off, pointing. 'Look.' The sun had just begun to dip beyond the horizon, flooding the sky with a great aura of orange light.

'It's stunning.'

'I have been many places,' he said, 'but I have never

seen sunsets like these.' He watched for a moment longer, absorbed by the sight.

Julia turned to him. 'When Robert did come here, did he and Grace make an effort to get along?'

'He didn't come often. He never liked Acapulco, you see. He was only here for tax reasons. Did they try to get along? She was so unpredictable it was impossible. You could never tell how she was going to behave. At one dinner party I attended they had the chairman of Bancomer, one of our biggest banks. It was important for Robert. Halfway through dinner Robert and this man began discussing a joint project. Grace, who'd had too much to drink – a not unusual occurrence – suddenly snapped: "If you two are going to bore the rest of us talking about money, I'm leaving the table. Hasn't anyone here read a book, or seen a play, or done anything remotely interesting?" Everyone was embarrassed. They felt terrible for Robert. But it was always like that. She would tear people to shreds, call them posturing idiots and mealy-mouthed mediocrities, people who were frequent guests at her house. She even rips into that man she sleeps with now and again.'

'Who's that?' Julia was immediately interested.

'I don't know his name. Lives in Los Angeles, I think. They say she bankrolls his projects.'

Julia was puzzled. 'If she was so awful why would people go to her dinner parties?'

'This is Acapulco, Julia. A small town with an even smaller social world. People have to go somewhere and Brand's kind of money was a great attraction.' He smiled. 'And the food was always good.'

Sitting high up on the darkening mountain, watching as lights began to come on along the bay, Julia felt some of her earlier nervousness abating. She finished her wine. Should she tell Voytek she was pregnant? She looked at his wide, honest face and buccaneer's beard. Yes, she decided, she should.

'Did Robert say I was having his baby?'

Voytek's face broke into a wide smile. 'I wondered if you would tell me. Yes, he did. He called me the night before he died. He was elated. It was the first thing he said, "My friend, I'm going to be a father again. Congratulate me." '

For a moment Julia was puzzled. '*Again?*' Then she remembered. 'Of course. Jane Summerwood was pregnant.'

The burly sculptor frowned. 'That's not what he meant, Julia. He was talking about Daniel.'

'Daniel?'

'His son. The one he had with Grace.'

Julia felt an odd constriction around her throat. She sat totally still.

'Robert had a son?'

'He didn't tell you?'

Seeing the look of bewilderment on Julia's face Voytek reached out a hand. She took it. For a long moment she stared down the mountain. The whole sky was flooded with colour now; reds and oranges and blues.

'*You have no children?*'

'*We decided against it. We were both wrapped up in our careers ... A mistake, perhaps ...*'

God in heaven, she thought, was that mad woman right after all? Was Robert Brand the liar she claimed? She turned back to the sculptor who was watching her, a look of concern on his face.

'Where is he now? Daniel?'

'He's dead, Julia.'

'Dead?' She put her hand to her throat. 'What happened?'

'He was kidnapped. Twenty years ago.' Voytek shook his head. 'I can't believe Robert never told you ...'

'Will you tell me?'

'He'd gone to the lagoon swimming, with his bodyguard. They killed the bodyguard and grabbed Daniel.'

'They wanted ransom?'

'Ten million dollars.'

'But they didn't release him?'

'Robert didn't pay. He said it was useless. They would never have released the child. The kidnappers weren't Mexicans, you see. Mexicans would have settled for the money. These people were Germans. Robert contacted a group in North Carolina, a security firm. They've had success in the past recovering kidnapped children. They tracked down the men to Cuernavaca. But by that time they had already killed Daniel. Grace never forgave him. She was convinced he should have paid. Shortly afterwards she had a breakdown. She was in a clinic for months.'

'What about the police?'

'They weren't contacted. Robert knew that would make things worse. It would have been in the newspapers; there would have been hoax calls.'

'But when the child was found? Didn't that get in the papers?'

'Money can buy anything here. It was hushed up.'

Julia sat absolutely still, conscious only of the beating of her heart. 'Their friends . . . didn't they wonder where he was?'

'He was just a kid. Eight years old. They dine late at Casa Shalimar. Ten o'clock, usually. The child was always in bed by then. People who did enquire were told he had been sent to school in France.' He shook his head. 'Robert told you nothing of this?'

'He said they had decided not to have children.'

Voytek looked away.

Julia slumped in her chair. 'So that's why she's crazy. She lost her only child. That poor, demented woman.'

'Stop that.' Voytek's voice was firm. 'Grace Brand does not deserve your sympathy. She made Robert's life hell. It would have made no difference if he had paid the ransom. The child had been dead all along. Robert guessed right.'

Shocked and bewildered, Julia got to her feet. The sculptor rose too.

188

'It's ironic. I came to see you because Grace Brand made me doubt my feelings about Robert. You've done the same thing.'

'I'm sorry. You asked me to tell you.' He took her arm. 'Don't judge Robert too harshly. He did what he thought was right.'

'He lied about it,' Julia said flatly.

'Perhaps he thought it would upset you,' Voytek said.

'It has,' Julia said. 'More than I can tell you.'

They walked through the cluttered studio. Pieces of sculpture were everywhere: on the floor, on tables, on the whitewashed walls – a brass horse's head, a giant fish, a peasant's hand, a clock face. He watched as she descended the steps. She turned at the bottom. He waved once and went back inside. She got into the waiting taxi.

Grace Brand was still in bed in her all-white bedroom when the phone rang.

'Hello, Grace.'

'Oh, it's you.'

'I was wondering how it went.'

'I saw her. It was not pleasant. An impertinent woman.'

'Was she surprised you knew she was there?'

'Hard to tell. Anyway, she's gone now.'

'There's something I know will interest you. Among Robert's things at the hotel were three books. Would you like me to read you the titles?'

'Go ahead.'

'*Childbirth Made Easy. Your First Child. Coping with Pregnancy.*'

Grace Brand took a deep breath and let it out slowly. 'So she's pregnant?'

'Why else would Robert have bought the books?'

'The bastard,' Grace said. Her voice rose. 'The rotten bastard . . .'

'He's dead, Grace.'

'And good riddance. Good riddance.' She slammed

down the phone without saying goodbye. For a long time she lay supine, her eyes closed.

Why had she not guessed the truth? Julia Lang *had* to be pregnant. Robert would never have agreed to pay so much money to an unimportant mistress.

She groaned. Here it was: the Jane Summerwood story all over again.

Chapter 31

'This is downright scary,' Lisa said. 'How did Grace Brand find out about you? And how did she know you were *there*?'

'I still don't know,' Julia said. 'Emma says she told nobody. I know you didn't.'

Lisa thought for a moment. 'Robert could have mentioned your name by accident. But someone else had to tell her you were in Acapulco.'

'I've gone over it a hundred times,' Julia said. 'I have no answer.'

It was a raw afternoon with gusts of rain. They were lunching in the Villa Basque, a Soho restaurant that Lisa liked, both glad to be warm and dry. Julia had been home for a week. She had told Lisa everything about her trip to Acapulco, omitting only one detail – the kidnapping of Robert's son. She would keep that to herself. Lisa would only use it as an excuse to attack Robert. Still shattered by what she had learned from Voytek, she was not in the mood for that.

Julia sipped her coffee. It had been a dreary morning, she was in no hurry to return to the hotel, and Lisa was a genuine friend, sympathetic and concerned.

'Look,' Lisa said, 'let's go over this. Only two people knew you were going, right? Emma and myself.'

'And the TTRA people.'

'It couldn't have been them,' Lisa said. 'That's just too far-fetched. You're sure no one else knew?'

'Positive.'

'Then Grace Brand has someone here who reports on your movements.'

Julia paled. 'You think she's having me watched?'

'It looks like it.'

'But why? Robert's dead. I'm no threat to her.'

'You're carrying Robert's child.'

'She can't know that.'

'She seems to know everything.' Lisa poured herself more wine. 'I think you should have one more stab at getting the money. Then lie low for a while.'

'What more can I do? I can't go back to that bank.'

'Get someone to help you.'

'You mean a lawyer?'

'Forget about lawyers. It would take years to challenge the bank in the Swiss courts. Anyway, what proof have you got? A dead man's promise . . .'

'Then what?'

'There's an American I know, Guy Ravenel. The Prince used him once when he was having problems.'

'What sort of person is he?'

'He's a fixer.'

'What does that mean?'

'He helps solve other people's problems.'

'He's probably terribly expensive.'

'That's something you'd have to work out with him.'

'I don't know,' Julia said. 'What can he do that I haven't?'

'Why don't you see him and find out?' Lisa said. 'He's due in London soon.'

'You think I should?'

'I *know* you should,' Lisa said firmly. 'You have only two choices. Either you fight for the money or you forget about it.'

'And you'd fight?'

'For $20 million? You bet your life I'd fight.'

At that moment a man paused in front of their table. They both looked up. It was Jeremy Orde, the newspaper columnist who had written the story about Chantal Ricci that had so enraged Moscato. Julia had met him at several functions at the hotel. She did not like him but she knew Lisa did. He frequently wrote items about her. He shook hands with both of them, managing at the same time to look around the restaurant, nodding and smiling. He seemed to know a lot of the people there.

'What are you two hatching up?' he asked.

'Nothing for your inquisitive ears,' Lisa chuckled.

'I doubt that,' Orde said. His eyes narrowed. 'What's all this I hear about you and that little Sultan? You were seen at Annabel's recently.'

Lisa looked at Julia. 'You can't keep secrets from Jeremy,' she said.

'Well,' Orde said, 'are you having it off with him?' He pronounced it 'orf'.

'Jeremy,' Lisa said reprovingly. 'There's a sultana.'

'That's not a very good raisin,' Orde said. He smirked at Julia to make sure she saw the joke. She smiled dutifully.

'I've only just met him,' Lisa said. 'Julia knows him far better than I do.'

'No doubt,' Orde said. 'He's her boss.' He turned to Julia. 'There are rumours floating around about you too.'

'Oh really?' Julia met his gaze.

'One of our photographers swears he saw you and Robert Brand together at Nice Airport.'

At that moment a pretty young woman passed their table and greeted Orde effusively. 'Darling,' she gushed. 'Such a funny piece this morning. You really hit home.'

Orde acknowledged this with a nod.

'We must lunch soon,' the young woman said, moving away. She had not even glanced at Lisa or Julia.

'You know Diana, I'm sure,' Orde said. 'Bunny Rutherford's girl. Loves it when I take a crack at the Royals. I expect you saw it.'

'No,' Julia said. She saw no reason to humour him.

'I did,' Lisa said. 'I read you every morning.'

Orde acknowledged the tribute with another smirk. He returned his gaze to Julia. 'So it wasn't you?'

'I don't know what you're talking about,' she said. She prayed he would go away.

193

'Who could it have been?' Orde went on. 'Some bint Brand picked up, I suppose – ' He broke off. 'Ah, here comes my guest. I'll see you two.' He hurried towards the door to greet a man Julia recognized as a Member of Parliament.

Julia reached for her coffee. 'You think he knows?' she asked quietly.

'Of course not,' Lisa said. 'He was fishing.' She put her hand on Julia's arm. 'Promise me you'll think about my friend Guy.'

'He sounds like my last hope.'

'Had he ever asked me for a divorce he could have had it at any time . . .'

Julia sat at her office desk trying to concentrate on a business letter she was writing. It wasn't easy. She was restless and unsettled. Since her return from Mexico she had thought a lot about Grace Brand's words. The more she thought about them the more distressed she became.

Robert Brand, the man she had fallen in love with, had struck her from the beginning as honourable and straightforward. Now she was not so sure. He had dismissed his command of German, which she had heard him speaking on the yacht. Now she knew he had lied about having had no children. Why? What possible difference would it have made to their relationship? What other lies had he told her? Was the story of the $20 million also untrue? Perhaps the Banque Eberhardt was right in claiming there was no such account. Surely a man in Brand's position would not have had to wait an extra day to get the number of a new account. Bankers would have tripped over themselves to accommodate him. But he had seemed so sincere, so delighted, when he learned of her pregnancy. He could easily have just written her a cheque and left it at that. Why the rigmarole about a Swiss account unless it was true?

She glanced at the slip of paper Lisa had given her at

lunch the day before: *Guy Ravenel. Berkeley Hotel. Arriving the 23rd.*

Well, she thought, why not?

It was Cristiani's last day at the Federal Banking Commission. He felt twinges of nostalgia at the prospect of leaving after so many years, but he was now anxious to get started on his own. He liked the little office he had picked out on the Quai Wilson. And he knew he had enough contacts to keep him busy for a while. His only frustration was the thought that he would have to abandon his surveillance of Paul Eberhardt just when it was becoming really interesting.

At one o'clock Bonnet took him out for a farewell lunch.

'I'm going to miss you,' the portly Commissioner said. 'Things are going to be quiet around here when you've gone.'

'What are you going to do about the Banque Eberhardt?'

'What can I do? The Lang woman hasn't come to us with a complaint. We've got no grounds to interfere.'

'We know he's breaking the law.'

'We do,' Bonnet agreed. 'But would you mind telling me how you came to learn that? Are you going to admit you asked your pal at the Justice Department to set up an unauthorized phone tap? If you do they'll whip away your investigator's licence before you can say Mont Blanc. Think about that.'

'I have thought about that,' Cristiani said. 'It depresses the hell out of me.'

Chapter 32

'Ravenel.'

The man who stood in the doorway of Julia's flat was short and stocky, his dark hair brushed straight back. He was wearing an unpressed suit, a white shirt and blue tie. He looked to be in his late forties but it was hard to tell; the shadows under his eyes could well have been caused by weariness. His complexion was sallow, his forehead heavily lined. He carried a raincoat over his left arm.

Julia held out her hand. 'Thank you for coming, Mr Ravenel. I hope this won't prove to be a waste of your time.'

'I hope so too, Miss Lang.'

He followed her into the living room, tossed the raincoat over a chair, took out a packet of 555s and lit one. He glanced around for an ashtray in which to place the dead match. 'What shall I do with this?'

The fact that he had not asked permission to smoke irked Julia. 'I'll get a saucer,' she said. 'I don't have any ashtrays.'

'A saucer will do fine,' he said.

When she returned from the kitchen he was sprawled on the sofa, his head back, looking up at the ceiling. 'High ceilings,' he said. 'You get them only in these old mansion flats. Been here long?'

'Several years,' she said brusquely. 'Would you care for some coffee?'

'I would,' he said. 'Black.'

A rude man, Julia decided, as she poured the already percolated coffee. When she returned he was staring out of the window at the street below. 'Noisy here, isn't it?' he said taking the coffee without comment.

'You get used to it,' Julia said. She sat down in the armchair; Ravenel returned to the sofa.

'Well, Miss Lang?'

'My friend Lisa Faraday felt you might be able to help me.'

'That depends on the problem.'

Julia took a deep breath. 'Mr Ravenel, just before he died a man with whom I was involved arranged for $20 million to be paid into an account at the Banque Eberhardt in Geneva to take care of my future. The bank denies any knowledge of the account.'

Ravenel blew a stream of cigarette smoke and watched it rise towards the ceiling. 'Have you anything in writing?'

'No. My friend died before it could be done.'

Ravenel leaned forward and stubbed out his cigarette in the saucer. To Julia's dismay he lit another one immediately.

'The man was Robert Brand. Your friend told me.'

'I see.'

'Brand was married?'

'Yes.'

Ravenel took a sip of his coffee. 'There's no sugar,' he said.

'You didn't say . . .' She got up and fetched the sugar basin from the kitchen.

'Did you often discuss money with Brand?'

'Never.'

'What do you live on?'

'I have a job at a hotel. I have my own money.'

Ravenel took two lumps of sugar and tried his coffee again. 'That's better,' he said. He blew out another stream of smoke.

'As I understand it you want me to help you gain access to a large sum of money you claim has been deposited in your name in a bank in Geneva. You have no evidence that this is so. There is only your word for it.'

197

'It's hardly the sort of story any woman would make up.'

'Wrong, Miss Lang. It's exactly the sort of story some woman would make up. I am not saying you have. But these sort of claims are being made every other day in the US.'

'Without proof?'

'Sometimes.'

'Then it's hopeless. I can't prove a thing. I have nothing but a piece of paper with the bank's name written by Robert.'

'No letters? No notes?'

'Nothing.'

Ravenel looked at her thoughtfully. 'You could probably sue the estate if you came to America. Make a fuss in the newspapers. A smart lawyer would get you some sort of settlement.'

'I won't do that, Mr Ravenel. I will not descend to the tactics of the gutter.'

Ravenel kept his eyes on her. 'Have you ever met Mrs Brand?'

'Yes. In Acapulco. I was there for a conference. She invited me to tea.'

'Was it a cordial meeting?'

'It was horrendous, Mr Ravenel. I believe Grace Brand to be mad.'

'Why do you say that?'

'The things she said to me. She was like a demented woman. Robert had told me she was mentally disturbed. That was an understatement.'

'What sort of things did she say?'

'She claimed to have had a woman killed.'

Ravenel's eyebrows rose. 'Who was that?'

'A woman named Jane Summerwood. She was murdered in Hyde Park last year. Robert had hoped to marry her. She was pregnant.'

'Did you believe Mrs Brand? Or did you think she was just trying to frighten you?'

'I believed her.'

Ravenel drank his coffee. His eyes never left Julia. 'She sounds like a dangerous woman.'

'I believe she is.'

He was silent for a moment. 'You realize that getting information from a Swiss bank is almost impossible?'

'I know that. I've already been to Geneva.' She told him about her conversation with Alain Charrier.

'Has it occurred to you that Charrier could have been telling the truth?' Ravenel said. 'Perhaps there is no account there.'

'Robert assured me there was.'

'Miss Lang, I did not know Robert Brand. But I can tell you that, faced with a pregnant mistress, men have been known to lie.'

Julia flushed. 'You know?'

'That you are having a child? Lisa told me.'

'She had no right.'

'I doubt I would have come to see you otherwise, Miss Lang. Discarded mistresses seeking redress do not interest me.' Once again Ravenel exhaled a cloud of smoke. 'You're sure the Banque Eberhardt was the bank?'

'Yes. But Mr Charrier would not verify it.'

'He wouldn't, would he?' He held out his cup. 'I'd like another if that's possible?'

Julia got up and went into the kitchen. Ravenel's rudeness appalled her. And yet there was something about him that generated trust. She returned with the coffee.

Ravenel looked at her intently. 'I have one more question. How determined are you to get this money?'

'What do you mean?'

'Do you care how you get it? Or how I get it for you?'

'If the money's mine – You mean you'll help me?'

'Miss Lang, if you had jumped at my suggestion that you sue the Brand estate in America I would have taken my leave. As it is,' he nodded wearily, 'yes, I will try to help.'

'I don't have much money.'

'I take ten percent of whatever money I recover.'

Julia was astonished. 'Two million dollars.'

'That's right.'

'That's a great deal of money.'

'I agree with you. But $18 million is better than no millions at all.'

'Would we have a contract or something?'

'A handshake will suffice.'

'I'd like to think about it.'

'I'll be in London another three days. Then I'm off to Switzerland to see a friend in Geneva.'

He stubbed out his cigarette and got to his feet, picking up his raincoat. Julia walked with him to the door.

'I wish you luck,' he said.

Julia made up her mind then. 'I accept your terms,' she said.

'I will do my best for you.' He gripped her hand firmly.

Albert-Jean Cristiani was feeling frustrated. Four times now he had instructed his new secretary, Yvette, that he wanted coffee available all day. He had bought the hot plate in the corner for that very purpose, he explained. All she had to do was switch it on before he arrived and make sure the coffee pot was always full.

She kept forgetting.

'I can't think of everything,' she grumbled. 'I've got to get all these files of yours in order. Everything's a mess. And there's all this dust. When are you going to get a carpet?'

'Soon,' Cristiani said.

'Anyway,' she said. 'Too much coffee is bad for you. All that caffeine.'

'Let me worry about that,' Cristiani said. 'Just keep the plate hot and the pot full.'

She nodded. She was a plump, ugly girl with minimal secretarial skills. He wasn't paying her much.

'There's a message,' she said sullenly. 'Someone called

Guy Ravenel called from London. Says he's coming here next week. Wants you to keep an evening free.'

'Which evening?'

'He didn't say.' She waddled off down the passage.

Chapter 33

Ravenel knew Geneva well. He did not like it. Bankers might claim that it was an international city but to him it seemed a middle-size town with a deeply provincial outlook. As far as he was concerned it had never really escaped the harsh strictures of John Calvin who, in his determination to turn the city into a saintly place in the sixteenth century, had given the church police the right to enter anyone's home day or night to make sure the Lord was being honoured properly. In those days a smile during a church sermon could land you in prison for three days. It was a wonder the entire population had not fled.

Looking out of the taxi as it sped through the morning traffic into town he reflected that these solid citizens going about their business were descendants of those who had stayed. And were, in their own way, just as censorious and prim-minded. And obsessed with money.

Zurich, of course, was the home of the commercial banks but it was here in Geneva that Switzerland's highly prestigious private banks were found. Among them the Banque Eberhardt.

Ravenel registered at the Hôtel Bristol and went to his room to freshen up. The shower helped a little but not much. His eyes felt gritty from lack of sleep. He had slept less than five hours in the past two days. It was catching up on him.

He put on a clean shirt and underwear and changed into a sports jacket and flannels. Then, slipping on a raincoat, he set off for the Quai Wilson.

On the third floor he stopped at a door marked only with a small brass plate: *'Cristiani et Cie'*. He smiled at the '*et Cie*'. The 'and Company' was there only to impress clients, he knew. Cristiani was on his own. He pressed the buzzer. The door was opened by a plump secretary.

'Mr Ravenel? Good morning. He's expecting you.' She hung his raincoat on a hook and led the way down a tiny corridor to a glass-fronted door.

Albert-Jean Cristiani was sitting behind a plain wooden desk working a calculator. The walls of his office were bare, as was the floor. The desk was piled high with files and papers. As Ravenel walked in he smiled widely, indicating a chair in front of the desk. Ravenel collapsed into it.

'You look terrible,' Cristiani said cordially.

'I'm tired,' Ravenel said. 'I need some sleep.'

'Don't we all. You want coffee?' He poured two cups. 'I was sorry to hear about your wife.'

'Thanks.'

'Good lady.'

Ravenel nodded. He lit a cigarette.

'You should cut that out,' Cristiani said. 'It will kill you.'

Ravenel shrugged. 'One of my few pleasures,' he said.

'You are not old enough to say that,' Cristiani admonished. 'Anyway, I don't believe you.' He sipped his coffee. 'I must say I'm surprised to see you here again. Some people in this city are not too fond of you after that last affair. Someone must have made this visit worthwhile?'

'Perhaps.'

'Anyone know you're here?'

'I just arrived.'

'Word reaches the *Groupement* quickly.'

'So I'm told.'

Cristiani held out both hands, palms upwards. 'So what do you think of my new quarters?'

'A carpet would help.'

'Give me a chance. I just moved in.' Cristiani drank his coffee noisily. 'So what is it this time?'

'A difficult one,' Ravenel said.

'More difficult than last time?'

'Perhaps.'

Certainly Ravenel's last venture – trying to recover some of the millions lost in the Credit Suisse disaster at Chiasso – had not been easy. But with help from Cristiani and a mutual friend he had finally retrieved some of the money for a grateful client and been suitably rewarded. Cristiani, as a Government employee, had asked for nothing. But Ravenel had found a way to thank him. A painting Cristiani had long admired in a Geneva gallery had suddenly come on sale at a ridiculously low price. Cristiani had snapped it up. The balance, which exceeded $10,000, had been secretly paid to the gallery by Ravenel.

'Go on.' Cristiani leaned forward.

'I need information about the Banque Eberhardt.'

Cristiani sighed. 'You too, huh?'

'What's that mean?'

'I spent my last weeks at the Commission trying to dig up something on that bank.'

Ravenel's eyebrows rose. 'Why the interest?'

'A couple of deaths.'

'Deaths?'

'You know. When people stop breathing.' Cristiani related his suspicions about di Marco and Leber. Ravenel listened intently.

'This di Marco – how long had he been with the bank?'

'Almost from the start. Worked his way up. You want some more coffee?'

'It's pretty grim stuff,' Ravenel said.

'Thanks. You're always so polite.' Cristiani got up and refilled their cups.

'And you think di Marco knew something?'

Cristiani nodded. 'And he was going to talk about it. We planned to meet but he got killed first.'

Ravenel lit another cigarette.

'I wish you wouldn't do that,' Cristiani said. He waved the smoke away with both hands.

'What's the story on Eberhardt?'

'He's Swiss. Late seventies. Started with the Hamburger Bank in Germany. Later joined the Deutsche Bank. Opened his own bank here just before the war. Stayed friendly with the Nazis.'

'When you Swiss believed Hitler was going to win the war.'

Cristiani looked glum. 'Not a glorious chapter in our history, I agree.'

'And this di Marco was his partner? Who's he got now?'

'A man named Alain Charrier.'

'Any good?'

'Not as good as di Marco.' He glared at Ravenel. 'Are you going to tell me why you need all this?'

'It's to do with Robert Brand.'

'Who just died.'

'Right. Eberhardt was his banker here. Brand was involved with a young woman in London. She became pregnant. He told her he was putting $20 million into an account for her here. She's contacted the bank. They deny all knowledge.'

Cristiani smiled slyly. He opened the centre drawer of his desk and took out a sheet of paper. He glanced down at it.

'Her name wouldn't be Julia Lang?'

Ravenel's eyebrows went up again. 'That's a good trick,' he said. 'How'd you know that?'

'We tapped Eberhardt's phone for a month. One of the calls we monitored was to Brand's widow in Mexico. She made it clear she'd have Eberhardt's guts for garters if he paid out that money.'

Ravenel drew in a breath. 'So there is an account there?'

'Seems so. She's told Eberhardt to deny it. He's breaking Swiss law. But I can't prove it. The phone tap wasn't strictly kosher.'

Ravenel thought for a moment. 'Why would Eberhardt do as she says? What's she got on him?'

'That's what I'd like to know.'

Ravenel thought for a minute. 'How easy is it to get into a bank like Eberhardt's?'

'No problem at all. You just walk in and plonk down a minimum of half a million dollars. They're not interested in less.'

'I mean out of office hours.'

Cristiani spluttered over his coffee. 'Are you serious?'

'Perfectly,' Ravenel said.

'You must be mad. Nobody breaks into a private Swiss bank.'

'There's always a first time,' Ravenel said.

'I can't believe I'm hearing this. What good would it do?'

'I'd get to look at the files.'

'Look,' Cristiani said, 'I like you, Guy. You're an interesting fellow. But I have no intention of coming to visit you once a month in Bois-Mermet Prison.'

'I'm going to try to get in,' Ravenel said. 'There's a lot of money at stake here.'

'It would take a fortune to make me even consider it,' Cristiani said.

'This is a fortune. A small one but a fortune.' Ravenel put out his cigarette. 'First, though, let's try something else. Know anything about Eberhardt's secretary?'

'Not a thing.'

'See what you can find out. Make some enquiries. There might be something in her background we can use to put on some pressure; persuade her to let us look at the file.'

'Not a chance,' Cristiani said.

'Worth a try.'

'Okay. Give me a couple of days.' He shook his head doubtfully. 'But, Guy, please, forget about the other idea. There's just no way.'

'I hear you,' Ravenel said.

They both rose.

'Can you amuse yourself while I'm making these enquiries?'

'I thought I'd go over to Montreux to see Marie Corbat.'

'Ah, Marie. You've kept in touch?'

'Of course.' Ravenel smiled. 'I'll be back Saturday. You free for dinner then?'

'I thought you'd never ask,' Cristiani said.

Ravenel had an hour to kill before meeting Marie Corbat for lunch at his favourite Montreux restaurant, François Doyen. After checking into the Palace Hotel, Ravenel wandered through the town, which had played host to people like Byron and Rousseau when it was little more than a clutch of lake villages. They would not like it now, he reflected, any more than he did. Too commercial, too obviously aimed at tourists. He preferred lakefront Vevey, which lay to the west.

Ravenel's decision to visit Marie Corbat had not been just for personal reasons. True, they had once enjoyed a brief romantic interlude and stayed good friends. But now he needed her help. Marie Corbat had been executive secretary to the presidents of two of Switzerland's most important banks – Credit Suisse and the Union Bank. She knew everyone and had extensive contacts in the banking business. She was fluent in German and Farsi, and had worked for three years with the Shah of Iran's personal Bank Omran through which he had funnelled millions of dollars to private banks in Switzerland and elsewhere. It was she who had helped Ravenel recover some of his client's money after the Chiasso disaster.

And, Ravenel surmised, she would almost certainly know people who worked at the Banque Eberhardt.

Marie was already there when he arrived, somewhat out of breath from his walk. She greeted him warmly. A tall, statuesque woman in her late forties, Marie Corbat had a haughty exterior which, Ravenel suspected, tended to intimidate would-be suitors. She had never married but was never at a loss for lovers.

'Ah, Guy,' she said, embracing him. 'What a pleasure.'

He kissed her on both cheeks and took a seat beside her on the banquette. They ordered the lunch and wine, with champagne cocktails to start.

'It's been too long,' she said taking his hand. 'I was so sorry to learn about your wife. You got my note?'

'Thanks.'

'And Louise? How is she?'

'Growing up fast. Five already.'

'Give her lots of love.'

'I do.' He sipped his drink. 'How is Mama?'

'Old now. Eighty-four. Still in good health, though. She walks every day. She sends her love.'

'And you?'

'Better than I deserve. I drink too much, the doctor says.'

'No great romance?'

Marie shrugged. 'It becomes more difficult the older you get. Men want young girls, firm flesh. They are revolted by middle-aged women.'

'You'll never be middle-aged,' Ravenel said.

'Dear Guy, it happens to us all. We don't believe that when we are young, but it does.' She smiled at him. 'What brings you back to Switzerland?'

Ravenel put down his glass. 'I need your help again.'

'If I can.'

They lapsed into silence when the waiter came over with the food. Both ate in contented silence for a while.

'Marie, I need to find out something about the Banque Eberhardt.'

'Some big accounts there: Armand de Plessy, Francine Rochas . . . people like that.'

'You know Paul Eberhardt?'

'Of course. He's old now. But very much in charge.'

'What about his secretary?'

Marie laughed. 'Don't tell me you're after her? She's even older than I am.'

'What's her name?'

'Marte Teske. Been with him for years. Not your type at all.'

'What can you tell me about her?'

'Sixtyish. Never married. Devoted to Eberhardt.' She glanced at Ravenel enquiringly. 'What's this all about?'

'A transaction took place recently. Twenty million dollars was deposited in a woman's account there by Robert Brand, the American billionaire. The bank denies it took place.'

'And Brand's dead so she can't prove it?'

'Unless there's some paperwork.'

'Bound to be. What do you hope to do? Subpoena them? Forget it.'

'I need to gain access to the bank.'

Marie's burst of laughter was so loud that people at the surrounding tables turned their heads. 'Are you serious? You want to break into the Banque Eberhardt?'

'Why not?'

'Why *not*? Because it can't be done. It's impossible. And even if you got in – what then?'

'I'd get to look at the files.'

'For a start everything's on computers.' She thought for a moment. 'Though they probably keep files too; they're old-fashioned there. But you wouldn't know where to look.'

'I would if you came with me.'

'Me?' Marie put down her knife and fork and stared at him incredulously.

'Why not?'

'Because I'm a respectable citizen, you idiot, not a bank robber.'

Ravenel lowered his voice. 'We're not going to rob the bank. Just look at some files.'

Marie shook her head. 'Do you know the penalty for breaking into a bank here? Prison for life. *For life*. The Swiss take their money seriously.'

Ravenel picked at his salad, took another sip of wine. 'It's a private bank, right? Not a commercial one?'

'What difference does that make?'

'They don't have vaults full of money.'

'But they do have alarms and monitors.'

'Look, the Brand private fortune is stashed away at the Banque Eberhardt. If the bank is refusing to pay my client, refusing to even admit the money's there, there's got to be a reason.'

'You're sure the money *is* there?'

'I'm sure.'

'Based on what?'

'Inside information.'

'So?'

'I've got to take a look at the paperwork in the bank.'

'What do you want me to do? Go out and buy a gun and a mask?'

'First I'm going to see if there's some way I can put pressure on Marte Teske; persuade her to dig out the file. Maybe there's something in her background. Maybe she has an illegitimate child. Maybe she's cheating on her taxes. There's got to be something.'

Marie chuckled. 'Guy, you judge everyone by your own moral standards. There doesn't have to be anything. She's a dull, dreary, devoted secretary who's given her whole life to the Banque Eberhardt. I doubt she's ever had a man in her life.' She held out her glass for Ravenel to pour more wine. 'This isn't bad. Gets better with every glass.'

'You've noticed.'

She giggled. 'Tell me about this client of yours.'

'She's English.'

'How boring.'

'I rather like her.'

'Why did Brand leave her this money?'

'She's pregnant.'

'Good reason.' She pushed her plate away. 'What are you doing this afternoon?'

'Making love to you.'

Marie smiled slowly. 'What a great idea. It's such a dreary day.'

At 5.30 p.m. that Thursday evening Albert-Jean Cristiani parked a rented Citroën on the opposite side of the street from the Banque Eberhardt. There, as he waited for the white-haired banker to emerge, he pondered the problem Ravenel faced. There was, he knew, no way the American could probe the secrets of a private Swiss bank. Even he, with the clout of the Federal Banking Commission behind him, had found himself up against a blank wall many times during his years as an investigator. True, Ravenel had had luck with the Chiasso business but only because his friend Marie Corbat had shown him how to break into Credit Suisse's Chiasso computer to find out where the funds had gone.

This was different.

Eberhardt emerged from the bank shortly after six and drove through the streets to the Pont du Mont-Blanc and out onto the Lausanne road. Keeping his distance, Cristiani followed.

About a mile past the town of Nyon, Eberhardt's Renault slowed and turned up a small lane to the left. Cristiani pulled his own car off the road and waited.

His heart was thumping in his chest. He knew the lane well, knew where it led.

An hour later he saw the Renault turn back onto the main road heading for Geneva. When the tail lights finally disappeared Cristiani pulled out and drove slowly up to the house of Madame Valdoni.

Chapter 34

The rating of the world's top ten hotels, issued by the journal of the International World Travellers' Association, was eagerly awaited by all great hoteliers. For them it was the equivalent of Michelin's three-star rating for restaurants.

Heading the list for many years had been the Oriental in Bangkok. The Hôtel du Cap in Antibes on the Riviera and the Ritz in Paris usually vied for second place. Other great hotels – the Dolder Grand in Zurich, the Mansion on Turtle Creek in Dallas and the Regent in Hong Kong took up the other slots. It was rare for a British hotel to figure on the list, but the year before the Burlington had made fifth place.

Julia had sent out a press release at the time, though none of the London newspapers had picked it up. She had not been surprised. A list of the world's top hotels, their lowest prices around the £250-a-night mark, was hardly likely to cause much excitement in a news editor's breast. Mentions had appeared, though, in several travel magazines and Andrew Lattimer had been well satisfied. To celebrate he had thrown a small cocktail party in his office.

Four days after her meeting with Ravenel, when Julia walked into her office, Emma's face was grim.

'Get ready for a shock,' she said.

'What is it now?'

'We're off the list.'

Emma picked up a copy of the IWTA journal open at a marked page. Julia scanned the list. In fifth place, where the Burlington had been a year earlier, was the Plaza-Athénée in Paris.

Julia slumped into her chair. Had it happened during Andrew Lattimer's term she would have been dismayed both for herself and the hotel. But now she felt a sense of secret satisfaction that this had happened to the man she despised so much. She even found herself hoping that the Sultan, who had been so proud of his hotel's inclusion on the list, might reassess his opinion of Moscato. Others in the hotel, she knew, would react similarly, though the decision to remove the hotel would have been made long before his arrival.

But it had happened during his tenure. That was satisfaction enough.

'Serves the bastard right,' Bryan Penrose said when Julia saw him in the lobby. 'He runs this place like a labour camp. Maybe the Sultan will kick him out.'

'It won't happen,' Julia said wistfully. 'But don't I wish it would.'

That afternoon, Julia saw that Emma was looking worried.

'You know you asked if I'd told anyone you'd gone to Acapulco?'

Julia sank into her chair. 'You said you hadn't.'

'I've remembered something. Two days after you'd gone, Mr Koenig came in to see you. I said you were away and wouldn't be back for a week. He wanted to know where you'd gone so I said it was a holiday somewhere; I wasn't sure. Then the phone rang and I had to go to my own room to look up some notes. When I came back he was standing beside your desk. That letter from the TTRA people was lying there.' Emma hesitated. 'I think he saw it . . .'

Julia sat perfectly still. Stricken. She remembered then what Voytek Konopka had said in Acapulco. *She even rips into that man she sleeps with now and again . . . Lives in Los Angeles, I think. They say she bankrolls his projects.*

Bobby Koenig. Was he the conduit to Grace Brand?

*　　*　　*

Julia sat alone in her office as the day ended, trying to come to terms with what she had learned. Bobby Koenig was the man who had betrayed her and Robert?

It seemed inconceivable to her that he could have done such a thing. But who else knew about her trip to Mexico?

She pushed aside her cup and, straightening up, crossed to the window and pressed her forehead against the cold glass, looking out at the small, flagstoned courtyard beyond. The trees, leafless now, stood silhouetted against the darkening sky.

Why had Koenig done this? Robert had trusted him completely; had told him everything. They were *friends*. Was it for money? Was that it? Was it because Grace Brand had come up with the financing for his latest film? Was he really that base?

Wearily she locked her desk. No wonder Grace Brand had known everything that Robert did. She had the best of all sources: his close friend.

Chapter 35

Cristiani had an apartment in one of the quieter streets in Geneva, just off the rue Voltaire. The floor was polished hardwood, the furniture functional, the curtains heavy. But he liked it a lot, particularly the two balconies overlooking the street. He had two bedrooms, a decent-sized living room and a tiny kitchen. He used it only to sleep. He ate all his meals out.

Since the arrival in town of Guy Ravenel he had been sleeping badly. And the morning after his visit to Madame Valdoni – when, for old times' sake, he had availed himself of her hospitality in the shape of a rather stunning beauty named Karen – he awoke feeling exhausted. Staring at his face in the bathroom mirror as he shaved he decided he needed a break. What he needed was a little pampering. He knew exactly where to get it.

Three hours away by lake steamer was the town of Evian-les-Bains on the French side of the lake. There, at the Royal Hotel, was the finest spa in the region. Cristiani had been there often and always returned refreshed and rested after being steamed and sweated, pummelled and pulled about.

An hour later he was on the lake steamer, sitting on the main deck watching winter sunshine dappling the snow-covered mountains in the distance. Feeling the tension slowly ebbing from his body he picked up the new murder mystery he had bought earlier that week and began reading.

Bonnet was right, he decided. He had become too preoccupied with the Eberhardt case. He had just spent two frustrating days trying to dig up something on

Eberhardt's secretary, Marte Teske. It had all come to nothing. She had never been with a man, never been involved in any scandal, never taken dope, never said a word out of place. She lived at home with her aged mother. The perfect secretary, Cristiani thought glumly; why can't I find someone like that?

Ravenel was due back next day. He would have to tell him to forget it; there was nothing he could do.

Three hours of cossetting at the spa helped to revive Cristiani's spirits. Wearing a white robe over his swimming trunks he adjourned to the sun room to relax over a cup of herbal tea before catching the steamer back. Although he had planned to read, soon he drifted off to sleep. When he awoke he saw with a start that he had barely fifteen minutes in which to board the last boat.

He dressed hurriedly, paid his bill and went out to catch a taxi down to the lakeside. Others, also late, were hurrying too. One of them cried out, 'Monsieur!' Cristiani, about to step into a cab, turned. The man was pointing to the ground. Cristiani retraced his steps and looked down. Trampled into the soft ground where he had dropped them were his keys. He retrieved them, thanked the man, and stood for a moment looking down at the perfect impression they had made.

He was still holding the muddied keys in his hand when he boarded the steamer with just a few moments to spare.

The visit to Evian had been a great idea. Now he knew how he could help Ravenel.

'There may be a way,' Cristiani said. He sat back, his hands together as if in prayer, looking at Ravenel.

'You got something on the secretary?'

'Forget about the secretary.' Cristiani tilted his chair back. 'Every Thursday evening Paul Eberhardt takes a little trip along the Lausanne road to a house near Nyon.

216

It belongs to a certain Madame Valdoni, well known for her stable of beautiful whores.'

'I thought Eberhardt was in his late seventies.'

'He is.'

'There's hope for us all, then.'

Cristiani scowled. 'I drove up to see Valdoni. I know her. She's made a lot of money at the game. Used to bank most of it with the Leclerc Bank in Geneva. Seemed a safe enough place to her. She knew I was with the Commission . . .'

'You were one of her customers?'

'Any objection?'

'None at all.'

'So she asked me about this bank. I warned her it was shaky and might go bankrupt – *sursis concordataire*, we call it. She got her money out just in time and put it safely in the Union Bank. So she owes me a favour.'

'What's this got to do with Eberhardt?'

'I'm coming to that. Why are you so damned impatient?'

'It's my nature,' Ravenel said.

'He usually has the same girl. Valdoni says she hates his guts.'

'So?'

'Eberhardt carries the key to the door of the bank on him. Do you follow me?'

'No.'

'I think I can persuade this girl to take an impression.'

'He may have a lot of keys. How will she know which is the right one?'

'It doesn't look like an ordinary key. It's coded. Electronic sensors built into the lock read the key. Anyone using the wrong key triggers an alarm at the police station.'

'Terrific.'

'I'm glad you think so.'

'If it's coded an impression won't help.'

'It will if we know the code.'

'But we don't.'

'Baume-Stromberg installed the locks and alarms fifteen years ago. I have a cousin who works there. He'll look it up.'

'You can encode this substitute key?'

'If you know what you're doing,' Cristiani said.

Ravenel sighed. 'I thought you Swiss were supposed to be so virtuous.'

'You thought wrong.'

'One thing: how will this girl get the key? Doesn't he undress in the room in front of her?'

'Apparently not. His tastes are somewhat bizarre. He undresses in one room and takes his pleasure in another while watching a film. I've worked out what to do with Valdoni. She'll give him another girl when we're ready. The girl who hates him – I forget her name – will creep into the room next door and get his keys.'

'You think it'll work.'

'You have a better idea?'

'No.'

'Then let's concentrate on this one.'

'What about alarms?'

'I've checked all that out. I know the Baume-Stromberg systems. There are standard beam alarms on the floor and contact alarms on the windows. There's a TV monitor in the hall linked to the police station. The vaults, of course, will have time locks. But the offices should be wide open.'

'I thought private banks didn't have vaults.'

'Sure they do. They don't carry large sums of money; not like the commercial banks. People aren't dropping in all day to cash fifty-franc cheques. But they do keep some money there. A million or so.'

Excited suddenly, Ravenel got up and paced the room. 'Have you got a floor plan of the alarms?'

'You want it on a plate, don't you?'

'If possible.'

'Well, I haven't. Though knowing Baume-Stromberg

there'll be a beam alarm just inside the entrance two feet from the floor.'

'The TV monitor that's linked to the police. Is that on all the time?'

'No. It's activated by pressure pads in the entrance.'

'Then we'd see it go on,' Ravenel said. 'A little red light. Give us time to get out.'

'No little red lights on Baume-Stromberg monitors,' Cristiani said.

'Any other good news?'

'That's about it.'

'I think I can handle the alarms,' Ravenel said optimistically.

'You'll have to,' Cristiani said. 'I'm damn sure I'm not coming with you.'

Ravenel helped himself to a cup of coffee. 'What time does Eberhardt leave the bank?'

'Around 6 p.m. I've timed him. Punctual fellow.'

'Where's his home?'

'In the Old City. Rue des Granges. Very respectable. His car is a Renault, by the way. I have the number.'

'You're sure he goes to Nyon every Thursday?'

'That's what Valdoni says. He's a creature of habit. Tells her he's a doctor. She knows he's lying. She took a look at his wallet one time.'

'Nice friend you've got.'

Cristiani said nothing.

Ravenel stubbed out his cigarette. 'How long will it take to get this key made and encoded?'

'A couple of days. Three at the outside.'

'So I could go in next Wednesday?'

'If you're so inclined.' Cristiani was suddenly serious. 'There's one thing you've got to remember, Guy. If this key doesn't work – and I don't promise it will – you won't get another chance. Eberhardt will know someone tried to break in. The lock will be changed.'

'I'll have to take that chance,' Ravenel said.

'That's right,' Cristiani agreed. 'You will.'

'I'll wait in London,' Ravenel decided. 'I don't want to be seen hanging around here. I'll be back next Tuesday. You'll be here?'

'Key in hand,' Cristiani said. 'By the way, how much are you paying me for all this?'

'Fifty thousand.'

'Sounds fair,' Cristiani said. 'I'll be able to buy a carpet . . .'

'You can't be serious?' Julia stared at Ravenel, seated on her sofa. 'It's out of the question.'

'I'm going to do it,' Ravenel repeated.

'But a Swiss bank? You'll go to prison forever if you're caught.'

'I don't plan on getting caught,' Ravenel said.

'But even if you do find proof of the account what good will that do? You can't admit how you got it.'

'A little ammunition can be highly effective when fired in the right direction.'

Julia faced him squarely. 'Mr Ravenel, this frightens me. I won't be responsible for you getting in serious trouble.'

'It's not your responsibility. It's my decision. We are partners now. If I choose to risk my neck that's my problem.'

He lit a cigarette and blew out a cloud of smoke. She waved her hand in front of her face to dissipate it. He seemed not to notice.

'When will you do this?'

'As soon as I get the key to the bank door. We're working on that now. Next Wednesday's my guess.'

Julia thought about this. 'Look,' she said, 'you got into this because of me. I'm not going to let you do it alone. I'm going to help.'

'Out of the question,' he said firmly. 'You're having a child. Too risky. Anyway, I've got an assistant, a friend of mine. Swiss.'

'What can he do I can't?'

'It's a she.'

Julia's eyes widened. 'A woman? Then let me come too.'

'There's nothing you can do,' Ravenel said.

Chapter 36

Late the following afternoon, as Julia worked on her newsletter, Emma buzzed her. 'There's a call from Acapulco,' she announced. 'Some man. The name sounds like Konopka.'

'Put him through,' she said quickly.

'Julia.' On the phone the Polish accent was even more pronounced. 'How are you, my dear?'

'I'm fine, Voytek. I've thought about you often.'

'I'm calling to tell you something interesting,' the Pole said without preamble. 'Last night I was invited to dinner by Grace Brand. I was reluctant to go but she told me a French art critic, Pierre Cousins, would be at the dinner and had asked to meet me.'

'How was she?' Julia asked.

'On her best behaviour. Hardly drinking. I got the impression she was interested in the critic. He's quite handsome. Anyway, I thought you might be interested in one of the guests who seemed quite at home there, someone you probably know.'

'Bobby Koenig,' she said quietly.

'Koenig?' Voytek sounded surprised. 'Why do you say that? He was Robert's friend. He would never go there.'

Julia switched the receiver to her other hand. 'Who then?'

'Jill Bannister.'

Julia was so stunned she slumped back in her chair. For a moment her mind simply refused to accept what she had just been told. Then, as reality sank in, she felt a lurching sensation in her stomach. She sat perfectly still, her mind racing. Jill Bannister. Not Bobby Koenig as she had suspected. *Jill Bannister*. That was Grace Brand's source; that was how she knew everything Robert was doing. Her informant was his own personal assistant; someone who knew every move he made. Julia felt sick.

Why? Had Grace Brand bought her? Or was there another reason? Had she herself been in love with Robert and seen Julia as a serious threat? He had been dining with her that night at the Connaught Hotel. At the time Julia had thought nothing of it. Now she felt a surge of anger.

Of course. That was how Grace Brand knew she was in Acapulco. She had told Robert the date of the conference and he would have written it in his diary. Jill Bannister would have seen it.

'Julia? Are you all right?' The sculptor's voice was full of concern.

'I'm sorry, Voytek. It was such a shock.'

'For me, too. They are obviously old friends. They sat beside each other at the table.'

'I can hardly believe it.'

'There's something else,' Voytek said. 'It may not be important, but you should know. This art critic invited Grace to Paris to see the new Matisse exhibition. She leaves in a week. I asked where she was staying. It's the Plaza-Athénée.'

'Why did she tell you that?' Now, Julia realized, she was suspicious of everyone.

'I asked her,' the Pole said simply. 'She doesn't know you and I ever met. She felt quite safe.'

'Of course. I'm sorry.'

'Watch out for yourself, Julia. This is a dangerous woman. You must take great care.'

'I will, Voytek.'

Long after the receiver at the other end had been hung up she sat at her desk, perfectly still, holding the phone in her hand.

Sitting up in bed at Casa Shalimar, Grace Brand was feeling jubilant. Her decision to fly to Paris for the Matisse exhibition had been a marvellous idea. Paul Eberhardt would be there attending some conference. He was even staying at the same hotel, she had discovered.

Two days before, he had called her about the Julia Lang account, talking about possible consequences. Here was the perfect opportunity to put the fear of God into the old fool. Face to face she was sure he would crumble.

She was looking forward to spending time in France with her new friend, Pierre Cousins. Her suggestion that after the exhibition they fly to the South of France and take a cruise on *The White Dolphin* had been well received. This was going to be an interesting trip . . .

The duplicity of Jill Bannister had stunned Julia. Even more startling was the depth of her own anger. She felt she understood for the first time the urge people had to strike out at an enemy. My God, she thought, what's happened to me? I'm filled with rage. I would cheerfully kill that woman.

Leafing through her file she took out the card with Jill Bannister's home address that Robert Brand had given her. Then she dialled the office in Grosvenor Square.

The call was answered on the second ring by a woman. 'The Brand Corporation.'

'Put me through to Jill Bannister, please.'

'Who is calling?'

'Julia Lang.'

'One minute, please.'

There was a long wait. Finally the woman came back on the line. 'I'm sorry, Miss Lang. Miss Bannister is not available. Can I help in some way?'

'No,' Julia said. 'It's Jill Bannister I want.'

'I told you,' the woman said. 'She is not available.'

'You mean she's not here, in London?'

'Not at the moment.'

'Where is she? In Acapulco?'

'I'm afraid I cannot give out that information.'

'Well here's some information you can give out,' Julia

said. 'Tell her I have her address in Hyde Park Square and intend coming round one of these nights to have a long talk with her about her friend Grace Brand. Have you got that?'

'I'll tell her,' the woman said.

Julia put down the phone. Now she knows I know, she thought. Maybe that will give her a few sleepless nights.

Chapter 37

Standing by his bedroom window Paul Eberhardt looked down at the darkened, tree-lined street below. The rue des Granges. The best address in Geneva. *His* street. He loved it the same way he loved the town.

Geneva was his favourite city. The Old Town, the beautiful lake with its fountain – the *jet d'eau* – spewing water 400 feet into the air, the great Cathedral of St Pierre, the ancient Russian church with its golden domes, the fine restaurants, which equalled those of Paris. Above all he liked its cleanliness. After the squalor of London and New York he was always glad to get back.

But some of the pleasure he had always taken from the city was now vitiated by recent events. More and more he found himself in a state of acute depression. He knew the reason: Grace Stansfield Brand. It was ironic, he thought. For months he had been haunted by fear that his partner, Georges di Marco, would carry out his threat to go to the authorities, bringing ruin to his bank. That threat was over. Now a new one had come along in the shape of an insane woman. In many ways Grace Brand posed an even greater threat than di Marco. The old man might have been laughed at had he gone with his story to Bern. He was feeble and foolish. Why would his word have been taken against that of one of Geneva's most eminent bankers?

Grace Brand was different. She was crazy. If he clashed with her again over the Julia Lang account there was no knowing what she might do. Now she had telephoned to say she would be in Paris while he was at a Bankers' Conference there and wanted to see him.

The prospect horrified him. It was bad enough to have

to cope with her shouted insults on the telephone; to come face to face with her in the same hotel, perhaps to suffer her abuse while some of his colleagues were around, that was unthinkable.

As he donned his dark blue blazer he came to a decision. If Grace Brand refused to change her mind over the Julia Lang account he would bring the situation to an end. It had gone on quite long enough. In the safe of his office at the bank was the number of the man who could solve the problem for him.

He debated whether to wait until morning to get it. But suppose the man was away? He had to find out. He would get it that night, he decided.

Eberhardt rarely returned to the bank at night because it meant deactivating the elaborate alarm system. But now he was motivated by a sense of urgency. Who knew what Grace Brand would do in Paris? With the man's services lined up he would feel armed against her. The man! He always thought of him as 'the man'. He did not know his real name. He had never seen him. The 40,000 Swiss francs were placed in a blank envelope and left in a locker at Cointrin Airport. The key was sent to a box number in Geneva. And the job was done.

Thank God for 'the man'. Tonight Eberhardt would alert him; tell him to be ready. A week's notice – he hoped that would be enough.

For five days Albert-Jean Cristiani had followed every move Eberhardt made. He watched him leave his house each morning and drive to the bank; he saw him return each night around 6 p.m. At 8.30 p.m., having changed from his formal banking attire, he would emerge wearing a dark blazer and grey slacks and drive to the Lion d'Or where he dined alone at a corner table. By 10.30 he was back home.

Only on Thursdays, when he drove to Madame Valdoni's, did he break his routine.

Cristiani was encouraged. He liked people to be

227

predictable in their movements. It made his life easier.

On the final night of his surveillance he got a shock. Instead of driving to the Lion d'Or as usual, Eberhardt headed back to the bank. He remained there for half an hour while Cristiani, his car parked at one end of the street behind some others, waited impatiently. When the banker finally emerged and drove home, Cristiani was filled with dismay. What had happened? Why had Eberhardt returned to the bank? Suppose this happened on the night Ravenel and Marie planned to break in? The prospect chilled him. He drove quickly back to his apartment and put in a call to London.

The telephone rang just as Julia was getting into bed. It was Ravenel.

'Change of plan,' he said. 'I'm going to need you after all.'

'You are?' She was delighted. 'What do you want me to do?'

'You're going to pose as a journalist and interview Eberhardt.'

'What?'

Speaking quietly, Ravenel told her about Eberhardt's return to the bank the night before.

'We can't risk that happening again,' he said. 'So we need you to keep him occupied.'

Julia sank to the edge of the bed. Was he serious? He wanted her to sit down with this Swiss banker and pretend to be somebody else? The idea petrified her. She tried to calm herself. She had volunteered to help; she could not back out now.

'I'm not sure I can do that,' she said slowly.

'Of course you can.' Ravenel's tone was brisk. 'Here's what you do. Tomorrow morning you call Eberhardt and say you're Hilary Bennett of the *Wall Street Journal*, based in London. There really is a Hilary Bennett, by the way; he may even recognize the name. Tell him your paper wants to profile him. He'll be flattered.'

'Suppose he checks up on me?'

'Tell him this is a rush assignment. You can only do it on Wednesday. Suggest dinner with him that night – let him come up with the place. But you pay, right? That's what he'll expect. You're on expenses. Keep him there as long as you can.'

'What if he's not free for dinner?'

'I'm sure he will be. I've had someone tailing him for five nights. He always dines alone.'

'But what if he isn't?'

'Sound crestfallen. Tell him how much you'd looked forward to meeting him.'

'He may want some identification.'

'I'll have some cards printed and get them to you tomorrow. Have you got a tape recorder?'

'A Sony.'

'Take that and a notepad with you.'

Julia's apprehension increased. 'You really think I can pull this off?'

'Positive,' Ravenel said easily. 'It's all going to be fine. Call him in the morning. Tell him you'll catch an afternoon flight Wednesday. When you get in call me. I've booked you at the Bristol. I'm at the Richemond. By then you'll know where you're dining. If you don't, leave a message with the concierge of the hotel. As soon as we're through I'll call you at the restaurant. Tell him it's your office. Then get out of there.'

'I'm going to be scared stiff,' Julia said.

'You won't. Think of him as an old fool you're trying to charm,' Ravenel said. 'He'll eat it up.'

'You're sure?'

'Pretty sure,' Ravenel said drily. He hung up.

Julia put down the phone and steadied herself. What have I let myself in for? she thought.

Chapter 38

By the time Wednesday arrived Julia was nervous and apprehensive. Paul Eberhardt had been gracious enough on the telephone, agreeing to dine with her that night at a restaurant called Olympe, but the thought of actually sitting face to face with the banker petrified her. Surely he would see through her? He would know she knew nothing about banking and finance. She had no chance of passing herself off as Hilary Bennett. The whole thing would be a disaster.

But she knew Ravenel was counting on her to do her part. She had already booked a flight for that afternoon and sent a memo to Moscato saying she was going on a quick promotional trip.

Feeling like a condemned woman she looked into her office just before lunch. Emma was in a high state of excitement.

'Want to hear the latest?'

'Gustave Plesset's quit?'

'Nothing like that. It's about Bryan Penrose.'

The Burlington's Director of Sales and Marketing was now married to Pam Helmore, the hotel's chief cashier. Julia had been invited to the wedding but that was the week she'd flown to Mexico.

'Well,' Emma said, 'last Sunday they drove to the Cotswolds for lunch. Upper Slaughter. There's a terrific hotel there – the Old Red House. Pam's sister, Sarah, is the cashier. You met her once.'

'I remember.'

'They'd just sat down in the bar for a drink when guess who they saw going into the dining room?'

'No idea.'

'Mr Moscato and Chantal Ricci. Holding hands.'

'I don't believe it.'

'It's true.'

'What did Pam and Bryan do?'

'They finished their drink and left. They didn't want Mr Moscato to see them. On their way out they took a look at the visitors' book. The lovebirds were signed in as Mr and Mrs Guido Moscato of Milan, Italy.'

'That wasn't very discreet.'

'They probably felt safe,' Emma said. 'They'd never dream they'd be spotted there.'

'I should have guessed,' Julia said. 'It explains everything. I can't believe I didn't see it. It's so obvious now.'

'He must have something,' Emma said. 'Though personally I can't see it.'

'He's an important hotel manager,' Julia said. 'And young Miss Ricci is very ambitious.'

'I suppose that's it.' Emma handed her the day's mail and turned to leave. 'What time are you off?'

'Three o'clock. I've got to pack first.'

'Enjoy yourself in Switzerland,' Emma said. 'Don't do anything I wouldn't do.'

Julia gave her a long look. 'Don't hold me to that,' she said.

As soon as Julia arrived in Geneva she telephoned Ravenel and told him she was dining with Eberhardt that night at Olympe. 'I made it as late as I could. Nine o'clock.'

'Any problems?' he asked.

'None. He seemed delighted.'

'You all right?'

'I'm terrified. I keep thinking he'll recognize me; realize I'm a phoney.'

'Relax, Julia.' It was the first time he had called her by her given name, she realized. 'He can't recognize you. He's never seen you. He'll be much too busy talking about himself and trying to impress you to be suspicious.

231

Put the tape recorder on the table. Ask if he minds. Then keep on plying him with questions.'

'I can't think of any. My mind's gone blank.'

'Ask him lots of personal stuff. Get him talking about the European Currency Unit, speculators, that sort of thing. Ask him if he thinks the dollar will go up or down – I'd like to know that myself. Keep him talking.'

'What time do you go in?'

'Ten o'clock. I'll call you the minute we're through.' He paused. 'Good luck.'

'I'm going to need it,' Julia said.

Chapter 39

Cristiani had come through as promised. Ravenel had the duplicate key in his pocket. Now all he needed was the nerve.

In his life he had done some risky things. But what he contemplated doing this time was crazy: illegally entering a bank to search for a file that might no longer exist. How absurd, how quixotic, to suppose he could get away with it. Then why do it? Was it the prospect of $2 million? Or the challenge of doing something that had never been done before – gaining unauthorized access to a private Swiss bank?

To help calm their nerves he had arranged to take Marie to dinner before leaving for the rue de Hesse. He had made reservations at Le Duc on the Quai du Mont-Blanc. A good dinner, he reasoned, might ease the sinking feeling in his stomach. But half an hour before he was due to leave for the restaurant Marie called. She was delayed in Montreux. Her mother was unwell. She would have to skip dinner but would meet him at 10 p.m. at the Café des Banques.

So Ravenel dined alone in the hotel restaurant, concerned about Julia, concerned about Marie, concerned about himself. He ate little and immediately afterwards went up to his room and put on a dark blue business suit. His only concession to his nocturnal plan was to wear a dark blue shirt, rather than a white one, and an even darker tie. Determined to have nothing incriminating on him he carried only a mini Maglite – innocent enough – and a Minox camera. In his pocket he slipped a small packet of needles.

At 9.45 p.m. exactly he put on a raincoat and took a

taxi to the corner of the rue de Hesse and the Boulevard
Georges Favon. There were only a few people in the Café
des Banques. He ordered a brandy. Nobody paid any
attention to him but a couple of men looked up when
Marie arrived a few moments later. She was wearing a
long black skirt, a frilly black and white check blouse and
black boots. No coat. She looked spectacular.

Ravenel glowered. 'I told you to come dressed like a
hooker.'

'That way we'd be sure to be picked up,' she said.
'Brandy for me too, please.'

'How's Mama?'

'A little better. It's flu, I think. Julia all right?'

'They're having dinner now.'

They downed their drinks quickly, and went out into
the cold night. The rain had stopped but the streets were
still damp. Ravenel glanced up and down the rue de
Hesse. It was deserted. Hand in hand, trying to look like
trysting lovers, they walked up the street. In Ravenel's
pocket was the key. If it didn't fit . . . well, he knew the
answer to that one. They would have to run for it or they
would both spend the rest of their lives in one of
Switzerland's maximum security prisons. And from what
he had heard about them he knew he didn't want to be
in one.

'Coming up,' he said quietly.

'I see it,' Marie replied.

in the darkness the wrought-iron door of the Banque
Eberhardt looked massive and forbidding, the sort that
would yield to nothing less than a frontal assault by an
M1 tank. Unless you had the key.

He had *a* key. But would it fit?

They walked straight past the bank looking up at the
darkened windows for signs of life. Nothing. Nor were
there lights visible in the buildings on either side. This
was a business district. The good burghers of the area
were all home, watching TV, boring their wives, lying to
their mistresses.

Ravenel and Marie crossed the street.

'You stay here,' he said. 'If the key fits, come in quickly after me and stand quite still. If it doesn't, take off. I don't know how long it will take the police to get here but we shouldn't be together.'

Marie nodded. 'If it goes wrong, dump the key. You can't be found with it on you.'

Ravenel walked quickly across the street. He hesitated for just a moment, his throat constricted, his guts knotted, then inserted the key in the brass lock of the door. It slid in easily. It turned. The door swung open. He started to breathe again, confidence returning with a rush.

Ravenel turned but Marie was already behind him. They stepped inside, closing the door, and stood there listening. There was no sound. Gradually their eyes became used to the darkness.

'I feel like a burglar,' he said.

'You are a burglar,' she said.

Ravenel turned on the Maglite and looked around for the source of the invisible beam. It was exactly where Cristiani had predicted, halfway into the entrance hall. He took off his raincoat and dumped it on the floor. 'I'll go first,' he whispered.

Carefully he stepped over the beam, poised for a quick retreat if he triggered the alarm. Then he remembered the alarm would ring at the police station – not at the bank. He wouldn't hear it.

He turned to Marie. 'Now you.'

She moved forward.

'Lift your skirt,' he hissed.

'Is that a proposition?' She was nervous; trying not to show it. She hoisted her skirt and stepped over the beam.

'Watch out for pressure pads,' he whispered. 'Keep to the side.' He glanced at the TV camera above the reception desk. It seemed to be aimed straight at them. Were the police even now piling into their cars? He tried not to think about it.

Moving the Maglite from side to side they crept slowly up the steps leading to the reception area, pausing every few seconds to listen.

No sound.

Ahead of them were two elevators with curved stairs on either side leading to the next floor. They took the right staircase, keeping to one side, hoping to bypass any pressure pad alarms. On the second floor was another beam. This time Marie lifted her skirt high, exposing white thighs and black panties.

'Any offers?' she said.

Nervous as he was, Ravenel smiled. He looked around. 'Let's try this corridor.'

'Trust me,' she said. 'The next floor.'

Carefully they climbed to the third floor, which was carpeted. Marie led the way along a corridor to the right, stopping at an unmarked door. 'This is Eberhardt's office,' she said.

'How can you be sure?'

'I came to see him while you were enjoying yourself in London. I said I was looking for a job.'

'What did he say?'

'He's thinking about it.'

Ravenel chuckled. Thank God for Marie. He turned the handle of Eberhardt's door. It was unlocked. He walked in flashing the light around. The office was mahogany panelled, with paintings on two of the walls. In one corner, by the window, was an ornate French desk with a high-backed gilt chair behind it. In front was a smaller chair; also gilt. Along one wall was an antique table on which lay a collection of financial newspapers and magazines. Everything in the office was designed to instil confidence, to make you feel: *Your money is safe with us. Have no fear.*

'Next room,' Marie said. She beckoned him towards a doorway leading to an adjacent office, obviously a secretary's. There was a wooden desk against one wall with a computer on it. Next to it stood an electric typewriter. There was a filing cabinet against the opposite wall.

Marie took the Maglite and tried the cabinet.

It was unlocked.

She pulled out a drawer, flicked through some files. 'Personal letters,' she said. 'No use.'

'Let's try the computer,' Ravenel suggested.

'You know the access code?'

'No.'

'Then forget it.'

'What now?'

'We'll try the next room.'

They went back into the corridor and crept along to the room next door. Inside was a long table. On either side were filing cabinets.

'Eureka,' Marie said. She tried one of the cabinets. It was locked. '*Merde*,' she breathed. She tried the others. All were locked.

'Fucked by the fickle finger of fate,' Ravenel said.

He went over to the window and looked down at the street below, expecting at any moment to see the flashing lights of a police car. Everything was quiet. He took the packet of steel needles from his pocket.

'Losing a button?' Marie enquired.

'Hold this light.'

While she did so, he examined the lock on the first filing cabinet.

'Which one should we try?'

'His name was Brand. How about the one marked A-D?'

'Don't be so smart,' Ravenel said. He went to work on the lock, holding the needle between his thumb and forefinger, twisting it gently inside the lock. There was a click. The lock slid out half an inch, opening the cabinet.

'Where did you learn that trick?' Marie asked.

'FBI Academy,' he said.

'You're really a menace.'

She opened the drawer and flicked quickly through

the green-coloured files while Ravenel held the light for her. Finally she withdrew one and put it on the table.

'This seems to be the most recent,' she said.

There were sheaves of papers in the file, in French, German and English. As far as Ravenel could see they were lists of investments and deposits around the world.

'The man's loaded,' Marie muttered.

'Was,' Ravenel said.

She continued going through the papers. There seemed to be nothing useful. Then, towards the end of the file, she found it. 'Look.' She took the light and shone it on Robert Brand's note, written on Burlington Hotel notepaper and signed, ordering the setting up of a $20 million account for Julia Lang.

'Got him,' Ravenel said. He took the Minox from his pocket and positioned it carefully above the file paper. He took two photos. 'Now let's get out of here.'

'Wait,' she said. An idea had occurred to her. 'Let's look at the other files.'

'What other files?'

'There are two other Brand files in there,' she said. She went across to the cabinet and brought them back.

'We don't need any more,' Ravenel said.'

'Just an idea,' Marie said. She began leafing through the files, turning over ancient papers dating back, as far as Ravenel could see, to the late thirties. All were in German. What the devil was she doing? She was calmly going through the files as though it were the most normal thing in the world for them to be there. Suddenly she paused and flicked back to a previous sheet.

'That's interesting,' she said.

'What?'

'Take a picture.'

Ravenel looked at the paper. 'That's dated 1938,' he said. 'Can't be the same guy.'

'Take a picture,' she said.

He positioned the Minox again. 'Now let's go.'

'Not yet. Open the next cabinet. The E-H.'

'Dammit, Marie, we've got what we wanted.'

He was becoming more and more agitated. If they'd accidentally tripped one of the beams, he thought, the police would be on the way. He could see himself in the courtyard trudging round with the other lifers.

'Open it.' Her face was serious now.

Full of misgivings Ravenel worked the needle again. The lock slid out. Marie searched through until she found an early file marked 'Eberhardt', the papers yellow with age, and began leafing through it.

'What are you looking for?' Ravenel hissed.

'Clues,' she said. 'You know what clues are, don't you?'

'Sweet Jesus,' he breathed. 'Let's get out of here.'

'Aha!' She slid a page from the file. 'Take a picture,' she said.

He positioned the camera.

She produced another sheet.

'One more,' she said.

'Marie . . .'

'One more.'

She held the yellowing sheet down while he positioned the camera.

'Now come on,' he hissed. 'I think I heard sirens.'

They both listened.

'Far away,' she said.

'Not far enough.'

'All right,' she said. 'That'll do.'

She replaced the files in the cabinets, closed them and made sure they were locked.

'I'll go first,' Ravenel whispered. They crept along the corridor and down the stairs, keeping to the side again. When they reached the entrance lobby she turned to him.

'Let's leave a note,' she said. '*Kilroy was here.*'

'For Christ's sake . . .'

They stepped over the beam in the entrance hall. Ravenel picked up his raincoat and cracked open the front door. He looked out. The street was deserted.

'All clear.'

They moved out, pulling the door shut behind them, and walked quickly towards the Boulevard Georges Favon. Giddy with success, near to hysteria, Ravenel put his arm around Marie.

'We did it,' he said. 'We really did it.'

'Oh my God,' she said excitedly, snuggling up to him. 'Wasn't that a turn-on? I feel like doing it all over again. I feel like . . . you know what I feel like?'

'No,' he said.

'Some passionate sex.'

He looked at her. 'We can't,' he said. 'I've got to call Julia at Olympe.'

'Oh *merde*. I'd forgotten.' She squeezed his arm. 'Maybe she'd like to join in?'

'Marie.' Ravenel was genuinely shocked. 'She's English. And she's pregnant.'

Marie was still glum-faced when they reached the end of the street and waved down a cruising taxi. But she brightened when they got back to the hotel. While Ravenel made the call she went up to the room he had reserved for her to freshen up. Then they adjourned to the bar to await Julia.

Over brandies.

Chapter 40

After her initial nervousness Julia was surprised to find herself enjoying her dinner with Paul Eberhardt. The restaurant was elegant and charming, with superb Art-Deco décor and delicious food. Eberhardt, distinguished-looking in a light suit and discreet tie, proved to be an amusing and entertaining companion. She realized he was enjoying being interviewed.

He spoke at length about his early days in Germany with the Deutsche Bank. 'It was so different then,' he said. 'We wore top hats and striped trousers.' He talked about the great private banks of Geneva – Lombard Odier, Pictet, Rothschild, Darier and Hentsch – some of them founded during the Napoleonic era to handle the investments of the Emperor. 'Now there are only twenty left,' he said. He told her how the *Groupement* underwrote the bonds issued by the City of Geneva – 'But of course you know all this.'

She was surprised that he talked so frankly about the death of his wife, Hilde, from cancer; about his concern for the bank's future after he had gone. 'I have a good partner, a man named Alain Charrier,' he said. 'He is splendid but not as good as Georges di Marco. He was a great loss. That was a nice obituary your paper carried.'

'Thank you,' Julia said. She had no idea what he was talking about.

'I should probably have retired long ago,' Eberhardt continued. 'But, as I say, I am concerned for the bank. I have no immediate heirs. Anyway, what would I do with my life? I enjoy my day-to-day work at the bank. I look after the fortunes of some very prominent people. I like to think I am respected in the banking community.'

He smiled self-consciously, as if mildly embarrassed to have talked so much. 'Now let me ask you some questions. How long have you been with the *Journal*?'

'Forever, it seems,' Julia said, hoping this would satisfy him.

'I've been reading you for quite some time,' Eberhardt said.

'That's because I write such a lot,' she said. Her laugh sounded hollow even to herself.

'Where were you before?'

'The *Financial Times*. I'm English.'

'I realize that. Is it usual for an American paper to employ a British journalist?'

'It does happen,' Julia said. 'They needed someone in London so they came to me.'

'They made a good choice, I'm sure,' Eberhardt said. 'Remind me of your editor's name?'

Julia's calm abandoned her briefly. She dropped her pen on the floor and made a great business of picking it up.

'The man I deal with is Walter Bushell,' she said. 'He's terrific. I'm sure you've come across him.'

'I don't believe so.'

'I'm surprised. He comes here a lot. Geneva is one of his favourite cities.'

'To be honest with you I don't have much contact with journalists,' Eberhardt said. 'I have not given an interview in years. It was only because I know your work that I agreed to meet you this evening.'

'I'm glad,' Julia said, relieved that he had let it go at that. When Eberhardt looked away to order more coffee she stole a quick glance at her watch. It was 10.30 p.m. Ravenel had to be out of the bank by now. What was keeping him?

Eberhardt turned back to her. 'Can you stay over tomorrow?'

She shook her head. 'I have to go back to London in the morning.'

'Stay until lunchtime. I could show you round the bank. You'd find it interesting. We could lunch nearby before you leave for the airport.'

'That's kind of you, Monsieur Eberhardt.' Julia reached across and shut off the tape recorder. She slipped it into her purse together with the notebook. 'Perhaps another time . . .'

'There is a great deal to see and enjoy in Geneva,' he said. 'We have fine theatre, a great orchestra . . .' He was silent while the new coffees were served. 'When do you propose to run this story?'

'I'll write it tomorrow,' Julia said. 'After that it's up to them.'

'You said there was some kind of rush.'

'But I don't know the exact day they'll use it.'

At that moment the maitre d' came over. 'Mademoiselle Bennett? Telephone for you.'

Eberhardt looked puzzled.

'My office,' Julia said. 'I told them where I'd be.'

She took the call in the booth by the entrance.

'Get to the Richemond as soon as you can,' Ravenel said. He hung up.

She returned to the table. 'That settles it,' she said. 'They want the story as soon as possible. I'll have to start writing tonight.'

She held up her hand for the bill. Eberhardt made no protest. She took out her Visa card and then, dismayed, realized he would see her name on it. She slid it back into her wallet and took out the sheaf of Swiss bank notes she had bought at the airport.

'Please,' Eberhardt said. He picked up the bill. 'This has been so enjoyable. Allow me.'

He escorted her to the door, his hand beneath her elbow. 'Where are you staying, Hilary?'

'The Bristol,' she said.

'I will drop you off,' he said. 'It's not out of my way. You'll never find a taxi.'

Her nervousness returned. What if he wants to come

in, she thought. Or hears them call me 'Miss Lang'?

'I'll have to transcribe my notes right away,' she said.

'I understand.' He opened the passenger door and helped her slide into the Renault. Five minutes later he dropped her off at the hotel.

'Thank you for a most interesting evening,' Julia said. 'But it should have been my bill.'

'Now you will feel obliged to return,' Eberhardt said. 'I hope you do.' He kissed her hand. 'Goodbye, Hilary.'

When Julia rushed into the Richemond, Marie and Ravenel were on their third brandies.

She looked from one to the other. 'So tell me.'

'We got it,' Ravenel said. 'Verification. The bank lied.'

A smile spread slowly across Julia's face. 'You are two of the most extraordinary people I've ever known,' she said. She hugged them both. 'You did it. You got in.' She looked incredulous.

'More important,' Marie said. 'We got out.'

'I never thought you'd do it.'

'I had my own doubts,' Ravenel said. 'Breaking into banks was not part of my training.'

'Were you scared? I bet you were.'

She's more interested in the fact that we got into the bank than the money, Ravenel thought. His estimation of Julia Lang went up another notch.

'I was petrified. I don't know about Marie.'

'I was too,' Marie said.

'What's next?' Julia asked.

'We get the pictures developed,' Ravenel said. 'Cristiani will pick them up in the morning.'

Julia shook her head in wonderment. 'I can scarcely believe it. It's incredible, what you did.'

'I think so too,' Marie said.

Ravenel put his hand on Julia's arm. 'What about you? How did it go with Eberhardt?'

'Incredibly well. He couldn't have been nicer. He wanted me to stay over to go round the bank tomorrow.'

'I guessed the old bastard would turn on the charm,' Ravenel said.

Marie nodded. 'Don't be fooled by him. He's a cold-nosed Swiss banker with ice-water in his veins.'

'Maybe so,' Julia said. 'But he was very gracious to me.'

'He thought you were an important journalist,' Marie said. 'Why wouldn't he be? Don't forget, he's the man who tried to do you out of your money.' She finished her brandy and yawned extravagantly. 'I'm ready for bed.' She gave Ravenel a long look.

'Me too,' he said.

'Not yet,' Julia said. 'I fly home tomorrow. Stay with me for a while.'

Marie and Ravenel exchanged glances.

'You stay.' Marie gave Ravenel a wooden smile. 'I'll go call Cristiani about picking up the film.'

Ravenel ordered another brandy.

Paul Eberhardt found himself smiling over his breakfast toast and coffee, something he had not done for a long time. What a delightful evening! And what a charming woman. Hilary Bennett. He had been much taken with her. She was the kind of woman who appealed to him; beautiful, intelligent and warm. Although the food had been good at Olympe he now wished he had suggested the Lion d'Or for dinner. He would like some of his friends there to have seen him with her. Perhaps next time. She would have enjoyed looking round his bank; he had noticed the look in her eyes when he suggested it. She had seemed genuinely sorry that she had to rush back so quickly. But he knew something about journalists and their deadlines. He wondered if she were married – he had not wanted to ask her that – and where in London she lived.

He would find out, he decided; send her some flowers; thank her for making the interview so pleasant; let her know how much he was looking forward to her return visit.

245

He thought back over the interview. Then he remembered. Damn. He had forgotten to tell her he was to chair the International Bankers' Conference in Vienna. A high honour. That should be in the article; it was even more important than the upcoming conference in Paris. He glanced at his watch and rose from the table. It was just past nine o'clock. Surely she would not have left the Bristol yet? He went into his study and called the hotel.

Chapter 41

The negatives were developed and enlarged in a private lab owned by a friend of Cristiani's. Studying them the next morning the investigator was startled. He picked up the telephone and called the Richemond.

Ravenel was still in bed with Marie, sleeping off their delayed lovemaking of the night before. It had been after 2 a.m. when he had finally got away from Julia.

'They're ready,' Cristiani told him.

'I'll pick them up later,' Ravenel said.

'I suggest you stop what you're doing and come by now,' Cristiani said. 'Two of these photographs are particularly interesting.'

'Half an hour then,' Ravenel said. He hung up and turned to Marie. 'Cristiani says a couple of those photographs are very interesting.'

Marie smiled contentedly. 'I told you,' she said softly.

When they arrived at Cristiani's office they found him pacing the room, the photographs in his hand.

'You speak German?' he asked Ravenel.

'Hardly any.'

'Too bad.' He flopped into his desk chair. 'Eberhardt must have been mad to keep these in the files,' he said.

Ravenel looked at Marie. She had a big grin on her face. 'Why?'

'They don't tell us everything,' Cristiani said. 'But they tell us a lot. Eh, Marie?' He handed her the photos. She picked up a magnifying glass from the desk and studied them intently.

'Incredible,' she said after a moment. 'I couldn't believe

it when I saw them. You're right. He was crazy not to destroy these.'

Ravenel looked first at him, then at Marie. 'Would you mind telling me what you're talking about?'

'These file papers show how Eberhardt's bank got started.'

'What's interesting about that?'

'It was Nazi money.'

Ravenel stared at him. '*Nazi* money?'

'It's there in the files.' Cristiani sat back, putting his hands together, interlocking his fingers. 'Remember I told you Eberhardt was pro-German? Went to Germany all the time during the war? Nothing wrong with that. A lot of Swiss businessmen did. From 1940 until 1944 the Nazis had us ringed. We were dependent on them for our fuel supplies.'

'So?'

'It seems Eberhardt had different reasons for visiting Germany. Someone there was secretly depositing funds in his bank.'

'Who?'

'We might have found out,' Marie said drily, 'if you hadn't hurried me out of that place. There were dozens of other papers in the files.'

'I thought I heard sirens,' Ravenel said.

'You heard ringing in your ears,' Marie scoffed. 'There were no sirens.' She handed the photos back to Cristiani.

'You saw the signatures of the two executives who witnessed the deposits?' Cristiani said.

Marie nodded. 'André Leber and Georges di Marco. Both knew about the Nazi money. Both are now conveniently dead.'

'Gets more and more interesting, doesn't it?' Cristiani studied the photos again. 'At least we've got one name here.'

'There was another on the next page,' Marie said. 'But Guy kept pushing me to leave so I missed it.'

'A pity,' Cristiani said. 'That would have given us the complete picture.'

Ravenel, sulky, looked at them both. 'How can you tell it was Nazi money?'

Cristiani held up the first photo and, using the magnifying glass, read from it. 'First entry. *May 1938. Five hundred thousand dollars deposited in account number 845-090. Origin: Berlin. Hand-delivered by Lt Heinz Linge.*' He looked up. 'Wouldn't you say that was fairly conclusive?'

'But money transfers must have been going on all the time?'

'Official ones, yes. That's how the Germans paid their agents operating overseas. And paid for vital materials. The Reichsbank asked us to transmit money to this or that country and we complied. We were neutral, remember.'

'So I've heard.'

Cristiani ignored this.

'What makes you so sure this wasn't an official transfer?' Ravenel asked.

'Because the Reichsbank didn't send money out of the country with couriers. Nor was it paid into private accounts.'

'So this was a secret arrangement?'

'Right.'

'Look,' Ravenel said. 'I'm grateful to you both. But I've got what I was looking for. This other stuff is your affair.'

Cristiani eyed him thoughtfully. He held out the photo of Brand's letter. 'This shows that $20 million was supposed to have been credited to an account set up for Julia Lang. What's your next move? You write to Eberhardt that you have it. He does not reply. What do you do? Sue him?'

'I could send it to the Federal Banking Commission.'

'That's right. You could. I'll give you their address. The first thing they'll want to know is how you obtained this photo. What will you tell them? "I broke into the bank ..."'

Ravenel sighed.

'If I were you,' Cristiani said, 'though I thank God I'm not, I would try to track down this Heinz Linge. If he's still alive and he'll talk to you, then you'll really have something to threaten Eberhardt with. A private bank has only one thing going for it – a reputation for absolute integrity. If it can be shown that Banque Eberhardt was started with Nazi money, money probably stolen from Jews, there would be an outcry.'

'Suppose we do go looking for Linge . . .'

'Not "we". You.'

'. . . and he's dead?'

'You could always go back into the bank and get the next sheet on the file,' Marie said. 'The one you wouldn't let me wait to read. "I think I heard sirens . . ."' she mimicked, pulling a face.

Ravenel glared at her.

'He may well be dead,' Cristiani said. 'Who knows?' He went over to the cabinet in the corner and looked through some papers. 'There's a man who specializes in keeping track of those sort of people,' he said.

'Someone at the Simon Wiesenthal Center?'

'No, they're only interested in war criminals. There's another man who keeps tabs on all the people who worked for the top Nazis, even their hairdressers. He might know where to find Linge.'

'What's his name?'

'That's what I'm looking for,' Cristiani said. 'Don't be so impatient.' He flicked through some more papers, cursing. 'That dumb secretary of mine. No idea of filing.' He pulled out a sheet. 'Here it is. Pierre Gautier.'

'The war ended years ago,' Ravenel said. 'I'm surprised he still bothers.'

Cristiani went back to his desk. 'Ever hear of Oradour sur Glane? Gautier evacuated his wife and daughter there during the war. A little village; nobody would bother with it. That's what he thought. But as punishment for the killing of a German officer in the area, the SS *Das Reich* Division drove all the local women and children into the village church, blew it up and set fire to the town. Six hundred women and children died, among them Gautier's wife and daughter.' He looked hard at Ravenel. 'Does that explain why he's carried his hate over the years?'

'Jesus.' Ravenel got up. 'Where can I find him?'

'He lives in Paris. Here's the address.' Cristiani held out the sheet.

'I'll call him tonight.'

Next day Ravenel said goodbye to Marie over a long lunch at Le Duc. Then he telephoned Julia in London.

'You won't hear from me for a day or two,' he said. 'I'm going to Paris.'

'I thought you'd already got what you need?'

'Part of it,' he said. 'It seems there's a whole lot more . . .'

'It's B-e-n-n-e-t-t.' Eberhardt spelled out the name for the reception clerk. He waited a moment. 'Of course I'm sure. I dropped her off at the hotel myself.'

'I'm sorry, Monsieur Eberhardt.' The clerk studied the computer console in front of him. 'I have no record of that name.'

'She checked in yesterday, from London.'

'No, sir, I'm sorry. Could she have used a married name?'

Eberhardt felt a twinge of disappointment. He had not considered that. Well, what if she were married? It meant nothing these days. She could be divorced; still using her married name . . .

'A young woman in her mid-thirties. Attractive. Blonde hair . . .'

'That doesn't help, sir. I was not on duty yesterday.'

'You know who I am? The Banque Eberhardt?'

'Of course, sir.'

'I have to get in touch with this lady most urgently. I know she stayed last night at your hotel. Give me the names of any guests who arrived yesterday afternoon from London and checked out this morning.'

He waited, standing by the telephone, finishing his coffee. He did not have long to wait.

'There was only one, Monsieur Eberhardt. A Miss Julia Lang.'

Julia Lang! He had dined with Julia Lang! The woman who had been in his thoughts for weeks now; whose very existence had caused so many of his recent problems.

Totally mystified, Eberhardt slumped back in his study chair. Why had she done this? What was the point? Was she hoping to trap him into saying something to her advantage? He racked his brains for an answer.

For years he had lived the life of a highly successful Swiss banker. Now everything seemed to be unravelling: Cristiani's probe into di Marco's death . . . the tapping of his telephone . . . Grace Brand's hysterical calls. And now this.

He tried to recall the conversation of the night before. What had he talked about? Had he said anything that she could use to incriminate him? He could think of nothing. It had been a perfectly ordinary interview. Now he saw why she had become flustered when asked the name of her editor.

He had her address in London. It would be a simple matter to obtain the phone number. But what then? What could he say to her – I know it was you. I just want to know why? He would seem like a gullible old fool.

The worst part was that he had liked her; had hoped to see her again. There had been eye contact there. She had responded to him.

Could it have been an innocent stratagem she had devised to meet him? He had refused to see her as Julia Lang so she had determined to meet him as Hilary

Bennett. But to what end? He sat perfectly still in his big leather chair searching for answers.

And found none.

Ravenel arrived late the following morning and took a taxi to his favourite small hotel, the Résidence du Bois in the rue Chalgrin. From there he telephoned Pierre Gautier. 'I am here,' he said.

'Do you know the Boulevard Raspail?'

'Very well.'

'There is a small street leading off it, the rue des Pierres. Come to number 75, apartment 4.'

Ravenel went down to find a cab. Traffic was heavy and it was forty-five minutes before he dropped off at the corner of the rue des Pierres, a narrow street lined with small shops and restaurants. He found Gautier's number easily and took the ancient lift to the fourth floor.

Gautier was waiting for him as he stepped out; a small man with a shock of white hair, bright piercing eyes and the look of someone who has spent his life suffering. They shook hands. Gautier led the way into a rambling apartment at the end of the corridor, a place of creaking floors and high ceilings with French windows looking out over the street. The walls were lined with bookcases, every shelf laden with bulging files and papers. Other files were piled on the floor. Many of them had pictures of men in uniform stuck to the covers with tape. The place looked a mess. Ravenel was immediately depressed.

Gautier gestured to a chair. 'I can offer you wine?'

'Thank you.'

The old man disappeared into the kitchen and returned a moment later with a tray holding two glasses and a bottle of Beaujolais.

'I didn't think people like you were still in business,' Ravenel said.

'In business?' Gautier said, glancing at him. 'A curious way of putting it. Yes, I am still in business.' He poured a measure of wine for both of them. 'You are trying to locate a former Nazi?'

'Yes.'

'Not a war criminal? For those you must go to the Public Prosecutor's Office in Frankfurt.'

'I understand that. As far as I know this man was not a war criminal.'

'What did he do?'

'He worked in Berlin. Probably for one of the top men.'

'His name?'

'Linge. Heinz Linge.' He held out the paper with Linge's name on it.

Gautier studied it carefully. 'Linge? Linge? I don't think I know this one.'

'He went into Switzerland at least once during the war.'

The old man sipped his wine. 'Probably took money out for someone. They all had accounts there, you know. I told the Americans that after the war. They weren't interested.'

'I'm interested,' Ravenel said. 'Do you think you might have something on him?'

'Why do you want to know about this man?'

'A friend of mine is trying to track down some money that is owed to her. I think this man may know something about it.'

Gautier glanced around. 'As you can see, everything's in a bit of a mess.'

'Perhaps I could help you?'

'You wouldn't know where to look.' He glanced back at Ravenel. 'People say I am crazy doing this. "Why?" they ask. "Why?" I tell them why. I lost my wife and child to those butchers. Oradour sur Glane. They were herded into the church there and blown to pieces. Gallant soldiers, eh? Men of the SS *Das Reich* Division; men who prided themselves on their fighting prowess. Not Nazi thugs, German soldiers.'

Ravenel listened silently.

'People forget,' Gautier said. 'I don't.' He glanced at the paper again. 'Heinz Linge,' he repeated. 'Let me take a look around.'

He wandered around the room, examining files, occasionally muttering to himself while Ravenel, watching, grew increasingly pessimistic. At the end of the search Gautier came back. 'Nothing here, I'm afraid.' He frowned. 'There's one more place.'

He disappeared down the hall. Ravenel looked around at the files wondering how Gautier ever found anything. He was a little mad, he judged. Everything about him suggested it; the way he talked, the look in his eyes, the movements of his hands. For years he had lived here alone, surrounded by his files, making calls, trying to track down the people who had destroyed his life.

'Aha!'

He heard a grunt of triumph. A moment later Gautier reappeared bearing a yellow file in his hand. 'Heinz Linge.' He held the file up for Ravenel to see the name on the top. There was a photograph too, of a young man in uniform looking very serious. 'Now,' he said, 'let's see what we have here.' He glanced at Ravenel. 'You see, one should never give up.'

'He's still alive, then?' Ravenel asked.

'Who knows? These files are not up to date. There's only me, you see.'

He opened the file and began reading, mumbling to himself. Finally he looked up. 'Nothing about Switzerland, I'm afraid. And nothing about who he worked for. It just shows that he served on the Russian front. Fought at Stalingrad. He was captured by the Russians and sent to a Siberian labour camp. In 1949 he was returned to Berlin.'

'Where is he now? Does it say?'

Gautier consulted the file again. 'He moved to Neuhaus in Bavaria in 1955. That's the last entry I have.'

'So he could be dead?'

'Yes.'

'Worth a try,' Ravenel said. He got up. 'Can I pay you for this?'

The old man looked offended. 'You think I do it for money?'

'I just thought . . .'

Gautier escorted Ravenel to the door. 'You know what people would like to forget?' he said. 'Adolf Hitler and Nazi Germany came about as the result of a free election.'

Ravenel nodded. 'I know.'

'Good luck,' Gautier said. He shut the door quietly.

Chapter 42

Ravenel spent fifteen minutes at the American Express office in Paris perusing a map of Germany. He wanted to find the exact location of Neuhaus. It lay, he discovered, northeast of Nuremberg on the way to Bayreuth. Satisfied, he booked himself on an Air France flight to Nuremberg at 3.30.

While the girl prepared his ticket, Ravenel went over to the cashiers' desk and drew $10,000 in cash against his credit card.

He was in Nuremberg by 5.15 p.m., by which time it was almost dusk. It was too late to drive to Neuhaus, he decided, so he checked into the Grand Hotel for the night.

In the morning he went into a men's store and bought a leather jacket, a blue sweater, jeans and a pair of loafers, reasoning that such an outfit would attract less attention in the countryside than his suit. Then he rented a BMW and set off on the short drive to Neuhaus.

It was very cold but the sky was bright blue and there was little wind. He felt invigorated as the car sped past small villages and picture-postcard churches nestling amid meadows. Everything looked as though it were straight out of a German tourist book, almost too pretty to be real.

Neuhaus proved to be a village of half-timbered houses, cow sheds and pig pens set amid dramatic hills and forests. Although there were two promising-looking inns he drove past them. At the end of the street he found a small *Gasthaus* and parked outside.

The proprietress, a plump and amiable woman named Greta, was delighted to welcome him and showed him to a cheerful room on the second floor. It was warm and comfortable, with a large double bed.

Had he come to visit Burg Veldenstein, she enquired. 'It's a great tourist attraction. Built on the site of an old fortress.'

'A castle?' Ravenel said.

'Yes,' Greta nodded vigorously. 'A castle.' She disappeared down the corridor to get fresh towels for him.

'Tell me,' Ravenel said when she returned, 'is there someone named Linge still living here?'

'Old Heinz. Yes. The cottage at the very end of the road, the one with a white fence. You know him?'

'A friend mentioned his name. Said he lived here.'

'Not for much longer,' Greta said shaking her head.

'He's dying?' Ravenel was immediately alarmed.

'They're kicking him out. The *Gemeinderat*.'

'What's that?'

'The people who run the town under the *Bürgermeister*. I don't – '

'You mean the council?'

She nodded. 'The council.'

'But why?'

'He cannot pay his *Grundsteuer*.' She sought the word in English. 'His house tax.'

'So he's got to go?'

'They don't like him,' Greta said. 'A pity. Such a brave man. Captured by the Russians during the war. He had a terrible time. A journalist from the *Nürnberger Nachrichten* was here just last month to talk to him about his experiences. He stayed here. Klaus Keppler.'

That sounded promising, Ravenel thought. 'Does Herr Linge still work?'

'Not any more. He was a gardener. Now he's too old.' She rubbed her hands together. 'You would like to eat supper here?'

'If it's possible.'

'There are no other guests but I will cook for you,' she said. 'You like venison?'

'Very much.'

'You shall have it. Straight from the forests. Eight o'clock is good?'

'Fine,' Ravenel said. 'What was the name of that journalist?'

'Keppler,' she said. 'Klaus Keppler.'

Ravenel unpacked and changed into the clothes he had bought in Nuremberg. Then he took a brisk walk through the village. Linge's cottage was easy to find. It lay back from the road at the far end of the main street with a battered picket fence around it. The cottage looked dilapidated, with the air of a place not deserted but shut tight against the world. The garden was wild and un- tended. Leaves were everywhere.

Some gardener, Ravenel thought to himself.

Just beyond the gate lay a sleek-coated Doberman, eyes wary. Ravenel walked past the cottage for half a mile, turned and walked back on the other side of the road.

When he got back to the *Gasthaus* he debated whether to telephone the *Nürnberger Nachrichten* and ask for Herr Keppler, or go there in person. Reasoning that it was only forty-five minutes away and he enjoyed driving the BMW, he got into the car and headed back towards Nuremberg.

An hour later he was in the lobby of the newspaper asking for Klaus Keppler.

'Tell him I'm a reporter with the *New York Times*,' Ravenel said. 'I'd like to pick his brains for five minutes.'

A moment later Klaus Keppler came bounding down the stairs. He was a young man brimming with en- thusiasm. He ushered Ravenel straight into a visiting room.

'You must know Mark Schindler?' he said. 'I work for him occasionally.'

'Of course,' Ravenel said. 'Splendid chap. I'll say hello for you.'

'Good paper, the *New York Times*,' Keppler said.

'We try,' Ravenel said modestly.

'How can I help you?'

'Last month you talked to an old man in Neuhaus – Heinz Linge.'

'I did.'

'I'm anxious to talk with him too.'

'Good luck. He's a difficult old bastard. He has a dog there that scared the hell out of me.'

'May I ask what you went to see him about?'

'We were planning a story about former prisoners of war. People who'd been held in Russian camps during and after the war. We wanted their feelings about Russians now that we're all pals again ... recollections ... you know the sort of thing.'

'Of course.'

'Wouldn't co-operate. Didn't want to know. Wouldn't even let us take his picture, the sour old swine. We abandoned the story – ' he broke off. 'Is that your line too?'

'More or less. Apparently the Russians gave him a bad time.'

'So I'm told. Now his own village is giving him problems. He wrote us a letter not long ago. Seems he's being chucked out of his house for not paying his rates.'

'You think he'll talk to me?'

'He might. An American paper. You never can tell.'

Ravenel thanked him.

'Watch out for that damn dog,' Keppler said.

Ravenel was back in Neuhaus by 3 p.m. He parked the car behind the *Gasthaus* and walked through the village to Linge's cottage.

The dog was still there in exactly the same position. He eyed it warily. He did not like Dobermans. He did not like the way they sized you up, sensing whether or not you were afraid. It wouldn't have to do much sizing up to know he was scared stiff.

He opened the front gate.

The dog half rose from its crouched position.

'*Guter Hund.*' Ravenel prayed the dog would make allowances for his accent. '*Sitz!*'

Warily he walked up the path to the front door. There was an iron knocker but no bell. He rapped once and waited. Rapped again.

The man who opened the door at the second knock stood there, peering at Ravenel through thick-lensed spectacles. He was a tall, gaunt man, a shade over six feet, very thin. His hair, what little there was, was pure white and brushed straight back. His skin was waxen. Only his eyes showed signs of life.

'*Was möchten Sie?*'

'*Ich bin ein amerikanischer Schriftsteller,*' Ravenel said. '*Ich hoffe Sie können mir helfen.*'

Part of the speech he had rehearsed so carefully was true, he reasoned. He wasn't an American writer but he did hope Linge could help him.

Linge stared at him for a moment longer. 'Go away,' he said in English.

'I've come a long way to talk to you,' Ravenel said.

'What's your name?'

'Ravenel.'

'Why do you come to me? What are you writing about?'

'The fall of Stalingrad,' Ravenel said. 'From the point of view of those who fought on both sides.'

Linge looked at him blankly. 'That's all been done,' he said. 'There's nothing more to say.'

'It's been written by historians,' Ravenel said, 'but never from the point of view of the ordinary soldier.'

There was no expression in the old man's eyes. 'I cannot help you.'

He closed the door in Ravenel's face.

After supper that night – the venison was followed by apple dumpling with two steins of Kulmbacher beer to wash it down – Ravenel invited Greta to sit with him.

'I went to see Herr Linge,' he said. 'He refused to talk to me.'

'I thought you knew a friend of his?'

'It made no difference.'

'He's a bitter old man,' she said. 'Something happened in the war, I think. He was a wreck when he returned.'

'He's been here ever since?'

'In that little cottage. He moved there with his wife and son. In the fifties, I remember.'

'Can't the son help him with money?'

'He was killed. An accident in America. That was years ago. The wife died soon afterwards.'

'And Linge has no money at all?'

'That's what he claims.'

By the time Ravenel went up to his bedroom that night he knew he had found the way to get Linge to talk.

He slept badly. The meal lay heavily in his stomach and he was not accustomed to such a soft bed. At 8 a.m. when Greta knocked and came in with a tray of breakfast, he was bleary-eyed. He felt better after the coffee. She had put a small flower on the tray, a touch he found oddly endearing.

By ten o'clock he was at Linge's cottage again. There was no sign of the Doberman, nor was there an immediate response to his knocking. He wondered if the old man was out or whether he was just refusing to open the door. Just as he was about to give up it cracked open.

'Go away,' Linge said. 'I will call the police.'

Ravenel held up his hands in a gesture of supplication. 'Hear me out, please. Then I will leave if you wish.'

The door opened a little wider and the old man stood looking at him uncertainly. Behind him was the Doberman. Ravenel took a deep breath and took out the bundle of $100 notes. 'I am authorized by my publisher to pay you $10,000 for any information you can give me.'

He fanned out the notes for Linge to see. The old man stared at the money as if mesmerized.

'Ten thousand dollars?'

Ravenel nodded.

The old man looked at him for a moment longer and then stood to one side, gesturing Ravenel to enter. He said something to the dog, which stalked away into the garden. The door opened straight on to a cosy raftered room filled with books and chintzy furnishings. There was a small fire burning in the hearth with two chairs in front of it.

'I was about to have coffee,' Linge said. 'You will join me?'

'Thanks.'

While Linge busied himself in the adjoining kitchen Ravenel looked around the room. On the mantel were some pictures, presumably family ones. From fading sepia prints a serious-looking man and woman stared into the camera with a smiling boy between them. To one side was a photograph of two young men in uniform. One of them Ravenel recognized as Linge.

When Linge returned with the coffee he took one of the chairs by the fire and gestured for Ravenel to sit in the other. 'This money, when would it be paid?'

'After we have talked.'

'Today?'

Ravenel nodded.

The old man looked suddenly apologetic. 'I'm sorry. I have forgotten your name.'

'Ravenel.'

'Herr Ravenel. This money could be a gift from God. I cannot pay my *Grundsteuer*, my house tax, and they are threatening to take away my home.'

'You have no money of your own?'

'For thirty years I was a gardener. Gardeners do not make much.'

Ravenel nodded. 'Can we talk about Stalingrad?' He took out the small tape recorder he had bought at Geneva airport and switched it on.

'It's a long time ago.'

'Whatever you remember.'

The old man laughed without humour. 'You want to know what I remember? Anger, that's what I remember. Anger at what had been done to me. Not the battle itself. I was a German officer anxious to do my bit. When the posting came through it never occurred to me *why* I'd been sent there. I had no chance to ask anyone. I had just one week to board the troop train.'

'You knew you were being sent to Stalingrad?'

'The Russian front, they said. That was bad enough, believe me. But it was Stalingrad. I was seconded to Friedrich Paulus' Sixth Army. It was hell on earth. Men were dying of frostbite, dysentery and typhus. We were no longer an army; just a collection of huddled groups trying to survive.' Linge shook his head as if still incredulous at the memory. 'General Paulus begged Hitler to let us evacuate. No, the Führer said, Stalingrad must be held. In the end, 300,000 of us were trapped there. Of those, 180,000 were taken captive; the rest died. Most of us perished of exhaustion on the long, icy roads of Siberia. Only 6,000 survived of the original 300,000.'

The old man stirred his coffee. 'You Americans like to think you won the war. Let me tell you something. The Russians won the war. Germany lost forty-one divisions in Russia – more than one million casualties – between July and October of 1943 alone. Four months. Even after the Normandy invasion our casualties on the Russian front were four times greater than in the West. Did you know that?'

'No,' Ravenel said.

'Not many Americans do,' Linge said.

'Where were you before you were sent to the Russian front?'

'Berlin.'

'You didn't fight in France? Or in any of the other occupied countries?'

'No.'

'Why was that?'

'My duties were in Berlin.'

'What exactly were you doing?'

Linge looked at him suspiciously. 'I thought you were writing about Stalingrad?'

'I am. But I need some background.'

'I was aide to Reichsmarschall Hermann Goering. He was brought up here. Did you know that? At the Burg Veldenstein. It was given to him by his mother's lover, Baron von Epenstein. It's a historic site.'

Ravenel leaned forward. 'If you were the Reichsmarschall's aide why were you sent to the Russian front in 1942? Could he not have prevented it?'

Linge looked at him. 'Of course he could have prevented it.' He got up from his chair and went over to a tiny bureau in the corner and searched through a drawer. A moment later he came back with a faded photograph. 'You want to see what that fat bastard gave me when I was posted?'

It was a picture of Hermann Goering in full uniform holding aloft his field marshal's baton. Written at the bottom was: *Die besten Wünsche und viel Glück.*

Linge took back the picture. 'Best wishes and good luck,' he said contemptuously, 'and he was letting me go to my death.'

'But why?'

The old man looked up sharply. 'What has this to do with your book?'

'Herr Linge, I missed the war. I was a boy at the time. And your story is so interesting . . .'

'I have told you nothing.'

'You've told me a lot. Except why you were sent to fight at Stalingrad.'

'Goering wanted rid of me.'

'Why?'

'I knew about his secret bank account in Switzerland.'

Ravenel let his breath out slowly. Dame Fortune was not just smiling at him this day; she was positively grinning.

Linge leaned forward. 'You have a certain image of Hermann Goering – am I right? You see him as a jovial, fat man, a sort of court jester to Hitler?'

'I suppose so.'

Linge's face seemed to contort a little. 'He was the most corrupt of them all. While others fought and died Goering looted the museums and art houses of Europe for treasures to hang in his country home. He lived there like a feudal king, he and his wife, Emmy, even when Germany was losing the war.'

'How did you know about the Swiss bank account?'

Linge looked at him fiercely. 'I was one of two people who set it up for him.'

'And for that you were sent to Russia?'

'For that.'

Stay cool, Ravenel told himself. Otherwise he'll guess the real reason you came here. Sit on your hands; look into the fire; anything. But don't seem so interested.

'You actually went to Switzerland to set it up? Incredible.'

'I knew the banker, you see. He was Swiss. He met the Reichsmarschall at a cocktail party at the Adlon Hotel hosted by some German bank. They hit it off and he was invited to Goering's home.

'He went there several times. One day the Reichsmarschall made him a proposition. From time to time he wished to deposit sums of money in this man's bank in Switzerland. It was not that he feared for the future, he said, but with Europe soon to be plunged into war it paid to be prudent.'

'How did the banker react to that?' Ravenel asked.

'He was flattered, of course; flattered to be taken into the confidence of the Reichsmarschall. Who wouldn't have been?'

'Wasn't this banker worried that someone in his own bank would talk?'

Linge shook his head. 'He knew nobody would. The Swiss Banking Act sets down harsh penalties for that.'

Ravenel nodded. He knew the act. 'What was the banker's name?'

'You want a lot for your money,' Linge said. 'His name was Eberhardt. He was an admirer of ours. From 1938 until 1942 I and another aide made ten trips to Geneva. We deposited more than $200 million in an account for Goering at his bank.'

'Good God,' Ravenel said. 'Dollars? Not Reichsmarks?'

'Dollars,' Linge repeated. 'He had his eye on the future. Most of it was money seized from wealthy Jews who had been forced to flee the country or who were sent to the camps.'

'How did you take the money into Switzerland?'

'In suitcases. We wore civilian clothes. We had to be careful, even with passes signed by the Reichsmarschall. Switzerland was full of agents trying to identify German holders of bank accounts. It was against the law, you see. After 1936 holders of undeclared assets abroad could be hanged.'

'What was your reward for doing this?'

'We were simply doing our duty. But we got to spend a week's leave in Switzerland. Drink some decent coffee. Bring back some of the things we couldn't get at home.'

'And Eberhardt was happy to do all this?'

'Happy?' Linge laughed drily. 'He was overjoyed. Until 1945 the Swiss were convinced that Germany would win the war. Eberhardt welcomed the money. He knew it would ensure him a place in the Reichs-marschall's good books after the war.'

'Then Goering was hanged at Nuremberg – '

'No. The night before the execution he committed suicide.'

'What happened to the money?'

'What do you think? It stayed in the bank. Unclaimed.'

'You could have gone to the authorities.'

'What authorities? There were no authorities. Germany was in ruins.'

'What about the bank? Did you contact them?'

'I tried. Eberhardt called the police and had me deported.'

'It's an incredible story,' Ravenel said. 'Absolutely incredible. You've never told it before?'

'I've told it often,' Linge said testily. 'Nobody believes me. Why should they? It's all in the past. And there's no evidence.'

Except at the Banque Eberhardt, Ravenel thought. And I have that.

He glanced again at the photograph of the two young officers on the mantelpiece. He took out the sheaf of $100 bills.

'I have one more question,' he said.

Ravenel waited until he got back to Nuremberg before calling Cristiani.

'How's it going?' the investigator asked.

'I've just had a talk with Heinz Linge.'

'He's still alive, then? That's a piece of luck. Was he co-operative?'

'It's amazing how much co-operation you can get for $10,000,' Ravenel said.

There was a snort at the end of the line. 'You paid him that much?'

'I didn't want to waste time.'

'I hope it was worth it?'

'It was,' Ravenel assured him. 'Can you take short-hand?'

'No,' Cristiani growled. 'That's why I have a secretary.'

'I don't want to involve her. You'll have to take it down in long hand,' Ravenel said. 'This is a letter I want you to hand deliver to Eberhardt tomorrow morning.'

Chapter 43

Paul Eberhardt resisted the impulse to slam down the phone on Grace Brand. But he was determined to give her one last chance to change her mind.

'What developments? What are you talking about?' Her voice was cold, the line to Mexico very clear.

'I have received a most disturbing letter, Madame Brand. A man named Ravenel, acting for Mademoiselle Lang.'

'I have already made my position clear with regard to this matter. I am not interested in further discussion.'

'But this letter – '

'Some rapacious lawyer. Ignore it.'

'Madame Brand, I cannot do that. He warns that if payment is not made to Mademoiselle Lang he will contact the *New York Times*. He knows about – '

'He knows nothing. How could he? There was one written note.'

'He has a copy, he claims.'

'Impossible. You still have the original?'

'Of course.'

'Then he's bluffing. Why are you wasting my time?'

'Madame Brand. I cannot take that risk . . .'

'I will say this one last time, Monsieur Eberhardt. Not one penny is to go to this woman. Now or ever.'

'It was Monsieur Brand's last wish.'

'He's dead, you fool. *Dead!* Can't you understand that?' Her voice rose. 'I control the Brand accounts now.'

'You don't seem to understand – '

'I will see you in Paris, Monsieur Eberhardt. I advise you not to go against my wishes.'

She hung up.

Eberhardt sat slumped at his desk, staring at the phone in his hand. He put it down slowly and picked up the letter that Cristiani had handed him. He read it again. This was no bluff. Guy Ravenel knew everything. And unless the money was paid immediately to Julia Lang he would go straight to the newspapers. The thought horrified Eberhardt. In two days' time he was due to fly to Paris. How could he do it with this threat hanging over him?

Grace Brand believed this man Ravenel was bluffing. But bluff could not explain the last, ominous sentence in the letter: *I send you best wishes from former Lt Heinz Linge who is sure you will remember him.*

Eberhardt read the sentence again, his hand trembling. How had they found *him*? He had thought him long dead.

There was no alternative. He would have to do what Ravenel demanded.

He toyed briefly with the idea of telephoning Julia Lang. Since his meeting with her he had found himself sympathizing with her more and more. She was up against a dangerous woman – did she realize that? He felt a need to explain his actions to her.

But that was foolish. She might not even listen to him. He sighed and picked up the phone and authorized payment of $20 million to Julia Lang through the Midland Bank in the Channel Islands.

The act gave him a feeling of satisfaction. Robert Brand had wanted her to have the money. Now she was getting it. Despite the machinations of that crazed woman in Acapulco.

Then, taking the black notebook from his pocket, he made his last call of the day.

For Julia the days dragged slowly. She had heard nothing from Ravenel since he announced he was going to Paris. Now some of the excitement generated by her Geneva adventure had begun to abate. If he had the evidence, what was he waiting for? Why could he not challenge the bank? Each night she awaited his call.

Some days she felt completely wiped out. She had put her fatigue down to emotional exhaustion but at her last visit to Dr Grierson he had taken her to task.

'You seem to forget, Julia, that you are nearly three months pregnant. Of course you get exhausted. All women carrying a child do. Your whole body is undergoing changes.' He completed his examination. 'Everything seems just fine,' he said. 'Still feeling nauseous?'

'Not so much.'

'That will pass. Anything else?'

'I get very depressed.'

'Mood swings are quite normal during pregnancy.' He scribbled something down in her file. 'Where do you plan to have the baby?'

'I thought the London Nursing Home.'

'Good idea,' he said. 'Better book now, though. They're busy.' He got up. 'Well, see you next month. Watch your diet.'

She had left his office plagued with feelings of guilt. Grierson had been right. She had been so racked with emotional upsets recently she had not been paying attention to the urgent signals her body was sending her.

Now she would.

Later that week she walked into her office to find Emma in tears. Closing the door she sat her down. 'What on earth's the matter?'

Emma looked at her with red-rimmed eyes. 'I've been fired,' she said.

'What?'

'Miss Ricci got me fired. She told Mr Moscato I was totally incompetent.'

Julia's temper flared. 'That bitch – who does she think she is? You work for me.'

'She claims there was a mistake in those photographs I gave her for the magazine; the ones of the original townhouse. One was of the old Connaught. It almost got

271

through to the finished magazine apparently. I know I captioned them correctly. I spent hours doing it. She must have mixed them up herself.'

'Wait here.'

Julia strode along the executive corridor and burst into Moscato's office without knocking. 'What's this about my secretary being fired?'

Moscato, sitting behind his desk, looked startled for a moment. His face darkened with anger. 'How dare you walk into my office like this?'

Julia was trembling with rage. 'Emma Carswell has been with this hotel for years. She is acknowledged by everyone to be the best secretary here. If you think I'm going to let that woman Ricci fire her you've got another think coming.'

Moscato seemed to recover some of his composure.

'I am not interested in debating the merits of your secretary, Miss Lang. Nor in arguing with you since you are clearly hysterical. The facts are that your secretary made a glaring mistake which would have made us look ridiculous had it not been caught in time. She is fired.' He paused. 'And that is the end of this conversation.'

'Oh no it isn't,' Julia snapped. She could hardly control herself. 'First of all, Emma assured me the photographs were captioned correctly. Second, I am the person to fire her if it ever becomes necessary.'

Moscato's voice was steely. 'Are you hard of hearing this morning or have I not made myself clear? Your secretary is fired.'

'I will not stand here and let you fire the best secretary I've ever had on the say-so of that woman.'

Moscato's face had gone very red. 'I am well aware of the hostility you have shown towards Miss Ricci since her arrival here. She is conscious of your jealousy but has chosen to ignore it. As editor of our new magazine she takes ultimate responsibility for its contents. When she told me about your secretary's mistake I agreed im-

272

mediately that she should be dismissed. I am amazed that you should be standing up for her.'

'I'm standing up for her because I believe she did not make a mistake.'

'This conversation is at an end, Miss Lang. If this is an ego thing and you want to be the one to fire your secretary then go ahead and do it. But you will do it today.' He rose. 'I cannot spend any more time on this. I have an important meeting tonight in Rome. I am already late for my flight.' He wagged a finger at Julia. 'We have given your secretary a month's notice. I consider that more than generous.'

Without another word Julia turned and marched from the room. She knew she had reached another crisis. If she let Moscato fire Emma because Chantal Ricci had slipped up she would forfeit the respect of everyone in the hotel. It would be a shameful act of betrayal to a decent, hard-working woman.

Seething with anger she returned to her office. When Emma came in she looked so crushed and defeated that Julia put her arms around her. 'Cheer up,' she said. 'I'm not letting you go without a fight.'

'She called me incompetent,' Emma said. It was almost a wail.

'Didn't you tell me that Pam Helmore's sister, Sarah, works at that hotel in Upper Slaughter? The Old Red House?'

'She's the cashier,' Emma said.

'Let me talk to her.'

There was a message on Julia's answering machine when she got home that night. Ravenel.

He was at Heathrow en route to Washington. He would be back in a couple of days. She was not to worry. She would get her money. He was convinced of that.

Ravenel put in a call to Cristiani the moment he arrived in Washington.

273

'You handed Eberhardt that letter?'

'He didn't open it immediately. Just nodded. He seemed highly nervous to see me. I told him I'd left the Commission and was now on my own. He relaxed a little then.'

'Anything else new?'

'A lot,' Cristiani said. 'I went to Zurich yesterday to see di Marco's sister. She'd called me. She's still very bitter about that suicide verdict on her brother. It seems he had a safe deposit box the police didn't know about. In it she found an old diary he'd kept during the war. She thought it might interest me.'

'Did it?'

'It explains why he was murdered. I'm sure he was going to blow the whistle on Eberhardt.'

'Can I get a look at this diary?'

'I'm having it translated for you now,' Cristiani said. 'I'll express it to you tonight.'

Chapter 44

The day Moscato returned from Rome, Julia went in to see him. In her hand she held an envelope.

'What is it?' He looked coldly at her.

Julia opened it and produced the copy of his overnight bill at the Old Red House together with three bills from previous stays. 'These came addressed to my office while you were away.' She put the bills, all made out to Mr and Mrs Moscato, in front of him. He looked down at them. When he saw the hotel heading he flushed. 'I was going to call Mrs Moscato to ask what she wanted done with them. My secretary suggested I wait until you returned.'

Moscato did not look at her. 'Why were these sent to you?'

'I've no idea. Obviously if you asked for copies of the bills they should have been sent directly to you. I am on the Old Red House's mailing list so I suppose there was a slip-up somewhere. Slip-ups do occur, as we both know.' Julia did not take her eyes from his face. 'I hope my secretary did the right thing in holding these for your return? She was most adamant they should not be sent on to your wife.'

Moscato seemed totally deflated. He nodded. 'She did exactly the right thing. I don't like to bother my wife with bills. They just confuse her.'

Julia turned to go. 'I'm sure these would have,' she said.

Later that afternoon Emma burst in to see her. 'You'll never guess,' she said. 'Mr Moscato has rescinded my notice. He says on reflection he acted too hastily. He even suggested there might be a salary increase for me.'

She clapped her hands together. 'Isn't that wonderful?'

Julia smiled. 'No more than you deserve, Emma dear. Now let's get on with some letters . . .'

Just as Julia was about to leave that evening the phone rang. It was Michael Chadwick.

'I've been meaning to call for weeks,' he said. 'I was so sorry to hear about your friend.'

'Thank you, Michael.'

'It must have been awful for you.'

'It was a terrible shock.'

'Do you need anything? If there is something I can do for you before I leave?'

The sympathy in his voice touched her.

'When are you off?'

'Monday.'

'Will I see you before you go?'

'How about dinner tonight? Are you free? We'll drink heavily. Tell each other how special we are.'

'I'm free,' she said, laughing. 'I'd like that.'

'I'll pick you up at eight.'

Michael had booked a table at Fabio's, the little Italian restaurant in Soho where they had gone on their first date. It was one of those old-fashioned restaurants with straw Chianti bottles hanging from whitewashed walls and framed posters of Capri and Venice. But the food was good and Fabio, whom they had not seen for some time, gave them a big welcome. He had the knack of remembering the names of almost everyone who had ever been to his restaurant.

'Mr Chadwick, Miss Lang. What a pleasure. How well you both look.' Beaming with pleasure he led the way to a corner table covered with a check tablecloth and lit by a sputtering candle. He handed them menus and bowed elaborately before disappearing to welcome other customers.

'I really love this place,' Michael said.

'Me too,' Julia said. 'It's like coming home.'

After much debate they ordered prosciutto and melon followed by lemon-marinated chicken. Fabio sent over a bottle of Orvieto, compliments of the house.

Julia had changed clothes three times on returning home, finally settling on a Chanel-style suit. She knew it was now too tight for her and hoped Michael would not notice. She had no intention of telling him she was pregnant.

He leaned forward. 'I behaved really badly last time we saw each other. I'm truly sorry.'

'All forgotten.'

'I was jealous, you know. I couldn't bear to think of you with someone else. But I want you to know I felt terrible afterwards.'

'So did I.'

'You've no idea how often I've walked past your flat and looked up at your windows.'

'You should have buzzed.'

'I wasn't sure . . . well, you know.' He reached across to pour her some wine.

'Just a drop for me,' Julia said.

'You love this stuff.'

'I know. It's just . . . I'm not feeling great.'

'You should have told me.'

She reached out a hand. 'I wanted to see you, Michael. It's been such a long time.'

He poured her half a glass and filled his own. Julia took a sip of the wine and immediately felt queasy. She picked up a slice of bread and chewed it. 'Maybe some water?' she said.

Michael waved his hand for the waiter. 'How are things at the hotel?'

'Not good.'

'Why's that?'

'Moscato's ruining the place. Everyone hates him. And we're not doing that well any more. The Sultan says he may sell.'

Michael looked surprised. 'That'll be a blow. He was so proud of the Burlington.'

'So were we all,' Julia said. 'Once.'

The food arrived and for several minutes they ate in silence, content with each other's company. When Julia looked up she saw a familiar figure approaching. It was Jeremy Orde, the columnist.

'Well, well,' he said. 'Look who's here.'

'Hello,' she said, without enthusiasm.

Orde nodded curtly to Michael before turning to Julia. 'What's going on at that hotel of yours?' he demanded. 'There are all sorts of rumours.'

'Oh really?'

'Yes, really,' he mimicked. 'I heard the other day the place may be sold. What's the matter? Is that randy little Sultan running out of money?'

'I've no idea,' Julia said tersely.

'Frankly I'm not surprised it got dropped from the Top Ten list. Last time I was there all I saw were glum faces. It's not doing well, they tell me.'

'You have better information than I do.'

'I hope so,' Orde said. 'I also have a pair of eyes.' He smirked. 'It's surprising, really. After Brand keeled over on top of that bimbo I felt sure the place would be packed. All that publicity we gave you.'

Julia said nothing.

'Who's running it, anyway?' Orde went on. 'Moscato or that Italian tart Ricci?'

'Why don't you ask them?' Julia said.

'I'm asking you.'

Michael put down his knife and fork and looked up. 'Get lost, chum,' he said.

Orde turned to look at him. 'What did you say?'

'I said take off. We're having dinner.'

'That had not escaped me,' Orde said.

'Here's something else that will not escape you,' Michael said, getting to his feet. At six feet two he towered above Orde. Taking hold of the journalist's tie,

Michael pulled him forward until their faces were almost touching across the table. Diners on either side watched in astonishment. 'When I'm having a quiet dinner I don't choose to have turds like you interrupting it. Is that clear?'

He released Orde, who pulled himself back sharply. Glaring at both of them he moved away to join some people at a table at the far end of the room. Fabio rushed over to Michael and Julia.

'I'm sorry, Fabio,' Michael said. 'A little misunderstanding. It's over now.'

He sat down again and turned to Julia who was pale-faced. 'Now,' he said briskly. 'What about some dessert?'

She shook her head.

'You're upset with me?' Michael asked.

'Upset?' she echoed. 'I've been longing for someone to put that little rat in his place.' She squeezed his hand. 'I loved what you did.'

Later, Michael dropped Julia off at her flat. 'I suppose this is it,' he said.

Julia kissed him on both cheeks. 'We'll see each other again, Michael. Somewhere.'

He smiled ruefully. 'I like your hellos better than your goodbyes.'

'There'll be other hellos for you,' Julia said, a little tearful.

'I suppose so.' He kissed her on the forehead, looked at her for a long moment, then turned and got back in the car.

'It's getting nasty around here,' Emma said the following afternoon.

'What's happened now?'

'Moscato's fired Pam Helmore. And Bryan Penrose resigned in protest.'

'But why?'

'Moscato says she's inefficient. Sound familiar? I think

that Ricci woman did some snooping and found out Pam's sister works at the Old Red House and that's how you got hold of those bills. Anyway, Pam's been sacked.'

Julia felt a wave of anger sweep over her. Her first instinct was to go straight to Moscato's office and confront him. But she knew she must calm down before doing that. She knew, too, in that moment, that she was through at the Burlington. The situation had become impossible. But first she had some things to do.

She sat down at her keyboard.

'What are you doing?' Emma asked.

'I have to send off a couple of news stories,' Julia said.

'I'll do them for you.'

'No, Emma. You're not to know anything about these.'

It took her thirty minutes to finish. She read the stories over carefully and slid them into envelopes addressed to Tony Vickers of the *Daily Express* and Arthur Brandon of the *Daily Mail*. She then wrote a long letter to the Sultan of Malacca, resigning and giving him the reasons.

At four o'clock, a time she knew Moscato was always alone and most people in the executive corridor were in their offices, Julia walked in ignoring the protest of Moscato's new young secretary.

She left the door wide open. 'So you've fired Pam Helmore, have you?' she demanded.

Moscato, who had been bent over his desk reading some papers, looked up angrily.

'Before you start protesting, the only way you'll get me out of here before I've said my piece is to throw me out physically. And I can tell you right now you won't find one person in this hotel who'll help you. You'll have to do it yourself. And if you lay one finger on me by God you'll regret it.'

Moscato looked wildly at her. 'You're fired. Leave this office at once.'

'You can't fire me. I have a contract. So just sit there and shut up.' Caught up in a wave of anger and overcome with revulsion for the man sitting in front of her, Julia stormed on. Her voice rose. 'You're a despicable little shit, Moscato. How I ever allowed myself to work for you I'll never understand. I should have spat in your face and walked out of here the day you walked in. But I'm going now and before I do you're going to listen to me.

'I've sent a story about what you've done to both the *Mail* and the *Express*. And when they print it, and print it they will, I'll make sure cuttings go off to the Sultan. I want him to know just what kind of a man he hired to ruin this wonderful hotel.'

The executive corridor, which usually hummed with activity at this hour, had now gone eerily quiet.

'You're scum, Moscato. You're not even, as I once thought, a decent hotel manager. A real hotelier does not tyrannize his employees as you do, or dismiss people for other people's mistakes. The way you were ready to fire my secretary to please your bedtime pal Ricci proved what a contemptible swine you really are.'

Moscato, his face pale, glanced towards the open door. He half rose from his chair, then sat down again.

'You've ruined this hotel, Moscato. You've betrayed everything that was fine and decent about it. When the Burlington was dropped from the list of top hotels there wasn't one person among the staff – not one – who wasn't glad because it was a slap in the face for you.' She paused, breathing hard.

'You're trash, Moscato. You raped me in Italy – ' she pitched her voice high – 'You *raped* me, a kid who trusted you and enjoyed working for you. What a gentleman. I nearly lost the sight of one eye – did you know that? – in my fight to keep your dirty hands off me. It took months for me to recover, months, and even now I can't look at you without wanting to vomit. I hope, I sincerely hope, that the Sultan kicks you out not only for what you did to me – I've written him the details – but for what you've done to this hotel. You're garbage, Moscato.'

She stood there, her heart thumping wildly, her face

flushed. There was a long silence. No sound came from any of the other offices in the executive corridor. With a last look of contempt at the man sitting slumped before her she turned and strode from the room.

Chapter 45

Paul Eberhardt had hoped to enjoy his stay in Paris. The conference was an important one. He knew the speech he was to give would be well received.

But he was on edge. Grace Brand was still in the hotel – he had caught sight of her for the first time the day before, getting into the elevator. How much longer was it going to take? It was already a week since he had made the final arrangement. What had happened to the man? He had a local number to make contact in an emergency. If nothing happened in the next twenty-four hours he would have to use it.

On the third day, as he emerged from the elevator, he came face to face with her. She was standing in the richly carpeted *salon de thé*, wearing a black suit with a deep V neck. He had forgotten how tall she was.

'So there you are,' she said. 'I wondered how much longer you'd keep avoiding me.'

'Good morning, Madame Brand. I'm afraid I am rather pressed for time . . .'

'I think you can spare a few minutes,' she said. 'I have something important I wish to discuss.'

'It will have to be quick, madame. I am attending an important conference.'

'Don't try my patience, Monsieur Eberhardt. Sit down and listen to what I have to say.'

Reluctantly Eberhardt went over to one of the ornate chairs. He sat down carefully.

She took a seat opposite him.

'First of all,' she said, 'I have decided to remove my accounts from your bank.'

'That is your privilege.'

'You don't have to tell me that,' she said sharply. 'I know very well what I can and cannot do. You will shortly be receiving instructions regarding the accounts.'

Eberhardt frowned. 'There are many investments.'

'You will be told what to do about those.'

Eberhardt took out a handkerchief and dabbed his lips. He felt exposed and vulnerable in front of this formidable woman. Two of his colleagues were standing talking not fifteen feet away. One of them glanced in his direction and nodded.

'I have looked after the Brand accounts for many years, Madame Brand. They have prospered under my steward-ship. I really feel – '

Her look was steely. 'You don't seem to understand. It no longer serves a useful purpose to bank with you. For reasons we both know, it suited Robert Brand to keep his private money with you. It does not suit me.'

Eberhardt, obliged to sit and listen, nodded stonily. 'Is there anything else?'

'You hinted on the telephone that, because of a letter you received, you were considering transferring money to an account my late husband ill-advisedly attempted to set up.'

'The account was set up before his death, Madame Brand. Under Swiss law – '

'I am not interested in your fucking Swiss law,' she said quietly. Eberhardt's face flushed. He looked around to see if they had been overheard. 'That account does not exist. Is that understood?' Even more quietly she said: 'It is within my power to ruin you. While my husband was alive I could not do that. Now I can. You would do well to remember it.'

Distressed, Eberhardt looked at his watch. 'I'm sorry. I have to leave. I will await your instructions regarding the accounts – '

'Stay where you are,' she said. 'I have not finished.'

Eberhardt tried one last time. 'I told you, Madame Brand, that a man named Ravenel had sent me a hand-delivered letter advising that he has obtained a copy of Robert Brand's instructions regarding the new account. He warned that unless the account is set up he will contact the *New York Times*.'

'And I told you the man is bluffing.'

'I don't think he is. He mentions a name in the letter which proves it.'

'What name? What are you talking about?'

'He mentions someone who was present when the Brand accounts were first set up. He clearly knows a great deal.'

'That is ancient history. It does not bother me.'

'Then it should, Madame Brand. It is the source of your present wealth.'

'You impertinent fool . . .'

Suddenly Eberhardt's desire to strike back at Grace Brand overcame his fear of her. He got to his feet. 'Since I am no longer your banker I do not have to tolerate your abuse and insults, madame. And, for your information, two days ago I signed the authority to pay $20 million from the Brand account to Julia Lang in accordance with the late Robert Brand's instructions.'

Grace Brand's face seemed to change. Her cheeks sagged, her eyes bulged, her lips turned down at the edges. She rose slowly to her feet.

'You treacherous bastard,' she shouted. She struck him viciously across the face. Caught off guard, he staggered and fell, clutching the side of one of the chairs, which toppled over. 'You dare go against my orders. You dare!' She made a wild lunge at him again as he clambered to his feet. 'You've thrown that money away, you stupid fool. You've given it to a dead woman . . .'

Suddenly everyone in the long salon was silent. There was the sound of running footsteps and two of the concierges rushed in from the front desk, eyes wide. No one spoke. Everyone stared aghast at the extraordinary tableau; the elderly Swiss banker clutching a chair for support; the elegantly dressed woman, a blue vein pulsating in her forehead, standing before him, eyes blazing.

Eberhardt straightened up. Turning, he walked unsteadily towards the elevators. When he reached his room he sat down on the bed for a few moments, trying to calm himself. Then he picked up the telephone.

Ravenel studied his face in the mirror of his hotel room in Washington, discouraged to see how pale he looked. There were dark circles under his eyes; a slight stubble on his chin. It was not surprising. He had spent two eight-hour days in the warehouse of the Central Office of the Immigration and Naturalization Service in suburban Maryland searching through files. He was exhausted. But he had found what he had come for, what he had suspected since talking with Heinz Linge. And with the arrival of the di Marco diary the pieces of the puzzle were now in place; there were no more questions.

He realized how hungry he was. He had sustained himself for the past twenty-four hours on cup after cup of black coffee. But it was finished now. He would catch the shuttle and take his daughter to an early dinner in New York. Then he would fly to London to give Julia the news.

Chapter 46

The day after her confrontation with Moscato, Julia walked out of her office for the last time. She had spent the afternoon clearing her desk and saying goodbye to friends at the hotel. Everyone seemed to have heard what had happened. People she barely knew came up to congratulate her. The story of the rape had circulated quickly. Moscato, she was told, had not put his face outside his office all day.

At 6 p.m. she took Emma out for a farewell drink. 'Your job is safe,' she assured her. 'Moscato won't dare touch you.'

'I don't care about that,' Emma said. 'It's you I'm worried about. What will you do?'

'It'll be fine,' Julia said with more confidence than she felt.

By the time she got home she was exhausted. Half of her could not believe what she had done. But she felt cleansed, relieved. Each day she had spent near Moscato had made her feel in some way contaminated. Now it was over.

Just as she was about to get in the shower the phone rang.

It was Lisa. 'I'm alone,' she said. 'The Prince is in town for a couple of days and has Deena. Want to share a pork chop?'

'I'll be there in half an hour. I've got something to tell you.'

'Incidentally,' Lisa said, 'your answering machine isn't picking up. I called you a couple of times already.'

'I'll have a look at it,' Julia said.

*   *   *

'You really said that?' Lisa clapped her hands together. 'And you wrote to George?'

Julia smiled at the 'George'. 'I even told him about the rape.'

Lisa nodded approval. 'I'd have given a lot to have seen Moscato's face when you marched in.'

'He just sat there. Hardly said a word.'

Lisa poured herself another glass of wine. 'Truthfully I'm surprised you lasted as long as you did with that slug.'

'It was at the cost of my pride. But I loved the hotel. Moscato turned it into a gulag.'

'Think, though, if you'd walked out when Moscato first got there you'd never have met Robert.'

'Maybe that would have been a good thing . . .'

'You must think positively,' Lisa said cheerfully. 'At least you'll have someone to bring in the firewood when you're an old hag. Any more news of Guy?'

Julia shook her head. 'No. I don't get it. He found the evidence that the bank lied. I thought that was it. Then he called to say he was going to Paris. Next there was a message saying he was off to Washington.'

'I can tell you one thing,' Lisa said, 'he won't be wasting time. That's something you can rely on.'

'He said I was sure to get the money. I won't believe it till the cheque's in my hand and I've paid him his share.'

'How much are you giving him?'

'Two million.'

'*What?* The Prince paid him only $100,000.'

'He asked for $2 million and I said yes. Look what he did for me. Without him I'd be nowhere.'

'I suppose you're right.'

'What did he do for the Prince? You never told me.'

Lisa chuckled. 'The Prince is sometimes a little indiscreet. Once in New York he was indiscreet with some diplomat's wife. The man found out and tried to blackmail him. He thought he had a chance to dip his fingers in the royal treasury. Then one night Guy called on him and explained how unwise he was being. That was the end of it.'

Julia smiled. She could just imagine it. Guy Ravenel could be a scary figure. But what exactly was he up to now?

Chapter 47

Friday afternoon is not the best time to arrive in London. Traffic was heavy and it was an hour and a quarter before Ravenel checked into the Berkeley. A light rain was falling; the hotel was sheathed in a fine mist.

There was a message at the desk: 'Call me urgently – Cristiani.' It had come in just after lunch.

Ravenel, gritty-eyed and tired, went straight to his room and put in the call.

'What's up, pal?'

'Jesus, Guy. Thank God you called.' There was an undercurrent of alarm in Cristiani's voice. 'I had the most extraordinary call this morning from Paul Eberhardt. He's in Paris. So is Grace Brand. They've had the most terrible confrontation in the Plaza-Athénée. She slapped his face in front of some of his colleagues. Screamed abuse at him. He went straight to his room and called me. Told me everything; how she tried to stop him opening the account for Julia; threatened him if he did . . .'

Ravenel sat down on the bed. 'Why call you?'

'He's scared,' Cristiani said. 'I could tell by his voice. He told me that when he got your letter he transferred the money to Julia immediately. A bank in the Channel Islands. He knows that if anything happens to her now there'll be hell to pay. The whole story will come out.'

Ravenel's voice rose. 'What do you mean – if anything happens to her?'

'When Eberhardt told Grace Brand he'd transferred the money, that's when she hit him. She screamed something like: "You've thrown that money away. You've given it to a dead woman." '

Ravenel was shaken. 'She said that?'

'She was deranged, Eberhardt says. He thinks she's crazy enough to do something terrible. He wants us to warn Julia. He likes her, he says – '

'Likes her?' Ravenel shot back. 'What's he talking about? He doesn't know her.'

'He knows it was her he had dinner with in Geneva. He found out somehow. He thinks she was just playing an innocent trick on him. He didn't seem resentful; just concerned about her. I've been calling her home number to warn her. There's no reply.'

Ravenel felt suddenly shaky. Fatigue mixed with fear. 'I'll call you later.'

He hung up and dialled Julia's number. There was no reply. He tried Lisa's number. There was no answer there either. He left a message on her machine to call him urgently and tried Julia's number again. Filled with dread he sat slumped on the edge of the bed, holding the receiver tightly while the phone rang and rang . . .

Julia had spent the day with Lisa, shopping at Harrods and lunching at a Knightsbridge restaurant renowned for its health food. When it began to drizzle Lisa suggested a French film that had been highly praised.

'We've got to do this often now you're free,' Lisa said.

Julia agreed. It had been so long since she'd taken a weekday off she was truly enjoying herself.

She was back in her flat by 6.30 p.m. There were some letters on the hall table, arranged in a neat pile by Rosie. She debated whether to go through them immediately or change into her tracksuit for a quick walk. The walk won. She had missed her regular exercise for several days. She knew how important it was not to become lazy. Picking up a torch she set off.

The park itself had closed at dusk so she was forced to circle it, striding along Cambridge Terrace and cutting down Chester Road. Because of the earlier rain the trees and bushes were dripping steadily. There was no sound anywhere, not even the barking of dogs. All she could hear was her own breathing as she walked along.

Suddenly she slowed, aware of a sound. She stopped and listened. Others used this route at night, joggers and walkers like herself. But no one else was about and she felt apprehensive.

'Hello,' she called.

Silence.

Looking back all she could see was an empty road, bordered on both sides by hedges. The sound, she felt sure, had come from inside the park itself. At that moment the weak moon was obscured by drifting cloud and the darkness intensified; the road now seemed like a black tunnel. She switched on her torch.

'Is anyone there?'

There was no reply.

By the time dusk settled over London, Ravenel was racked with worry. Where in God's name was she? Perhaps someone in her building would know? It was a long shot but anything was better than sitting cooped up in his hotel room. He left a message with the hotel switchboard operator in case Lisa called, and went down to find a taxi. By the time he reached Great Portland Street it was quite dark. He looked up at Julia's windows on the third floor. No lights. Still hopeful, he pressed her buzzer. There was no response. One by one he pressed the other buttons on the panel. Finally one of them answered: 'Hello.' A woman.

'I'm sorry to disturb you,' Ravenel had to yell to be heard above the noise of the traffic. 'I need your help. I'm trying to find Julia Lang.'

'She just went out,' the woman said. 'Ten minutes ago. I saw her at the door.'

'Do you know where she went?'

'She had on a tracksuit. My guess would be Regent's Park. She usually – '

Ravenel started running.

The streets around the park were dark and smelled of winter; rotting leaves, wet grass and weeping trees. It was cold. Ravenel shivered as he walked along, looking from left to right, feeling exposed and vulnerable. He did not know this area, where the streets led. All he knew was that down one of them Julia Lang was walking, unaware that in the darkness someone could be waiting for her.

To the right were the Georgian terraces, illuminated by hazy streetlights. He walked quickly, his heart thudding, his shoes echoing on the wet pavement. To the left was a smaller road, bisecting the park. Leafless trees lined either side. He turned down it, then stood still, listening, sure he had heard something, a rustling in the bushes. A squirrel ran across the road in front of him and vanished behind the hedge to the right. He shivered again.

At the end of the road were ornate iron gates, the entrance to the park proper. Closed, they looked dark and forbidding. Somewhere ahead of him he heard a twig snap. He froze. He sensed rather than saw a slight movement in the bushes. There was someone there. He was convinced of it. He moved between two of the trees trying to slow his rapid breathing.

Then he saw her, walking fast towards him, waving the beam of her torch from side to side.

He put his hand in the pocket of his raincoat and took out his black Swiss army knife. It was the largest one made, with all the right tools and a three-inch blade, honed razor sharp. He opened the blade carefully.

He heard the sound before he saw the movement. A figure leaped from the bushes. He heard Julia's cry as the man swung her round, raising something high in the air, bringing it hard down on her back. She groaned as she sank to her knees. Ravenel hurled himself forward, propelled by a burst of adrenalin. Then he was on the man, clawing at him, reaching for his neck. The assailant wheeled, cursing, raising some sort of bar in the air, thrusting at him. Ravenel held on desperately, caught up in a wave of fury, his left arm around the man's neck, pulling it back, the knife slicing deep through the jugular, the man's legs twitching, his arms flailing as the frothing blood gushed out and he slid slowly to the ground.

Gasping for breath, his heart beating wildly, his knees shaking, Ravenel lost his footing on the blood-soaked asphalt and fell, landing heavily on his shoulder. He turned painfully, looking at Julia who lay crumpled on the wet path, drenched in her attacker's still spurting blood.

It began to rain again.

Chapter 48

It was cold on top of the building. He was wearing a heavy overcoat and gloves but the freezing wind still cut right through him. He shivered, cursing the weather.

He did not usually operate this way. But the original plan to use a car would not work. As with many of the avenues in Paris, there was a secondary lane, a *contre-allée*, running parallel with the wide street allowing cars and taxis to turn in to pick up and discharge people using the hotels, stores and restaurants.

He had watched the woman for several days now. She always waited until her limousine had pulled up in front of the hotel before venturing out.

It had to be a rifle.

He had found what he wanted in Montmartre five days before; a Weatherby Mark V with a Pentax scope and a specially designed silencer which, he was assured, in no way detracted from its accuracy. He hoped this was true. He had had no chance to try it out.

Lying flat on the roof he scanned the avenue below. Posing as the dispatcher for the limousine company he had called the hotel to determine what time the driver was supposed to pick her up.

He had not long to wait.

On the roof two pigeons waddled past looking for scraps. The only sound was the hum of the generator on the far side of the stairwell housing. On the floors below residents of the expensive block were sitting down to breakfast, reading the paper, planning the day. It was Friday and people were starting to unwind in preparation for the weekend. From the open window of one of the apartments he could smell fresh coffee brewing. He tried to ignore it. He had eaten no breakfast that morning, preferring to come to an assignment hungry and alert. Afterwards, he would treat himself to a large *café au lait* at a nearby café. And some croissants with butter and jam.

From where he lay he commanded a perfect, uninterrupted view of the entrance to the Plaza-Athénée Hotel.

While he lay there an attractive young woman emerged from the hotel and stood for a moment looking around. She glanced upwards and for a moment he thought she had seen him or caught the glint from the rifle barrel. Then she was joined by a dark-haired man and together they set off up the avenue towards the Champs-Elysées.

Suddenly he froze. A black cat appeared on the roof and strolled towards him, miaowing. He shooed it away. The cat, without resentment, slunk over to a corner where an empty cola can was lying. With its right paw it dislodged the can, which rolled across the roof. Even above the hum of the generator the noise of the rolling can could clearly be heard. Putting down his rifle the sniper reached for the can and propped it upright.

At 9.30 a.m. precisely a black limousine pulled up in front of the hotel. The sniper snuggled the butt into his shoulder, wincing slightly as the concrete dug into his right elbow. He saw the woman emerge, nod to the doorman and approach the limo. He edged the rifle barrel slightly to the left so that the crosshairs of the scope were centred on her head. At this distance the power of the scope was so fine he could see the design on her silk scarf.

It happened in an instant!

As he squeezed the trigger the black cat suddenly shot in front of him. At that precise moment a tall man came rushing from the hotel, bumping into the woman. The bullet from the Weatherby smashed into the woman's head and continued on, less accurate now, ripping into the man's forehead. Both of them fell backwards, legs twitching, hands clawing the air, before slumping to the pavement.

He swore. Dammit. That fucking cat! He had nearly missed her. And he'd killed some other poor bastard. The man who had commissioned the hit had been quite specific; no one else was to get hurt. He hoped there would not be repercussions. He peered cautiously over the parapet. People were standing around in shock, staring at the inert bodies on the ground. Then the hotel doorman rushed back into the hotel. To call the police, he supposed.

Carefully he slotted the Weatherby into the contoured base of the carrying case. Spinning the coded lock he got up, brushed some cement dust from his overcoat and left the roof.

There was nobody on duty in the small office to the left of the entrance hall. The concierge, he had already established, went next door to the café for breakfast at this hour. Without a glance towards the hotel, he set off briskly for the Place de l'Alma, the gun case concealed beneath his copious overcoat. It would be at least twenty minutes before a police van came wailing up, he guessed. He was wrong. Police from the Eighth Arrondissement station, proud of their reputation for speed and efficiency, were there in half that time. But by then the rifle was embedded in the mud of the Seine beneath the Pont de l'Alma and the marksman was buttering the first of two croissants at Le Grand Corona, sitting in one of the window seats.

Next day the shooting made headlines in both *Le Monde* and *Le Figaro*. The stories described Grace Brand as the widow of the late billionaire Robert Brand, and Paul Eberhardt as one of Geneva's top bankers.

Police inquiries were continuing, they reported.

Chapter 49

Julia came to with a moan, her mouth dry, a dull, throbbing pain down her back. Blinking her eyes open, she breathed in slowly. The ceiling of the room seemed to be floating above her, moving in and out of focus. She sat up slowly, wincing at a sudden spasm of pain.

She looked around. She was lying on her own bed in her white bathrobe. She had on only her underwear underneath.

Bewildered, she let her head fall back on the pillow. What was she doing there? She had been walking. And then . . .

Instinctively her hand moved down to the swell of her stomach.

'Welcome back.'

Ravenel stood in the doorway of her bedroom. He was wearing nothing but a bath towel around his waist. She sat up, astonished.

'You?'

Ravenel nodded, smiling.

'How did you get here?'

'Rest now,' he said. His voice was gentle. 'I'll explain later.'

She sank back against the pillows, then looked towards the door again. He was still standing there, watching her.

Ravenel was back. She was in her own flat. She was safe.

She closed her eyes and slept.

'I carried you,' Ravenel said. 'Over my shoulder, firemen style. Luckily it was pouring with rain. The streets were deserted.'

'All that way?'

'I couldn't risk a taxi,' he said. 'I had blood on my clothes.'

They were sitting in the lounge of Julia's flat. Julia was still in her bathrobe and underclothes. Ravenel was wearing his shirt and trousers, washed and dried.

'Then you . . . you undressed me?' She was surprised at her own embarrassment.

'You were a bit of a mess,' Ravenel said. He glanced at her over the rim of his cup. 'I didn't want to ruin your bed so I stripped you in the bathroom and put you in your robe.' He chuckled. 'Then I took a shower with my clothes on. A first for me.'

'I don't remember a thing,' she said.

'You were out like a light,' Ravenel said. 'I had a hell of a job getting the flat key out of your pocket.'

Trying to adjust her position on the sofa, she winced.

'Still hurting?'

She nodded.

'Tomorrow you must see your doctor. Make sure you're all right. Check on the baby.'

'Who was it . . . who attacked me?'

'Someone sent by Grace Brand. Probably the same man who murdered Jane Summerwood.'

'Dear God.' Julia stared at him, horrified. 'He was sent to kill me?'

'Yes.'

'Then he'll try again.'

'No,' Ravenel said, 'he won't. He's dead.'

'You killed him?'

Ravenel nodded.

'What will we tell the police?'

'We don't involve the police. The man was a thug. They'll think he was killed by his own sort. That's the end of it.' He sneezed suddenly.

Hunched in one corner of the sofa Julia realized the front of her robe had opened slightly, revealing the tops of her breasts. She wrapped the robe more tightly around herself. Ravenel appeared not to have noticed. 'I'd better go and change,' she said.

'Relax,' he said. 'This is your home.'

'I don't understand.' She shook her head. 'How do you *know* it was her who sent him?'

Briefly Ravenel related the events that had led him to the park. Julia sat back, her legs tucked beneath her, shocked at what she was hearing.

'Why was Grace Brand even in Paris?'

'That I don't know,' Ravenel said. 'Maybe to see Eberhardt – she knew he was attending a conference there. Maybe for some other reason. In any event they had this confrontation at the hotel. When he told her he'd transferred the money to you she actually hit him. She said he'd thrown the money away. You were a dead duck. That's when Eberhardt called Cristiani. By that time he'd had enough of Grace Brand.'

She looked at him soberly. 'I could be dead by now,' she said. 'So could you.'

'I had one advantage,' Ravenel said. 'He didn't know I was there.'

'Even so . . .'

'Are you ready for the rest of the story?'

She nodded.

He sneezed again. 'Damn. I think I'm getting a cold.' He glanced around. 'Any chance of a brandy? Kill it at birth.'

She went over to the side-table and poured a cognac. Ravenel lit a cigarette – his first since they had begun talking.

Julia sat down again, watching him as he sipped the brandy.

'The story starts with Hermann Goering.'

'The fat Nazi? What's he got to do with all this?'

'Be patient. You'll find out. Although he seemed to be a jovial man he was a very sinister fellow. At the height of the war he lived like a rajah at his country estate outside Berlin. He was unscrupulous, immoral and very, very dangerous.

'All that is well documented. What is not documented is that from the late thirties until the early forties Goering secretly sent large amounts of money out of Germany into Switzerland. Most of it was money from the sale of properties belonging to Jews who'd been sent to concentration camps or forced to flee the country.

'This money was deposited in a bank in Geneva belonging to a friend of his.' Observing Julia's reaction, he nodded. 'The Banque Eberhardt. Eberhardt, you see, was the friend. To get the money *out* of Germany he recruited two young officers, who took it out in suitcases.

'By the early forties Goering had deposited $200 million in the bank. He had the two young men transferred to the Russian front. They were captured at Stalingrad and sent to prison camps in Siberia. Goering confidently expected them to perish there, and with them all traces of what he had done. That's how the money got to the Banque Eberhardt.'

'Incredible,' Julia said, still not sure where it was all leading.

Ravenel brushed back a lock of hair that had fallen over his forehead. 'When Paul Eberhardt received the news of Goering's suicide he waited a few years to see if Goering's family came forward or if the Allies stumbled across some reference to the money in captured papers. When they did not he relaxed. The money stayed in the vaults and over the years the Banque Eberhardt became one of the most successful private banks in Switzerland.

'Then one day in 1951 Eberhardt was told that a man was downstairs asking to see him. His name was Heinz Linge. He was one of the two officers who had brought out Goering's money. Linge had just been released by the Russians and had decided to put the squeeze on Eberhardt. But Linge was now a broken, pathetic figure and Eberhardt decided to bluff it out. He summoned the police and had Linge deported. And although his sudden appearance had momentarily unnerved Eberhardt, the banker's prestige and reputation were now so high he did not worry.

'But six months later the second officer involved in bringing out Goering's money showed up at the bank. He, too, had miraculously survived and just been released by the Russians. This man was not at all like Linge. Told that Eberhardt would not see him he sent up a note giving the number of Goering's secret account, a list of every trip he had made to the bank, details of where he had stayed and copies of two photographs showing Eberhardt and Goering together at the Field Marshal's estate outside Berlin. He warned that if Eberhardt still refused to see him he would go straight to the Justice Ministry in Bern.'

Ravenel leaned forward and stubbed out his cigarette. He lit another one. The smoke drifted towards Julia. She did not even notice. She realized she had edged forward and was sitting right at the edge of the sofa. She tried to relax.

'Eberhardt realized he could not send this man packing as he had Heinz Linge. So he saw him. The man told him his terms: $50 million to keep silent. Eberhardt knew he had no option. Washington was pressing the Swiss Government to reveal just how much Nazi money was being held in Swiss banks. He could not risk this man talking. He agreed to give the man the money on the understanding that it remained in an account with his bank. The man accepted the terms. After all, he could hardly lug $50 million in cash back to the ruins of Berlin.'

'How do you *know* all that?'

'Eberhardt's partner kept a diary. We got hold of it.'

'He *gave* it to you?'

'A gift from the grave,' Ravenel said. He put down his brandy glass. 'To continue – the former officer returned to Berlin. But it was too late for his new fortune to help him. His health had been ruined in captivity. His wife was already dead, killed in the bombing of Berlin. All he had was his son, now twenty-two. When the man died, the son inherited the millions. Two years later he emigrated to the United States for good.

'Once in America the young man determined to re-invent himself. He went to college. He worked as a trainee at Bankers' Trust, then joined Lehman Brothers for a shot at investment banking. He found he had the knack of making money. Soon he doubled, tripled, and quadrupled his original fortune. He became an American citizen. He dropped the last letter from his surname. He married an American woman . . .'

Ravenel looked at Julia. Her fingers, interlaced, were straining against each other. 'You know his name, of course.'

'Robert Brand.' It was almost a whisper.

'Robert Brand. His father's name was Walter Brandt. Once in America young Robert discovered there was a man named Roland "Fire" Brand who'd built his fortune on Texas oil. He let it be rumoured they were related. People accepted that. They were already intrigued by this young man who seemed to be building one of America's great fortunes.'

Julia sat motionless. Now nothing seemed too far-fetched or incredible. So many things that had perplexed her about Robert Brand suddenly made sense: his phobia about being photographed; his refusal to be interviewed. His whole success, she realized, had been based on a lie. The fortune he had inherited from his father had been stolen. He had been brought up by Nazis.

'*I didn't know you spoke German.*'

'*A smattering. It helps in business . . .*'

A life of lies.

She shivered.

'Are you all right?' Ravenel put a hand on her arm.

She nodded. 'All this was in that diary?'

'Not all. Some of it I found in files when we got into the bank. One of them had the name of Heinz Linge. I went to Germany to see him. He told me about Walter

Brandt and his son. It was too much of a coincidence. I went to Washington to check the names of German immigrants in the fifties. There it was: Robert Brandt.'

'Why didn't anybody find out about him? He was so well known . . .'

'In my country nobody probes a person's past unless there's a reason – they're running for office or something. It's un-American. And Brand was extremely careful. He was hardly ever photographed. He never gave interviews. He never talked about the past. He kept a very low profile. It's easier than you think to stay out of the spotlight if that's what you want.'

'But his wife . . . ?'

'She knew. It's not that easy to explain away $50 million when you're in your early twenties. And she had to know he wasn't a native-born American. In those days he'd have had an accent.'

Ravenel ran his hand over his chin. 'Think about it. Here we have a woman – Grace Standsfield Brand – who is widely accepted as one of America's top hostesses. The day after her husband dies, when calls of sympathy are coming in, she gets one that enrages her. Her banker in Switzerland tells her that before he died, Robert Brand instructed him to transfer $20 million to the account of Julia Lang. The banker *has* to inform her because the transfer order came in after Brand's death. She knows all about you already. Somebody here kept her informed.'

'I know who it was,' Julia said quietly. 'Robert's secretary, Jill Bannister.'

Ravenel's eyebrows rose slightly. 'Really? Anyway, Grace Brand tells Eberhardt: No way. Then, when she learns – from this Jill Bannister, I assume – that you're pregnant, she goes really crazy. She had never forgiven Brand for the death of their son – you know about that?' Julia nodded. 'She wasn't about to let him father another child. When she found out about Jane Summerwood she had her killed. She arranged the same end for you.'

'It's beyond belief.'

'Not really. People are always hiring hit men in my country.'

'You found out so much,' she said.

'I got a lot from Brand's friend, Bobby Koenig.'

'How did you get in touch with him?'

'Through the Chelsea police. Koenig was the one who took Brand's body back to New York.' He looked at her curiously. 'You didn't know?'

Julia shook her head. She realized with a pang just how little she did know.

'It was Koenig who filled me in about the kidnapping. It goes back to Linge. One day Linge came across a German magazine and saw a story about Robert Brand, the American multimillionaire. There was an old photograph of him taken in the street and even though it was blurred and indistinct Linge knew at once it was Walter Brandt's son. The article went on to detail Brand's luxurious lifestyle in New York and Mexico, and ran pictures of his wife and young son. Linge is not very bright but even he was able to figure out the probable origin of Brand's wealth. He knew, you see, that Walter Brandt had gone to Geneva to see Eberhardt just as he had. They'd discussed it. But Brandt had not told him the outcome.

'Linge told his son, Gerhardt, about the magazine story. Gerhardt was bitter. Here he was, the son of a gardener in Bavaria, and there was Brand, living in luxury in America. The resentment festered. He thought of different ways he could pressure Brand to help him. At length he hit upon a scheme. With two friends he would fly to Mexico and kidnap Brand's son and hold him to ransom. Gerhardt was always in trouble with the law. Old Heinz had long ago given up on him.

'They pulled it off. They got the boy, killing the bodyguard in the process. But then the unthinkable happened. Brand refused to pay the ransom demand. He guessed, and he was right, that his son was already dead. Gerhardt and the others panicked. They fled. But Brand had recruited a team of professionals to track them down. They followed them to Cuernavaca and in the shoot-out Gerhardt and the others were killed.'

'It's almost unbelievable,' Julia said.

'It happened.' Ravenel got to his feet and stretched. He walked across to the window and parted the curtains, looking out into the dark night.

'There are some things I don't understand,' Julia said. 'Why did Robert keep on using the Banque Eberhardt? Eberhardt couldn't have done anything to him without incriminating himself.'

'That's true,' Ravenel said, sitting down again. 'And Brand had done nothing illegal. He'd inherited the money from his father. He was an American citizen. The story of how he first accrued wealth would certainly have hurt him but it would have destroyed Eberhardt. He'd have gone to jail. I think Brand just kept his money there rather than take any chances. He needed a bank in Europe.'

'And that man you said had the diary; the one you found?'

'Georges di Marco.'

Julia leaned forward. 'I know that name. Paul Eberhardt mentioned him.'

'He was his partner. Been with him from the early days. He was a very proper Swiss banker and he'd kept notes of every deposit Goering made. Other people had to be involved, you see. Those two officers couldn't just hand a suitcase full of money to Eberhardt and say: "Put this in the vaults." It all had to be itemized properly. But di Marco went further. He made notes in his diary of actual conversations, including what took place when Walter Brandt turned up and demanded that $50 million.

'Di Marco was due to retire soon. I think his conscience had begun to trouble him. He'd supported Eberhardt and lied when Washington began making enquiries after the war about Nazi funds deposited in Switzerland. Now he wanted to confess. He didn't care about the consequences. When he ran across Cristiani he decided he was the man to talk to. He set up a meeting. A day or two later he was found floating in Lake Geneva. He was murdered.'

Julia put her hand to her mouth.

'Cristiani suspected it from the start. The police kept insisting it was suicide. Then di Marco's sister found his diary and got in touch with Cristiani. Once he saw that di Marco had been present each time Goering's money was delivered he saw the motive.'

'Then who killed him?'

'The one man who would be finished if di Marco talked. Paul Eberhardt. It had happened once before. There'd been another man involved during the Goering transactions. His name was André Leber. We know all this because both men's signatures were on receipts we found in the bank's files. Leber retired years ago but Eberhardt kept paying him money every month. Cristiani is convinced Leber was blackmailing him. It went on for a long time until Leber was run down by a car in a street in Zurich. Eberhardt ordered that too, I'm convinced.'

'Good God.'

'You've got to realize what was at stake: a top Swiss banker's reputation. Eberhardt is one of Switzerland's banking mandarins. Next year he's due to chair the International Bankers' Conference in Vienna. He is a very important man in banking circles, responsible for the fortunes of some of the richest people in the world. He had everything to lose. He would not have hesitated to have those two men killed.'

Julia raised her legs, resting her chin on her knees. In the darkness Ravenel caught a glimpse of her pale thighs. He had to remind himself that she was a client; one who would soon be paying him $2 million. As if aware of his thoughts, Julia lowered her legs, stretching them.

'It all seems so incredible. He seemed such a civilized man at that dinner.'

Ravenel nodded. 'They said the same thing about Hermann Goering.'

'Will you tell the Swiss police what you know?'

'Maybe Cristiani will. I don't know. They'd probably be afraid to touch it.'

'But he's a murderer.'

'Yes, he is.'

She frowned again. 'Why do you suppose he decided to pay me at last? If he has.'

'I had Cristiani hand deliver a letter to him. In it I warned him that if the money wasn't released to you immediately I would give the whole story to the *New York Times*. I mentioned Heinz Linge's name in the letter so he'd know I wasn't kidding. My guess is you'll get your money quite quickly.'

Struck by a sudden thought she got up and went into the hall. The small pile of letters was there on the entry table. She flicked through them. The last one was from the Midland Bank in Jersey acknowledging receipt of a draft in her favour for $20 million, payable by the Banque Eberhardt of Geneva.

'We require your instructions regarding this draft,' the letter read. 'Please contact us as soon as possible.'

She stared at it for a long time. 'Heavens,' she muttered. 'It's really true.' She returned to the lounge and showed it to Ravenel. 'Two million of that is yours,' she said. 'I don't even know how to write a cheque for that amount.'

'It's not difficult,' he said with a small smile. 'Just write a two with six zeros after it.'

She glanced at the black and white photograph of her mother and father on the table; the two of them sitting in the front of some tour bus, squinting a little in the bright sun, looking happy and relaxed. She remembered the day she had seen them off to Italy; her mother, concerned as always for her well-being while they were gone; her father, jokey and happy, arms full of newspapers and magazines, carrying the camera that he would never use and the umbrella they would never need. They had been killed in a plane crash while on holiday in Sicily. They had left her £12,000. She had thought that quite a lot. Now she had $18 million.

Ravenel held up his empty glass. 'Any more of this?'

'Of course.'

'I shouldn't be letting you wait on me,' he said. 'My daughter told me pregnant women should be pampered.'

'You have a daughter?'

'What's the matter? You think I'm not fit to have a child?'

'But you never talk about her.'

'I saw her just the other night in New York. Here.' He took a bulky wallet from his pocket and produced a picture of a little girl standing in the street, smiling at the camera.

'She's adorable,' Julia said. 'What's her name?'

'Louise.'

'How old is she?'

'Five.'

'Where's her mother?'

'She died. Eighteen months ago. Breast cancer.'

'Oh no. I'm so sorry.' She reached down and touched Ravenel's face lightly with her fingertips.

'Where was this taken?'

'Outside our apartment on West 57th Street. That's Carnegie Hall in the background.'

'Who looks after her?'

'I've got a nanny.'

Julia studied the picture again. 'You're a lucky little girl, Louise Ravenel. You've got the most remarkable daddy.' She refilled Ravenel's glass.

The phone rang. It was Cristiani. 'Are you all right?' he asked urgently. 'We've been trying to reach you for hours.'

'I'm fine,' she said.

'Thank God. Is Guy there?'

'Sitting right here.' She passed the receiver to Ravenel. He listened intently for several minutes, saying nothing.

'Thanks, Albert-Jean,' he said finally. 'I'll see you in a day or two.'

He put down the receiver. 'It's over, Julia,' he said. 'Eberhardt and Grace Brand were shot dead in Paris this morning.'

Chapter 50

A week had passed. Julia's back was still bruised but most of the pain had gone. The baby was all right. Dr Grierson had given her a thorough examination and reassured her. 'You're lucky,' he said. 'A fall like that. You must be careful.'

A story about the man found dead in the park was carried by several of the morning papers. According to the police he was a known underworld figure and a gangland revenge killing was suspected.

Guy Ravenel had been gone three days. He had flown first to Geneva, then on to New York. Julia had insisted on going with him to the airport.

He had bought himself a new, dark blue suit in Regent Street. She had grown so used to him in his crumpled outfits she found it odd to see him looking so dapper.

'I'll never be able to thank you enough,' she said.

He chuckled. 'Two million is a good start.'

'That's your fee. That doesn't count.'

'There is a way,' Ravenel said, suddenly earnest. 'Come with me to New York.'

She gave him a long look.

'I can't do that, Guy. Not right now.'

'Later?'

'I'll try.'

They said goodbye outside Passport Control. He took her hands in his and kissed her full on the lips.

'Look after yourself,' he said as he went through the door.

The knowledge that he would no longer be part of her life saddened her. For weeks she had been with him on a roller-coaster ride that had turned her days upside down. She realized with a pang how placid things would be from now on.

The fact that she was a wealthy woman had still not sunk in. She could go where she liked; do as she pleased.

'I still feel a bit uneasy about the money,' she told Lisa when they had lunch together. 'After all, it was Nazi money.'

'Don't be ridiculous,' Lisa said firmly. 'It was Robert's money. He made it and he wanted you to have it for the child.' She speared a piece of smoked salmon with her fork. 'You know what I've been wondering? Who'll inherit the Brand fortune? Some cousin twice removed living in a one-room apartment in Milwaukee, perhaps.'

'I neither know nor care,' Julia said. 'I was in love with Robert Brand for a very short while. Even if he'd lived I'm not sure it would have lasted. There were too many lies.'

'I think he was scared of losing you,' Lisa said. 'That's why he lied.'

'He lied to me from the beginning,' Julia said. She pushed aside her own smoked salmon. I shouldn't be eating all this, she decided. I'm big enough already.

Lisa studied her friend. 'You're going to miss Guy Ravenel, aren't you?'

'Very much.'

'Got to you, didn't he?'

'It's not that. It's just . . . oh, I don't know. He's such a fantastic man. I know I'll never meet anyone like him again.'

'He's certainly something,' Lisa said. 'Breaking into the bank like that. It took some nerve. But what about you? Calmly dining with Paul Eberhardt while he did it.'

'I wasn't so calm,' Julia said. 'I was petrified.'

'Now he's dead. So is Grace Brand.'

'No tears this side of the table.'

'There was a story in the *Herald Tribune*. The French police have no clues.'

'Guy thinks there was a mistake. He thinks Eberhardt

set up the hit and happened to get in the way.'

'You're lucky you got your money before he was knocked off.'

'I know it.'

'All Guy's doing.'

She nodded.

'Did he tell you he has a daughter?' Lisa asked.

'He showed me her picture.'

'I met her in New York last year. She's about the same age as Deena. Adorable.'

'I hope I meet her one day.'

'What's keeping you?' Lisa asked. 'You could go tomorrow.'

'I could,' Julia said. 'But I won't. Guy Ravenel may be the most exciting man I've ever met but I don't want to spend my nights worrying which bank he's breaking into.'

'He doesn't have to do that any more,' Lisa said with a chuckle. 'He's worth at least $2 million.'

'That won't change him,' Julia said. 'He's a risk taker. Always will be.'

'You may be right. And what about that woman – the one who went into the bank with him?'

'Marie. Marie Corbat.'

'She sounds like my kind of woman,' Lisa said.

'Guy flew back to see her before he went home,' Julia said. 'Took her a cheque. Albert-Jean Cristiani got one too. My way of saying thanks.'

Lisa smiled then. 'I like that, Julia Lang.'

She was home by 2.30 p.m. As she walked into the flat the phone was ringing.

It was Emma. 'I've been calling and calling,' she said. 'There was no answer . . .'

Damn, Julia thought. I forgot about the machine.

'I thought you'd be interested in the news. The *Mail* and the *Express* are running your stories tomorrow. Tony Vickers and Arthur Brandon called to tell me.'

Julia felt a strong sense of satisfaction. The stories, she knew, would give a lift to those still at the hotel.

'I wonder what Moscato's reaction will be,' she said.

'We'll never know, will we?' She could hear the suppressed excitement in Emma's voice. 'He's gone.'

'What do you mean, gone?'

'The Sultan fired him. Ricci too. He flew in yesterday. They were out by mid-afternoon.'

Julia felt suddenly weary. She sat down on the edge of the bed and kicked off her shoes.

'Wait till you hear the best news,' Emma went on. 'Tim Perrin takes over next month.'

Julia felt a surge of happiness. 'Tim? Really? That's wonderful . . .'

'There's more. The Sultan's secretary called this morning. He wants to know if you can come to tea this afternoon?'

'What for?'

'I've no idea.'

Julia glanced out of the window at the darkening sky. Rain was threatening. She swung her legs onto the bed and leaned back against the headboard.

'No,' she said.

'You're busy?'

'I'm just not coming, Emma.'

'Please.'

'Whose side are you on?'

'Yours, of course.'

'I've resigned, Emma.'

'Because of Moscato. But he's gone now.' She was silent for a moment. 'It wouldn't hurt just to come to tea.'

Julia sighed. 'All right, Emma. To please you I'll come. But don't read anything into it.'

'I made a mistake, Julia. You were right and I was wrong.' The Sultan of Malacca sat forward on the sofa of his suite, looking earnestly at Julia. 'I was so determined to save my hotel I chose badly.'

'He almost ruined the Burlington.'

'I know that. But now I've chosen well. Tim Perrin.'

'The best.'

'He's arriving here next month,' the Sultan said. 'I told him I would make every effort to get you to return to the hotel. He thinks so highly of you.'

I have money in the bank, Julia thought. In six months' time I'm having Robert's baby. I don't have to listen to this.

'Well, Julia?'

'It's not possible,' she said. 'I'm having a baby.'

The Sultan chuckled. 'I had noticed . . . well, that you had put on weight. Congratulations. That's wonderful news.'

'So you see . . .'

He leaned back. 'You can take off all the time you want. Have your baby. Come back when you're ready.'

'The same job?'

'Tim Perrin wants you as his number two.' He clasped his hands together. 'Will you at least consider it, Julia?'

She looked at his bald head and dark, flashing eyes. Only a few weeks ago, she reflected, he was sitting right there telling me to get along with Moscato or get out. Now, because Tim Perrin wants me, he's pleading.

'There are terms,' she began.

'I understand.'

'Pam Helmore and Bryan Penrose will have to be reinstated.'

'That's already done. Tim Perrin insisted on it.'

'You give us two years to prove ourselves. With no interference.'

He considered this for a long moment. Finally he nodded. 'Agreed.'

Surprised at the rush of confidence she felt, Julia could think of nothing more to say. She rose quickly. 'I'll give you my decision at the end of the week.'

'I'll be waiting,' he said.

On her way back to the executive corridor people

stopped to greet her with hugs and handshakes. Suddenly the Burlington seemed to be alive again with smiles everywhere. Had she been kidding herself in supposing she could walk away from this place which had been home for so long?

When she went into her old office Emma jumped up. 'Well?'

'He wants me back as Tim's number two.'

Emma danced around her. 'That's terrific. Do I come with you?'

'Of course. If I say yes.'

'You must say yes. You know the hotel business back to front. You'll be wonderful. And you mustn't worry. I'll look after things while you're off having your baby.'

Julia stared at her. 'Dammit, Emma, are there no secrets around here?'

Emma smiled. 'Even a barren old frump like me can tell when a woman is pregnant.' She put her hand on Julia's arm. 'Can I be godmother?'

'Only if you promise not to fuss.'

Julia slumped down in her old chair. Emma moved round to adjust a cushion behind her back. 'Does this mean welcome back?' she asked.

Julia smiled. 'Yes, Emma, I guess it means welcome back.'

Postscript

Letter from Lazarus, Ridley and Lenz of Madison Avenue, New York City

Dear Miss Lang,

The day before he died my friend and client Robert Brand wrote me a confidential letter expressing his delight at the prospect of becoming a father again and stating that he wished your child to be accepted as his sole heir and beneficiary.

While his wife, Grace, was still alive this posed numerous legal problems which I need not go into now, but with her recent demise there is no reason why Robert's last wish should not be granted.

The child of your union therefore becomes the sole heir to the assets of the Brand Corporation with you as guardian until he or she becomes of age.

In order to complete the necesssary legal documents perhaps we can arrange a meeting at a time and place suitable to yourself. I am available to come to London should you not wish to make the journey to New York.

Cordially,
Elliot Lenz

From *the Daily Telegraph*

The Burlington Hotel, one of London's best-known landmarks, was bought yesterday by a consortium headed by billionaire American industrialist Robert Brand Jnr, 27.

The Burlington, owned by the Sultan of Malacca until his death, and most recently a member of the Palace Group, has long been a favourite hotel of international travellers. The Primrose Ball, one of the social events of the London season, is held there.

'My mother was with the Burlington for many years,' Mr Brand said yesterday. 'So my family has a long association with the hotel. I am happy to continue it.'

Brand's mother, Mrs Guy Ravenel, the former Julia Lang, who now lives in the Bahamas, is expected in London next month to see her horse, the Derby favourite Shalimar, run. She was for many years the Burlington's Director of Publicity.